COOL JOE'S REDEMPTION

BETTY HERMELEE

outskirts press

Cool Joe's Redemption
All Rights Reserved.
Copyright © 2022 Betty Hermelee
v2.0

This is a work of fiction. Names, characters, businesses, places, events, locales, and incidents are either the products of the author's imagination or used in a fictitious manner. Any resemblance to actual persons, living or dead, or actual events is purely coincidental.

The opinions expressed in this manuscript are solely the opinions of the author and do not represent the opinions or thoughts of the publisher. The author has represented and warranted full ownership and/or legal right to publish all the materials in this book.

This book may not be reproduced, transmitted, or stored in whole or in part by any means, including graphic, electronic, or mechanical without the express written consent of the publisher except in the case of brief quotations embodied in critical articles and reviews.

Outskirts Press, Inc.
http://www.outskirtspress.com

ISBN: 978-1-9772-5077-3

Cover Image by Betty Hermelee

Outskirts Press and the "OP" logo are trademarks belonging to Outskirts Press, Inc.

PRINTED IN THE UNITED STATES OF AMERICA

To my husband, Norm
Supportive and patient

LIST OF MAIN CHARACTERS

JOE and TESS VALENTI- PARENTS

CHILDREN/SPOUSE:

PETE and VIV
TOMMY and ANGELA
FRANKIE and ANNA
ROBBIE and SYLVIA
MARGARET and TED
MARIA and JIM
DANNY

1

JOE

Cool Joe, as I am known, deal maker of the 1920's New York scene, a distant relative of a famous mobster. My real name is Joe Valenti, short, dark hair, mustache, overweight, but with a tall personality. I like to joke around, especially with my kids. But I'm not real proud of my genes. I'm not really a mobster. I just hang around with them; some of it happens to rub off on me.

Since the kids all moved out, I now live with my wife Tess in a rather small apartment in the Harlem section of Manhattan. It's of a typical size for that area; one bedroom, sitting room, closet kitchen, one bathroom, tub, and shower.

When I say closet kitchen, I mean it. You open a door, and there's your kitchen. But you should see what comes out of that closet; lots of good Italian food. Watch it, and you could easily knock into it.

I own a store front haberdashery, which attracts

many men and women of high fashion. Instead of putting it back in, I suck most of my money out of that business. It's a cash cow, money under the mattress, you know, that's how the family lives, and I mean all of us.

Me and Tess have eight grown children, mostly in their twenties and thirties. They all got married except one. After number five, we stop counting and sometimes can't recall all of their names cause they look very much alike.

One day, we get tragic news that Donny, the youngest, is killed by a bullet on the streets of Brooklyn, where he lives. Most likely, his body guards screw up, and Donny takes the punishment. This devasting news drives me to drink, in addition to which I hire different bodyguards.

I go to see my Boss to find out exactly who killed Donny; he doesn't say a word, but I consider retribution, of course. Tess is totally out of it, weeping day and night.

"Don't do it, Joe."

"What do you mean, Tess?"

"Don't go after the Boss. You'll get yourself killed. What are you, crazy?"

"Tess, I'm just so troubled and angry. I'll think on it, sweetheart, don't worry."

"One death is enough, our baby boy." I feel sick to my stomach.

"Okay, okay, just relax; you're very upset so let's not talk about it anymore?"

Tess looks at me and gives me a kiss on the lips.

"I love you, Joe, even though you're a crooked cookie sometimes."

As true Italians, the funeral is elaborate, and hundreds of mourners attend, family friends and a few "extended family members." The chapel smells like a flower garden. I pull my Boss over and have a few quiet words with him, just a warning.

I cry a river of tears when I see my youngest son dressed in his wedding suit with a red rose in his lapel, his face perfectly posed as if he is still breathing. I cross myself and say a quick prayer.

Back in the reception room, food flows like a fast-moving stream; everybody pitches in with the cooking. Tess is so broken up that she doesn't want to eat, covers her aging face with her beige lace veil, and sits in a corner, silent. Visitors respect her grief.

That evening, we gather to pray at church. My daughter-in-law, Linda, and her children look very sad. Dressed in a black silk suit, she wears her hair in a bun, pearls around her neck, a black lace veil, so sheer you could tell there is no face make-up.

She is very silent. I explain that I will get new bodyguards for her and warn them of extreme caution. She tries to smile as if thanking me.

After a long period of mourning, going to church services, and more family gatherings, me and the kids are pretty much back to our sketchy routine; I make a promise to pay more attention to the family and return to my store and my quasi-legal hobbies, of which Tess only knows the half of it.

Me and Tess live sort of a bumpy life, much of which is caused by my shady hobbies. I love to gamble, especially at the race track. Me and my cronies often take a beating, but the thrill of the sport and the chance to win big keeps all of us glued to it. I never discuss how much I win or lose.

As long as Tess is comfortable, I'm satisfied. Every Saturday, me and my buddies take the train to Queens with a stash of cash in our pockets. If I win big, which is pretty often, I dash home and take Tess out to dine, as she likes to be treated like a queen.

"How about a delicious dinner out tonight at Tony's?"

"That sounds wonderful. How much did you win today, Joe?"

"Oh, don't be silly, Tess, actually not that much, but we haven't been out in a while so let's go, eh?"

"Okay, boss, you lead the way. I'll follow."

"And guess what? We'll go in style in a taxi instead of the rail. How's that for a treat?"

"What a wonderful idea," says Tess with her coat half-buttoned.

Even though Tess loves to be pampered, she earns excellent ratings for her fine Italian cooking. On Sundays, the kids and the grandkids cram into our apartment, and out of the closet-kitchen comes a lasagna, steaming hot with extra thick mozzarella cheese, tempting the grandkids to ooze it around their tongues...and ask for more.

While they make strings of cheese, we adults drink wine from an Italian winery owned by one of my buddies. There is no business talk at the dining table, which stretches the length of the sitting room.

Prohibition doesn't stop my drinking habits. I find ways to get the gold and play poker simultaneously. My cronies and I take turns gambling big money at different venues around the city, while Tess thinks I am going to the silent movies with the guys.

One night I return late, so drunk that I collapse on the sitting room floor. Supposedly, I mumble some words and fall asleep. Tess leaves me there, figuring that I will wake up sober in the morning, which I do with some strong espresso.

"What were you doing last night, Joe?"

"Playing cards at Monte's place," I think she probably believes me.

Tess looks puzzled. "Really, Joe? Geez, you were very drunk last night."

"Well, I have to admit we all had a few whiskies. Boy, were they good."

"I'm glad you made it home alive. You could have fallen in the street, you know?"

"Yeah, I know, but I made it home drunk as a skunk."

Our lives finally calm down once we accept Donny's death, but we pray for him at home and in church every night. We spend more time with the grandkids; take them to the park, the zoo, the planetarium, and of course for ice cream, that being the best part of the day.

If you think I can't remember my kids' names, I certainly don't remember the grandkids' names; too many of them. But they're sweet kids, and we love them dearly.

As we age into our late seventies, life slows down to a more or less normal pace, and some of the Boss' lackeys are kicked off one at a time, a bullet at a time, and temporary peace follows, but probably not for long. He'll get new guards and henchmen, and the mess will linger. And, the Boss doesn't kid around.

Tess still loves to cook in our midget kitchen, but I don't complain. Her food is scrumptious.

"What's for dinner tonight, my sweet?"

"Your favorite, baked spaghetti. How about something to drink?"

"Good idea, Tess. How about a glass of red wine?"

"I'll take it, old man, good for what ails you."

"Listen, we're both getting old and cranky, right, not like the old days when we'd go dancing."

"But we're still pretty spry, don't you think? I mean, we're both seventy-five!" says Tess, laughing as she speaks.

"Yeah, we're pretty healthy, a few aches here and there, but not too bad."

One day, I wake up short of breath, and Tess is very scared. I blow it off as a common cold as I cough my guts out until I start spitting up blood. A doctor comes and says it's pneumonia.

In those days, there was no antibiotic to treat this illness. I soon develop a fever, which leads to my legs and body aching, and I get despondent, crabby, and don't want to move out of bed.

Tess tries hard to stay calm and nurse my sick, coughing body and certainly my crazy mind. She and the family take turns visiting regularly and spend time chatting with me.

At first, I am clear and talk a lot, but I become angry and stubborn as time passes. I refuse chest compresses and other medications available. They bring me gifts, read to me; Tess and the kids repeatedly try to humor me, but frankly, I don't want to be.

"Hey Tess, come on, no more visitors, just you and me. I mean, I love the kids, but it's too much blabbing all the time. I'm too tired."

"They love you, Joe, and are worried about your health, be nice to them, please."

"Okay, okay, but not too often. I need to rest to get better, I hope."

"You will," says Tess, trying her hardest to smile.

About a week later, on a clear, cool fall day, God speaks to me and pleads with me to end my suffering. I find it hard to breathe. I listen carefully and see the end coming, and, as a pious man, I speak to Him. I say I am ready to go and don't want to suffer further.

Then, I have a conversation with myself. I talk

about leaving my beloved family and how they will manage without me. Guilt-ridden and with much pain, I cry and fall asleep until I don't remember anymore.

When I wake up, I have a plan which is part of my dream, in which I remember almost every detail. Without too much doubt, I go to the bedroom window and look down at the street below. We are on floor eight, a sure death, and, frankly, I am petrified. I can't do this.

What if I die? Or become a paralyzed victim? Thoughts scramble through my mind. In a couple of hours, Tess will be awake, and I have little time to think over this plan.

I go to my armoire, pull out a scarf, sit on the bed's edge and carefully fold the scarf around my forehead and eyes, all the time crying, and then tie it in the back.

I carefully step toward the window, slowly finding my way with my hands. Weak as a sick dog, I can sit on the sill. I weep for a while, with tears on my cheeks, muttering the names of my family. Then in a split second, I fling myself out the window.

In less than a minute, death on the street. Before Tess awakens, there are screams of horror below.

2

PETE

It is all my fault!

I'm the eldest and should have been more supportive of our family.

It is stupid to think that mom and dad could raise eight kids alone without help and work in all of his businesses. And, when they aged and dad got sick, I failed to notice the severity of their circumstances. As a result, we've had two tragedies, both of which are horrific deaths.

It has taken me a long time to recover from these traumas. I'll never forget when my little brother Donny passed away. Yes, my adorable, funny, smart guy, who I believe, is my parents' favorite.

Donny, struck down by a vicious bullet to the chest in the middle of the street. He is dead at the scene, blood oozing down his limp body into the gutter. I'll never forget this sight for as long as I live. It haunts me day and night.

Our family still lives in fear every day. And, when my dad died as he did, I thought I would never recover. But, I'm still here and closer to my mom and the rest of the large family. We miss our beloveds, and now we stick together as a team.

I'm in the dock loading business in Brooklyn, N.Y. I work big rigs and take cargo off giant ships, usually from China. I just got a job promotion to assistant manager of loading and unloading. My boss is proud of me and sometimes stashes extra cash in my pocket.

I have my own bodyguards, just in case, but it's never enough because the bosses' hitmen are clever and watch for loopholes where they can do some bloody harm when you're not always in agreement with them. I'm in good standing with the bosses at the docks but not always in other trades. I'm getting a call right now.

"Hello, it's Pete here."

"Mo here. Hey, you know what the deal is, right?"

"Which one?"

"Stop f—kin' around with me."

"Oh, you mean the loan deal?"

"Hey, it's due in one week, pal."

See what I mean? They bug you to death.

I take a second loan to pay the mortgage on my house in Brooklyn. This guy is a loan shark who makes lots of money on the loan, a real crook. He's part of the mob and is a callous guy, but he's not a hit man.

I have to discuss this with my wife, Vivian, who has some money stashed under the mattress. I give her an anniversary gift and tell her to hide it. I feel bad about doing this, but otherwise, I'll keep getting phone calls and threats. I try to keep my business apart from my family affairs.

"I'm home, honey! How was your day?"

"Eh, same old thing. I'm tired of cooking Pete, let's go out to dinner tonight."

"I'm too tired Viv, let's do it another night. Hey! What about ordering a pizza? Where are the boys?"

"Playing soccer, won't be home 'til late. So I made P.B.J. sandwiches for them before they left."

"So, it's just you and me; we can get a small one and save bucks. You phone, and I'll pick it up."

On my way to the pizza place, I try to think about how to approach Vivian about the money under the mattress. I really prefer that she doesn't know how much we owe on the loan.

Let's see. I can tell her we need a new roof, as an expert told me. Or, I can say maybe we should send the kids to private school since there has been some trouble at their current school.

DAMN! Whatever I tell her, she's going to give me an argument or start bawling like she has a habit of doing. I'm on my way home now from the pizza place, and I'm just going to give it to her straight; tell her about the loan.

"Yum, that pizza is delish, eh?"

"I've had better," says Viv

We sat there eating our pizza, radio news on, but no talking. I'm getting up the courage to tell her. "Honey?"

"Yes, Pete, what is it; the tone in your voice is a bit suspicious."

Uh oh, she knows something's coming.

"Well, you know that promotion I got?" Well, it's not a whole lot of money; it's okay, but we will still need more money to pay our mortgage, the kid's expenses, and all. I couldn't ask mom. She only has enough to live on, and I want her to be comfortable, you know. So, I had to borrow money from Eddie, the loan shark, but it isn't enough."

"Eddie, the loan shark? He's a real mobster. I know you can't touch a real bank, but couldn't you have asked me first? I would have suggested a person of known repute, you know, in the real world. By the way, is he a hit man? We need some extra personnel (wink wink),"

"I gotta pay this loan off by next Monday, one week from today."

"Or else?"

"Or else it's one strike against me, three strikes, and you're dead."

"Can I think about it tonight?"

"While you're sleeping?"

"No dummy, while I'm up."

I can't wait for her response, so I step out of the house to take a walk. It's late, and the stars are out, a half-moon too. I find a bench to sit on cause my feet are killing me. I look up to the bright sky to find someone to help me.

I am a spiritual man; I pray to whoever will listen. I pray that Vivian lets me use her money (it's really my money after working so long). Vivian can be tough sometimes, real tough. But she has a soft side too, like when she buys me a gold chain to wear around my neck.

Heck, it isn't even real gold, but who cares; it was a kind thought. My mind wanders to my family. My brother and their wives all work hard to keep their families afloat. They're also involved with bosses, but much cleaner than me (I think).

I start to walk home, feel sick to my stomach, begin to sweat at the thought that Vivian may give me a fight about the money. I look up at the sky, see some fluffy clouds pass over the moon, a real pretty sight. I hope whoever I speak to up there will grant my wishes, and I won't have to worry about Eddie. Another call is coming in.

"Hey Pete, this is Eddie. You should know my voice by now, geez."

"Yes, Eddie, I know it's you."

"Well, I got something to tell ya."

"Yes?"

"Well, I called one of my buddies who has ties to, you know, loot."

"Yeah, Eddie, and?"

"And ya know these are hard times; this other Boss with all the loot is gonna try to pay off part your loan for ya, but I'm warnin' you, he may ask a favor of you some time; ya know that's just how it works; keep your guards. Okay, Pete, just remember what I told ya."

We hang up the call, and I have tears running down my face. I'm so happy. I walk faster so I can tell Vivian the good news. Man, I almost can't believe it!

I walk into the house all smiles and such. And, who is waiting with smiles on their faces?

Vivian and my two boys.

"Guess what, Viv?"

"What?"

"I got the part of the loan taken care of, not telling who, but we're okay. You can keep the money under your mattress."

"Well, I was thinking too, and I decided to give you the money under our mattress."

What a night! We all hug, rain falls down our cheeks. We decide to spend some of the mattress money on a trip to Atlantic City. "A little gambling, eh?"

Hey, this is what we, the Valenti's, do, you know.

Now, we're planning our trip to Atlantic City. We're picking a modest hotel 'cause we can't afford the deluxe ones. So we're going to splurge and get two rooms. I think to myself.

I just hope Eddie was right about someone kicking in the dough to pay off my loan. But you never know with these guys; they can be fickle. Anyway, we're going to celebrate a little. We owe ourselves a vacation.

"Hey, you guys, Michael, Paul and Viv, come here. I want to show you the hotel I picked out."

"Wow, dad, that looks great. Is it on the beach?" asks Paul.

"It sure is, and it has a rooftop swimming pool, though it may be too cold to use."

"Dad, I like swimming in cold water," says Michael, with a big grin on his face.

"Guess what? I booked it for Christmas!"

"Hey, mom, why were you gone for so long?"

"I'll tell you at another time. Let's all celebrate that I'm home."

3

TESS

I still can't get over my Joe's death. It's been three years of hell! Yeah, I know I should move on, but what does that mean? Move to another place? Move to get re-married? Move to get a job?

I still feel the guilt. If only I were up early that morning (I sleep like a log), Joe never would have jumped out of that window! As long as I live, I'll have nightmares about that accident. Was it really an accident?

I guess I'll never know how depressed Joe truly felt; I mean, I know he wasn't well because he had pneumonia and a hard feeling on his chest; some nights, he felt he couldn't breathe, so I put special compresses on his chest but did I think he'd ever jump out the window? Never.

I wake up to the sound of sirens and horns and screams, but I hear that all the time in Brooklyn, nothing new. I pop my head up, it's still dark, so I snore myself back to sleep.

My neighbor, Mrs. Fachiolo, knocks on the door screaming her head off at about seven am. Words cannot come out...she is breathing heavy. I can tell something is very wrong. She grabs me by the arm and points to the window.

I look down, see a body, and collapse. Everything after that is like a fog. Like I am in another world, and this is just a nightmare. I know it's true when Richie, the cop, who I know from the neighborhood, bursts into the apartment and puts his arm around me. My sobs are like rain falling from heaven. I can't stop bawling.

My kids come over to console me, other relatives, friends, and some of Joe's bodyguards and other underworld characters. Flowers and food take up the whole apartment. Joe's body is so damaged, we have to have a closed coffin. The priest comes to say some prayers, then slugs down a brandy

All I can say is the funeral is huge, and many have to stand outside and can't hear the sermon. I have to admit it is long, some of it in Latin, and pretty boring. But out of love and respect for my Joe, we live through it.

THREE YEARS LATER

Three years later, I still wear many black clothes and think of Joe often.

My kids are a comfort and visit a lot, but there's nothing like losing a husband; he was a real character, but a loving one.

Betty Hermelee

Lately, my kids have noticed that my memory isn't so good. They say that I repeat myself and forget where I am half the time; I really don't notice it, except once when I get into a cab and forget my address. So if others notice it, it must be true. Pete, my oldest, thinks that I should see a neurologist to check me out. He says he'll escort me, so I guess I'll go.

About a week after the doctor's appointment (where the doc makes me touch my nose and all kinds of counting and stuff, so annoying), the test results come back, and Pete reads the English version of the report. He has a stern look on his face.

"What's going on, Pete?"

"I'm still reading, ma."

"It's bad news, right?"

Minutes, which seem like hours, go by.

Pete looks me straight in the face.

"Ma, I'm no genius, but this looks to me like you got dementia."

"What does that mean, Pete?"

"It means your brain isn't acting right; it's a little off-kilter, ma."

"How could that be possible? It came on so fast? I'm not seeing double or nothing."

"Sometimes it just does, ma; we'll set you up for the best treatment, okay, ma?

I'm going call the other kids, and we'll have a plan for you."

"Yea, but whose gonna pay for it, Pete?"

"I'll take care of that part, ma. You just relax and don't worry. I got connections. Now I'm going take you home to rest, then Robbie will come over for a visit."

"Hey Eddie"

"Yeah, Pete?"

"I don't know if you know that my mom's got dementia."

"No, Pete, how would I know?"

"I just told you, that's how."

"Well, she needs expensive treatment, and honestly, I don't have the money. Her insurance won't cover all of it, ya know."

"Yeah, I know, so, what do ya want from me?"

"Well, I thought maybe you could give me a loan."

"Ah, come on, Pete, you already owe me."

"Well, I really owe the Boss, but he won't deal with me.

"Eddie, listen, you're in pretty good standing with the Boss, so I think he'll listen to you.

I'll get back to ya, Pete, after I speak to him, but don't count on it."

"Hey ma, Pete tells me he thinks he can get some dough from the Boss."

"For what, Robbie?"

"Remember, ma, you have dementia, and you need medical help; your insurance is not good enough, so we need to bargain with the Boss. We need some household help in here to keep you on the path."

"What path?"

"The path of getting better, ma."

"I'm so fed up with these Boss characters; they make things so hard for us. It's always something like I give to you, then you owe me with lots of interest; it's like funny money, which they keep under their mattresses." But my boys are so involved with loan sharks they better keep their cool, or they'll get bounced off, just like Donny. I can't say his name, or I'll start to bawl.

I try to keep myself busy. I have friends who meet every Tuesday to play cards. They don't notice my dementia; maybe they're as crazy as me. We don't play for real money, just chips. Near the end of our game, we all sip brandy.

It makes me feel good, so I slug more down. When I get home, I'm a little tipsy, so I lay down and take a nap. Between doing my paperwork and seeing my family, I keep pretty busy. But at night, before I go to sleep, I pray to Joe and Donny, may their souls rest in peace.

I decide to make an omelet for breakfast one day, something I don't often do. I usually stir up the eggs and put in a little milk to make them fluffy. I wear a housecoat in the mornings before I go out for errands. That's what people my age wear.

I get out the frying pan and turn on the gas stove. I stir the eggs, butter, and salt in the pan, and suddenly, I see that the sleeve of my housecoat is on fire, and it smells awful.

I scream and get some water, but it won't go out. I scream again, and my neighbor comes running in and beats me with a broom. Well, she put out the fire, but my arm and neck are burned. I fall to the floor in pain. She calls Robbie, my son.

The next thing I know, an ambulance comes and attends to me; I am on my way to the hospital emergency room. I can hardly talk anymore cause I have a mask on my whole face.

PETE

Hey, Pete here. Weeks go by painfully slow with ma in the burn unit. I didn't think it was this bad. My family prays to the saints. Doctors come and go; nurses change ma's bandages. The kids cry at different times, and there is no silence except for prayer. Even Eddie comes to visit, and he prays too. There is no enemy at this moment. All eyes are on Tess.

Ma slips into a coma. The doctors look worried. The family reads their faces.

A few more painful days pass and ma's heart stops beating. She lays there like an angel of death. We weep and whisper that we love her and that now she is in the hands of God.

We leave the hospital in disbelief. We've just lost three members of our family in a short amount of time.

Now, we have no parents, we're on our own, but we'll try to do the right things, make them proud of us. I, as the oldest, have to take more responsibility, make sure my siblings are doing well, keep them as clean as they can be, including myself. We are all religious people, and we go to church to pray at home and at other times, like now since we lost our dear ma.

After we split up, I walk home instead of taking the rail. Exercise is good for the mind and body. As I walk, I think about my future, my kids, and my wife. My head spins, and my pace gets faster. I guess I just want to be home with a drink of bourbon in my hand.

4

ROBBIE

After ma takes her last breath, we bawl like a bunch of babies. We all believed that she would die of dementia. But, the horrible burn accident? Never. This is so freaky that we are still in shock, paralyzed, and feel helpless, and now the tough work comes cause we have to bury her.

We've gone through this twice before with dad and sweet Donny. And, now ma, it's crazy! I got tears in my eyes thinking of her just lyin' there in the burn unit drugged up to stop the pain.

My siblings help dress ma for the casket. We decide on her wedding dress, and believe it or not, it still fits, which makes us happy. The service is in the same church where we buried dad and Donny.

We are slammed with people pushing to enter, and finally, the doors close, and the priest begins his long ceremony. We are sad and use a lot of tissues, especially me. I get very emotional at the church;

my big brother Pete gives a beautiful eulogy, tears in our eyes. The casket is open because they are able to put makeup over ma's neck burns, so we have a last glance at her, so pretty and peaceful.

After the ceremony, we ride to the burial site and pick out a lovely stone with engraving on it, "ma, you'll always be with us." Following that, we go back to Pete's house for some food and drink. I notice many visitors drinking whiskey, so I indulge. I'm feelin' a bit tipsy.

I guess that's a good thing. My body guards attend, Eddie and even Johnnie the Boss. They all behave, maybe a nasty word here or there, but mostly cordial. Johnnie asks about the loan and how it's going, and I say all is well. He gives me a dirty look, and I just ignore it; life goes on.

Now, about me. Well, I'm in the waste management business, based in Brooklyn. Most people know it as the garbage business, but I don't drive the trucks. I'm in management, responsible for overseeing the truck routes, like which days they go to this neighborhood or that one, and keeping them on schedule.

The dough is pretty good, enough to mostly pay my mortgage, with a little help from the boys. I don't owe as much as Pete, but I still owe, so I gotta be careful. There are hit men all over the damn place, and they wear plain clothes, so you don't know who they are, just wandering around to make trouble.

Sometimes you can catch them with a particular

license plate, but mostly they hide pretty well. I just heard of a friend of mine being kicked off for swearing at one of the Bosses. Boy, they don't fool around.

By the way, I forgot to say that my boss at the garbage company has a deal where he gets gas cheaper than anyone in the city; it's some kind of payoff, but hey, who cares; it has to do with oil off the ships, and he got lucky and so did we.

My wife is Sylvia, and she's the same age as me. She's pretty with long dark curly hair (though I see a few grays sneakin' in); she works as a sales person at Macy's in Manhattan and takes the rail every day back and forth.

We have one daughter, Simone, who is fourteen but thinks she's twenty-one. Aren't all teenagers nutty? I know you're thinking that Italians have lots of kids, but unfortunately, Sylvia couldn't have anymore. So, Simone is very spoiled, even bratty, if you wanna know.

She has a boyfriend, Charley, who we sort of like, but I think Simone is smarter than he is, so it's a bit disturbing. He's sixteen, and he brags a lot, still can't drive, but sometimes he sneaks out with his dad's old jalopy in the middle of the night and stops at our house, never comes in, but I know it, cause I'm a light sleeper. He just flashes his lights at Simone's window. Harmless, I think.

"Good morning, my beautiful family."
"Hi, dad."
Sylvia says nothing.

"What's up, pussy cat?" says I.

"Well, I didn't want to tell you last night when we were cuddling in bed, but I got laid off."

"What?"

"Yup, just like that after five long years standing on my feet eight hours a day,"

"I'm so sorry, pussy cat; you must feel awful. Now I feel awful cause we need your money to help pay off our mortgage."

"Dad, don't be so hard on mom, she sad."

"Yeah, I know. I'm just upset too. Do you think you can get another job, like in another department store?"

"I'll try. Can you get me a job with one of your boss men, like as a secretary or something?"

"Are you kidding?" says I. "I don't want you near them. Just pretend they don't exist, okay? We'll be good until next month, and then we'll need more dough comin' in."

"I'm off to school, mom and dad; don't fret, mom, you'll get another job, I know it. I'll ask around school too, you never know. Bye, see ya later."

"What a kid," I mumble, "she's pretty grown-up for her age, you know."

"Yes, she's my best friend."

"You mean I'm not?"

"Yes, I have two!"

"This Friday, I get my last paycheck. We'll survive."

"Yes, we will, pussy cat."

I take a deep breath.

That same night at dinner, we discuss possible jobs. There are a few openings. Meanwhile, Sylvia makes a delicious chicken cacciatore, and we gobble it up. She's such a great cook, wife, and mom too. I'm a lucky guy.

"Mom, can Charley come over later for a bit? We'll sit on the porch and gab."

"No nonsense, you're only fourteen years old."

"I know, but don't I look mature?"

"Sure, you do love, but just remember your real age," says Sylvia.

"Okay, I'll buzz Charley and let him know."

"Finish your dinner first," I demand, "you're too skinny."

So, Charley comes over, and like most parents, we're snoopin' around trying to listen to their conversation. They're speaking quite softly, and it's hard to hear, so I give up and go in the sitting room to listen to some news.

Sylvia joins me after she cleans the dishes. We listen to a comedy show and we both yawn and decide to go upstairs to bed, well not really to sleep, but you know, a little hanky panky. While I'm in bed, I think to myself. I hope Sylvia can find another job pretty quickly.

She doesn't know it, but our loan payment is due in two weeks, not a month. I lie to my wife. But what am I supposed to do, make her hysterical? Borrow again from one of them loan sharks who steal my money with their high illegal interest rates? My head is spinning now; I'll think about it and deal with it in the morning.

I have a nightmare that Eddie is strangling me 'cause I accidentally said a bad word to him. I wake up sweating like crazy at four am, sneak to the bathroom real quiet, then try my hardest to go back to sleep.

I think I'm in a half-sleep when my alarm screams at six-thirty am. I pop out of bed. Sylvia is still snoring like crazy, which she usually does right before she wakes up. It's the weirdest thing. I wake up Sylvia 'cause this is her last week of work, and every penny counts.

Oh, please get another job Sylvia, my pussy cat.

It's seven-thirty am now, and we're all sitting at the breakfast table, eating our eggs and bacon, when the doorbell rings.

"Just a minute, comin'," I say.

I open the door, and it's my Boss man and one of his assistants glaring at me.

My face turns blood red, and Sylvia and Simone's mouths are wide open with a horrified look.

"What can I do for you, fellas?"

In a throaty voice, the Boss man says, "You can come with us to the office. We got somethin' to talk about."

I start to sweat and tell Sylvia and Simone to relax. Everything will be okay. It's just a meeting.

The Bosses are silent. I grab my case, give my

sugar pies a kiss, and next thing I know, they're shoving me out the front door; I look behind and see my girls watching with horrifying looks on their pretty faces.

I try to talk to these guys, but they remain silent. I'm squeezed between two heavyweights who press against me. They keep me blindfolded, so I have no idea where I'm going. But I suspect it's to the Boss' mansion.

My poor wife and kid look so upset and frightened I could just cry, I hope this is just a meeting with Johnnie about I don't know what, but we'll see. The car stops, and two guys grab me and sort of push me into an entrance. Then they take me into a room that smells like rotten eggs. They sit down cause I can hear them breathing, and that's not too pleasant either.

I sit for quite a while, and they are silent. Finally, one more person comes in and takes off my blindfold. Now I can see where I am and am not too happy about it. I still try to figure out why I'm here. Look, nobody around our circle is perfectly honest.

At some point, I may have slipped some extra cash in my pocket, but nothing compared to the embezzling that goes on in other businesses. I'm a pretty honest guy, so what's the big deal here?

Well, we'll see when the Boss finally comes in. In the meantime, I think of my beautiful family, and I will assure them when I can that I'll be home shortly.

5

SYLVIA

Our mouths stay open a few minutes after Robbie is taken, shoved out the door by those damn henchmen. Once we can take a deep breath, we both start to cry, so Simone comes to sit on my lap and just bawl. I try to calm her by saying that dad will be back shortly.

They're having a meeting at the boss's house, that's all. She's so bright she doesn't believe me. I'm scared to death they'll hurt Robbie. If they think you've crossed them in any way, you're in trouble.

Everything is about money and loan sharks with these guys. It's all illegal anyway. They don't have bank accounts like ordinary people; the dough is hidden somewhere like all cash under the mattress. It's the way we live.

About an hour after they drag Robbie out, we get a call from him. He sounds muffled.

"Hey Sylvia, I can't talk loud cause I'm bein'

tapped, I'm sure, but the Boss wants to have a meeting with me; I think it's about the loan but not sure. I'll call you back in a few. Are you okay? And Simone? I feel terrible the way these clowns handled it this morning, but, you know, that's their style, rough and love tough. I love you, pussy cat; gotta get off now."

I think to myself: why are they taking him to a meeting? He's got a month to pay off the loan. I really don't get it, but I also kinda do 'cause they're all crooks. They think they can get away with anything and won't get caught by the cops. In fact, the cops get paid off by the mob who have their own phony legal system; what a joke.

Simone stops whimpering and leaves the comfort of my lap. I know she's worried sick about her dad. They are very close and often have "dates" together, like going to the movies, just the two of them.

"What's with these guys taking dad away like that?" says Simone with a query look on her face.

Well, honey, you know this business as well as I do."

How did dad get himself involved with these terrible people anyway?"

"It's very easy, sweetie; he's in a business crawling with bad people; they just suck you in with gifts and promises. He fell for it."

"Mom, do you think dad is like them?" says Simone, turning her head as if she doesn't want to hear.

"Dad has a very casual relationship, and no, it's not the same."

"Then why are they taking him away?"

"That's what we'll find out when dad calls back."

"In the meantime, get yourself ready. You're already late for school."

"Can't I stay home today?"

"Absolutely not!"

Simone gives me a "dirty" look and runs upstairs. About an hour later, I get a call. It's Robbie.

"Hello, pussy cat, not such good news."

"What is it, Robbie? Tell me!"

"Well, they say I stole money from the garbage business, which is owned by one of the Bosses; in other words, they're calling it embezzlement or something like that. But pussy cat, you know me, I wouldn't steal a dime from anyone. I may take out a loan but never steal. I think they're using me as a pawn in this nonsense cause I didn't do nothin'. I think they're tryin' to protect someone else higher up than me and sticking me with the blame."

"Oh, my lord, Robbie! That's terrible," and I begin to shed some tears: I think the worst because I fear being alone with Simone, and it's like death in a way. "I know you're not a thief, I swear, but what's going to happen? Are we all in danger?"

"I hope not. But just in case, I'll plead with Eddie to get an extra body guard to watch our house."

"That's so scary, Robbie; Simone will be devastated. What will they do with you?"

"Well, they can't call the cops because they're all guilty of various crimes, like knocking people off and such, so I don't know yet; they're tryin' to figure it out, but they're not too pleased I can tell you that."

"I'm sure of that, my poor Robbie."

"I don't know what to say, never been in trouble before, and I'm innocent, I swear."

"I believe you, Robbie, honest I do. It's just that my head is spinning right now. Will you lose your job?'

"They may put me on probation for a time, but I might still get some pay. It depends on the big guys and what they say, you know."

"What am I going to tell Simone when she gets home from school?"

"Just tell her I'm still meeting with the Boss, and I'll be home a little late, okay?"

"Okay, Robbie, I'm really scared to death, so don't forget to call when you know something."

I hang up the phone and run to the kitchen to get some red wine to soothe my mind. I am stunned and shaky and need to sort this out. All I can think of is Donny, who got killed because he crossed one of the bosses; is that how they punish people who wrong them?

I know they pay off the cops like crazy, so the cops turn a cheek. They usually stay out of each other's way. Did Robbie steal money from the company? He is always worried about loans and such.

No, he wouldn't do anything like that; or would he? My Robbie, the sweetest husband and father in the world? I drink some more wine and try to believe that Robbie is completely innocent. I will honor Robbie's words to me and say nothing to Simone.

"Hi, I'm home!"

"Oh, hi sweetheart, how was your day at school?"

"Fine, how come you're drinking wine in the afternoon, mom?" says Simone with a strange look on her face.

"Oh, I just feel like it; I've done this before. Did you have any tests today?"

"No, just lectures all day, pretty boring, I must say. What's for dinner tonight?"

"Actually, I forgot to take something from the freezer."

"You never do that, mom. What's going on? Are you drunk?" says Simone as she stares at the wine bottle.

"No, sweetheart, just worried about dad and busy trying to find a job."

"Any luck in the job market, mom?"

"Two possibilities. One at a women's shoe store, the other at a jewelry store."

"When will you know? Dad is already nervous about money."

"I know, Simone, but we'll all be okay. By the way, dad called and said he'd be late in these meetings and not to wait for him to eat dinner."

"Is he okay?" Cause those rotten guys were awful to him this morning," says Simone, with a look of fear.

"Yes dear, he's okay; he called twice, and he

seems pretty confident that The Boss won't be rough with him. How about since it's just you and me, we order a pizza and pick it up."

"Sounds good to me, mom. You still have a weird, worried look on your face. Hope everything is cool."

"What kind of pizza would you like, Simone? I'll call in for a pick-up."

"Since I know you're nervous and sad, mom, you pick the kind of pizza you like, okay?" Simone replies with a bit of a smile on her rosy cheeks.

"Okay, how about a large with olives, peppers, sausage, and extra cheese?"

"Wonderful, mom, great choice. I'll keep you company on the ride."

So, I call for the pizza, and it's about twenty minutes 'til it's ready. There is a rather long silence between us while waiting. I'm picking at my fingers, and Simone is reading a textbook.

"Maybe if we get a large one, we can save some for dad. How late did you say he would be home?"

"He didn't really say, but I'm guessing maybe nine or ten."

"Mom, what's the worst thing they can do to dad?" Simone queries, hands folded but shaky.

"I don't even want to think like that, Simone. It's too worrisome."

"Would they kill him?"

"Let's not talk about it, please."

"Now, where's my wine? I think I'll have another glass. We have to leave soon. I'll guzzle it up."

Simone finds it and pours me about a third. I know she doesn't want me driving tipsy.

We pick up the piping hot pizza and drive home. No word from Robbie yet. I feel sick to my stomach, and I only nibble at the pizza while Simone is starving and dives right in. After eating, we listen to some music, and then she excuses herself to do homework.

I'm still sipping my red wine and feeling calmer. But, by ten o'clock, still no word from Robbie, and there's no one to call; wait, maybe Eddie knows. I try to call, but no answer.

I pace the floor and light up a cigarette, which I rarely do. I go upstairs to find Simone, and she is fast asleep, light on, book in hand. I quietly take the book and turn out the light.

Now I'm alone in my dreadful thoughts, even more so than earlier in the day. It's midnight, and Robbie is not home yet, and no phone call. I don't even know where they took him.

I wait up until two am, smoking and pacing the floor, peeking out the window now and then to look for the car to pull up any minute, but it doesn't.

I think to myself: has he been in an accident? If so, then someone would call me or come to the house. Anyway, I go upstairs to the bathroom and decide to take a sleeping pill, hoping that Robbie will be by my side when I wake up.

6

MARIA

I wake up at seven am every single morning, just used to it. The kids are up anyway, all four of them, two in elementary school and two in middle school; a lot of noise around this house. I'm the second youngest of us eight kids, and boy did I get picked on when I was a mere child.

The older kids picked on the younger ones, so I got creamed on the second most. It's like "hand-me-down" clothes too; by the time they get to me, they're like rags. Now that we're all adults, I get protected a lot as the second "baby" of Joe and Tess, may they rest in peace.

My hubby, Jim, owns a dry-cleaning company on Staten Island and has about ten employees, friendly people, mostly Italians like us. We're the outcasts cause the rest of the family lives in Brooklyn and Harlem.

Jim is lucky that he doesn't have to commute to

Manhattan for work. Our family is very close, and we see each other a lot, switch off houses to have pot luck dinners on Sundays because we have so many people to feed. UH! The phone is ringing. Gotta get it.

"Hello!"

"Maria, this is Sylvia," she sniffles on the phone. "I'm sorry to bother you so early, but Robbie never came home last night. Two head guys picked him up yesterday morning and literally dragged him out of the house with me and Simone watching in horror. They pushed him into a black sedan and blasted off. I only heard from him twice, and he said he'd be home last night but never showed." Sylvia continues to sob intermittently.

"Oh no, that's awful, Sylvia dear," I say in a nervous tone. "Why are they after him, do you know?"

"Have no idea, but when he called, he said something about stealing money from his company. I'm so scared, but I don't want to show Simone my real feelings. She keeps asking for him and is horrified that they might kill him."

"Now, I want you to calm down. I'll stay on the phone," says I in a comforting tone. "I think the boys might just be questioning a whole bunch of people to see who the culprit really is. So, don't get into an uproar yet; this is standard stuff for them, you know that. It may take days before they really know something, right?"

"Right," says Sylvia in a weakened voice. "But

why didn't he call last night to tell me he's not coming home?"

"You know the deal here, Sylvia, we all know, so don't panic yet. I know you're in Brooklyn, but how about coming over, we can chat, and that may console you a bit. Take the rail, and I'll make lunch for both of us while we wait for a call. Bring your car phone with you."

"Well, I guess that might be a good idea," says Sylvia with a bit of hesitancy. "Simone has a key to the house, and I'll leave her a note. See you soon."

After Sylva hangs up, I start trembling a little, unsure what the deal is here with Robbie. Maybe it's just nothing, or maybe it's serious, hard to call the shots with the little I know. I wonder if Pete or the others know anything. I think I'll make a quick call to Pete before Sylvia gets here. I think I have his work number. Yup, I got it.

"Hello, this is Maria, Peter's sister. Is he there?"

"Yes, I believe he is; just a moment while I track him down."

"Thank you," says Maria waiting impatiently.

"Hello, sis?

"Yup, it's me; some kind of trouble is brewing around our family; Robbie is missing."

"What? What happened? Tell me." He seems distressed.

"I have few details, but I got a call from Sylvia this morning, practically in hysterics, that Robbie was dragged out of the house yesterday morning by two bosses and shoved into a car. He didn't return last night but did call twice. He's thinking embezzlement charges, that he stole money from his own company, which is part of the "group," you know?"

"I find it hard to believe that Robbie would do that," Pete paces the floor; "They're probably questioning him and maybe brain-washing him, who knows? That's really awful; I can imagine how Sylvia and Simone feel, probably terrified. I'll see what I can find out through the chain of command. I'll be in touch if I'm lucky. Say hi to Sylvia, and you take care."

"Thanks, Pete, you're such a great brother, you know that?"

"Well, this is a bit scary, so let's all be vigilant, okay?"

"Okay, Pete, thanks for your help, goodbye" and hangs up the phone with a quizzical look.

I'm feeling a little relieved that Pete has some positive influence on them, but maybe not enough; we'll just have to be patient, which is difficult for all of us.

I'm going to make a couple of salami sandwiches for lunch and, depending on Sylvia's state of mind, either sweet iced tea or a glass of red wine. I feel terrible for Simone, too, because I know she's scared and so close to her dad that it's probably hard to focus on her school work.

I'm just thinking, as well as I know my brother, you don't know what goes on in people's minds.

Sometimes they're desperate and want to protect their families and will do something stupid; I can't figure Robbie out.

We're all in the same boat in a way, and we're always looking over our backs too. I think I'll pray for Robbie tonight before bedtime.

The doorbell rings.

"I'm coming, just a minute." I don't know what to expect from Sylvia. "Hi sweetie, please come in and take off your coat."

Sylvia collapses in my arms, sniffling.

"Aw, come on now, we'll find Robbie soon enough. I know it's so scary, believe me." I keep patting Sylvia on the back, trying to reassure her. Frankly, I'm scared to death myself.

She clings to me for about five minutes, whimpering, then lifts her head, eyes red, cheeks flushed, just stares at me.

"I made lunch for us; your favorite sandwich, salami with mustard and a pickle on the side."

Sylvia says nothing, no reaction at all. She sits at the kitchen table with a blank face.

"Are you a little hungry? Maybe just eat half the sandwich. I made sweet iced tea, or would you like to have a glass of your favorite red wine. Which will it be?"

Sylvia sits at the table and fiddles with her sandwich, not really that interested in it.

"I'll have some red wine, please," she finally decides.

"Great, I'll open a new bottle, and I think I'll have some too."

Sylvia remains silent for about two or three minutes.

"I just don't know what to do about Robbie's absence," says Sylvia acting anxious and shaky.

"There is nothing we can do at the moment, and I do feel for you; if it were me, I'd be in hysterics, weeping all day. I think you're handling it better than me for sure. Have a sip of wine Syl...maybe that will calm you."

Sylvia looks in her purse, takes out a cigarette, and lights it. She blows rings of smoke around the kitchen. Then she slugs her wine rather hastily as if she wants more.

"Oh, guess what?"

No reply from Sylvia.

"I called Pete at work and told him what is going on with Robbie and all; naturally, he is distraught, but he promises he will speak to the Boss as soon as possible; can't promise anything, but he'll do his best to help. Look, we're all in this. We're a family who sticks together. I think Pete is owed favors, so this might help a lot."

Sylvia sighs and takes a deep breath while continuing to smoke her cigarette.

"How should I handle Simone, though?" Sylvia says with hesitation.

"I think she's old enough to understand some things about this disaster. But I wouldn't go into the gory details. It's too upsetting."

"Well, she saw the thugs drag Robbie out yesterday morning. She knows they're taking him somewhere, and it's not to the movies; she's very intuitive and scared to death."

"In my opinion, I would just say that he's in a conference all week with the big guys, in case he doesn't return tonight."

"She'll never believe me, Maria; I can't even talk about it anymore. It's so sickening."

While Maria answers the phone, Sylvia sneaks in another glass of wine.

"Hello! Oh, Pete, so happy you got back to me. What's up? What? No, they can't…"

Sylvia jumps up to get near the phone. She is visibly shaking.

"Well, aren't you owed some favors or something? Ah-ha, I see. Do you want to talk to Sylvia? she's right here near the phone."

Sylvia grabs the phone.

"Pete? Is it bad news?" She listens intently, hangs up, and drops to her knees. I sit on the floor with my arm around Sylvia's shoulder. We sit in silence for a while. I'm afraid to leave her alone at this moment. I hear whimpers and sniffles.

"Would you like some more wine, Syl?"

No answer; she may be in shock. I grab the phone and call Pete.

"Hello, Pete, it's me, Maria. Can you talk?"
"Not really; how is Sylvia?"
"In shock, what should I do?"

"Stay with her until she's better, the get cold washcloths for her forehead. I'll try to call soon."

I tell Sylvia that I'm coming right back with some cold washcloths. I don't see her move at all, just hunched over, hair surrounding her face.

7

FRANKIE

ONE WEEK LATER

Robbie is still missing, and we're waiting for some news, hopin' that it is good news. But I have to tell you that Sylvia is takin' it real hard, and so is our whole family. Simone is depressed and not eating.

We talk to them every day, and we take turns visitin', not a pretty scene. In my opinion, missing for a week is not a good sign, especially in the company of the bosses. I don't think they killed him, but they may be brain-washin' him and maiming him in some way. I know this cause I've seen it before in my company and with some acquaintances.

Speakin' of my company, I'm an assistant manager in the cement business in Brooklyn, where we live. My job is to ensure the trucks are correctly loaded and sent off to building sites. My pay is okay, nothin' to brag about, but I can pay the mortgage and feed my family, which by the way consists of my wife Anna and two kids, Frankie Jr, eleven, and Gracie, eight.

At the moment, me and Anna are not getting along so well, and we're thinking of separatin'. We know this will hurt the kids, but it's a friendly partin', so I don't think it will that bad. Neither of us has been happy together for the last several years, so we think it's for the best.

I, of course, will be the one to move out, so I'll have to start lookin' for a two-bedroom apartment near the house so the kids can walk to see me. They won't have to change schools, and my work is flexible, so I can pick them up sometimes.

"Anna! Is this clean or dirty laundry?"

"It's clean. You can fold your own laundry."

"Wow, things have changed around here. I used to get my laundry folded really nicely. What happened?"

"I think you should start learning how to do it yourself, right?"

"I guess so, Anna, but while we're still livin' together, can you please be nice to me?"

"We'll have to talk, Frankie; I think it's time to find a place and move out," says Anna with a scorned looked on her face.

"When do we tell the kids?"

Anna gives me a strange look. "Maybe at dinner tonight. What do you think?"

I think about it for a second. "Okay, Anna, tonight it is."

At the dinner table, we all pray before eatin', each child saying their own prayer.

"Dad," says Frankie Jr., "how is aunt Sylvia feeling? She must really be freaking out. Even I feel jittery and nervous about Uncle Robbie's mysterious whereabouts."

"We all do," says I, "but let's not dwell on it at dinner, okay?"

"Wait a minute there," says Anna as she pushes her plate away, "the kid is upset, Frankie, don't you have any feelings?"

"Listen, Anna, let's try to be civil at the dinner table, okay?" I can't believe she is pullin' this stuff.

We eat the rest of our dinner in silence. The kids are just pushin' their food around the plates.

Anna clears the dishes and kicks the door open to the kitchen cause I guess she's mad as hell. The kids and I look at each other with funny faces. Oops, here she comes, and we all straighten up in our seats.

"We're havin' a gelatin dessert with whipped cream." As she passes out the plates, Anna sits down and serves each of us some gelatin. The kids are not too happy with this dessert, and they delay picking up their spoons. The kids look at me and smirk.

"Okay then," says Anna with an assured look on her face. "Kids, mom and dad want to speak to you about something important."

Couldn't she have waited a bit longer, I'm thinkin'.

"Frankie, do you want to start first?"

The phone rings.

"I'll get it. Hello? Sylvia? Yes, really? Okay, I'll be right there."

"It's Sylvia on the phone, Simone is havin' a nervous breakdown, and she needs help. I'm leavin' now, don't know exactly what time I'll return."

"But..." says Anna in a loud voice.

"See ya later, guys." and I slam the door.

On the way over to Sylvia's, I'm thinkin' Anna's gonna screw up this whole separation thing if she's not careful. Kids are naïve and may not take it too well. We have to plan it at a better time.

I arrive at Sylvia's place, and she's standin' right at the entrance. She looks awful, very pale and skinny, and I just saw her three days ago.

"Thank the Lord you're here Frankie, Simone is in like a trance after bawlin' her head off for about thirty minutes. She's all balled up in her bed and won't speak."

"I'll go upstairs with you and see what I can do." I knock on the door, no answer, so I knock again. Then slowly, I open it and see Simone in a fetal position, moanin' and mutterin' to herself. I go over to her, sit on the bed, and gently put my hand on her hair, strokin' it.

"Uncle Frankie here Simone, can we talk?" No response. I wait another minute and repeat myself.

No response. Then she turns to look at me with red eyes and blotchy cheeks.

"My dad is gone forever, I know it," she says in a teary voice, snifflin' all the while. "They took him and threw him in the garbage dump," now cryin'. "That's what these guys do," more snifflin'.

"We don't know that for sure sweetie, he could be fine, just being questioned. I know it seems like a long time, but that's the way this system works. I'm sure he'll be calling any day now with some good news." I'm probably telling a lie, but she needs to calm down.

After a few minutes of snifflin' and blowin' her nose, Simone calms down. She sits on her bed in a yoga position with a very blank look on her face, almost like she's back in her trance. Sylvia sits next to her and strokes her hair. Every minute or two, she kisses her wet cheeks.

Simone begins to mutter some words: "I know he's dead. I know he's dead." Then she is back in her trance.

Sylvia decides to call the doctor to see if there is medicine she can get her that would help. I sit with her while Sylvia leaves the room. I think this is not the time to be talkin' about my separation with Anna when all this other stuff is going on.

Sylvia returns to Simone's room with information about some medicine, looking pale.

"What did the doc say?"

"Well, they're going to call in a prescription for a medicine, which will help her a lot."

"That's a good idea. Do you want me to stay a while?"

"No, that's okay. You need to get back home, Frankie. I was just really scared to death about Simone, and I guess I was feeling lonely without Robbie here." She begins to weep.

I hug Sylvia and pat her on the back, trying to soothe her for whatever it's worth.

"I know what you're goin' through, Sylvia, and it's real hard, but I think Robbie will be released soon cause I think he's innocent, didn't steal anythin' from the company. But the bosses have to find the culprit, and he's low on the ladder, so they're torturin' him."

"Oh no! How do you know this, Frankie?"

"Because I know how their organization works, that's how."

Sylvia begins to weep with hands over her eyes. I try to console her again, and then I get a glass of her favorite red wine.

"Here, try this. I know it will ease your sufferin', right?"

She sniffles, blows her nose, and takes the glass from my unsteady hand.

I tell her that I'll keep in touch every day, give her another kiss and leave. I don't know what else to tell them, but now I'm getting worried about Robbie

On the way home on the elevator, I think maybe I should give Pete a call this evening cause he might just have some new information on Robbie.

"Hi, I'm home, everybody."

Anna shouts out: "Yeah? So what!"

"That's a lovely greetin', my dear Anna, couldn't be more pleasant."

Anna shows up with a beer in her hand and one for me.

"Where are the kids?"

"Up in their rooms doing homework."

"How's Simone taking all of this terrible drama?"

"Not too well. She thinks they killed her father."

"Well, that could be true, right?"

"Don't ever talk like that, Anna! It's not true, and you don't know what's goin' on. You act as if you don't care. All you want is a separation from me. That's what's on your little mind. Well, let me tell you somethin', the most important thing right now is gettin' Robbie home alive! And I don't want to hear about our marriage until Robbie's situation is resolved, and if you don't like it, you can leave."

And I stomp out of the house, walk around the corner and go to our neighborhood bar to think and drink.

8

TOMMY

TWO WEEKS LATER

I hate to tell you, but Robbie has not come home, nor have we heard a word from him. Pete is doing everything he can, without getting into trouble, to get information on the whereabouts of Robbie. He's made phone calls to certain "people" and has even paid a visit to one of the big guys.

Unfortunately, we can't get much information, and it's so awful for our whole family, especially Sylvia and Simone. I talk to Sylvia almost every day, and she is in deep depression, thankfully taking some medicine for it.

Simone is also taking meds and still feels that her father is dead. What a horrible thought. Don't get me wrong, we're not negating that thought, but we're trying to push it away. I promise my family that this will conclude soon.

I live in Brooklyn with my wife Angela and five kids, too many to name. Don't get me wrong, they're all great kids, as far as kids go, you know. My wife is to die for, taller than me, short blonde hair (dyed, of course), a turned-up nose (that's not Italian), beautiful skin, and shapely legs, who could ask for more.

We're the same age, but she looks so young even our family can't believe it. Three of my kids look like her, and the other two look like me, poor things. Our row house is a little tight, so the kids have to double up on rooms, but they get along, so it's not so bad. We have a small backyard and a basketball hoop which the kids are crazy about, and they use it even in winter.

I own my own taxi, so my hours are flexible. Usually, I drive during the day when the kids are in school, at least some of them. It costs a chunk of money to get a cab license, but it's paying me back cause I have a lot of customers in New York City, and they tip well.

There are many Bosses in the taxi business, so you still gotta watch out for yourself. They're into everybody's business, especially in Brooklyn, but I can spot them like a hawk, so I just stay as clean as I can and out of their way.

One family hobby is fishing on one of the piers in Brooklyn. My oldest three spend Saturdays getting their poles ready, and off we go to the pier. I'm lucky cause I just drive my taxi right up to the parking area, no buses, subways, nothing.

Sometimes we even catch fish! I let the boys go up to the hot dog stand and buy lunch, which they enjoy. Unfortunately, Angela hates fish, so even when we catch some, we throw them back, or else I'm thrown out of the house.

Don't get me wrong, Angela is a great cook, and mostly she makes chicken, beef stew, or I can cook outdoors on our small grill, but she detests the smell of fish.

Phone rings.

"Hello, yo, Pete, what's going on?" Of course, I'm thinking the worst.

"Just checking in. How's my bro?"

"That's not why you're calling Pete. Come on. You got something to say, I know."

"Well," says Pete with a scratchy voice.

I'm starting to get some information on Robbie. Spoke to Johnnie, and all he told me was that Robbie is alive. Don't get too excited. We don't know what condition he's in, could be bad, but I'm still digging."

"Hey Pete, yeah, go on, tell me more." I feel very agitated.

"They're still questioning him, and I think he might have some injuries, but I'm not sure what."

"Who told you he might have some injuries?"

"Johnnie told me, but then he hung up," says Pete with remorse in his voice.

"Geez, that's awful, Pete. Now we'll be biting our nails until we know something true, right?"

"What should we tell Sylvia, Pete?"

"If you want to call her, I would just say that Robbie is alive, period, end of the report, even though she'll ask a million questions."

"You think it's okay if I call her?"

"Of course," says Pete, with some encouragement.

"Promise to call me the minute you know some more news, okay?"

"I will do that for sure, bro, don't worry. Think positive even though it's tough."

"Okay, Pete, thanks," and I hang up, thinking about my next maneuver. I feel an obligation to call Sylvia. It's the right thing to do, but I'll be very vague and not lead her to think the worst, but first I'll tell Angela.

My sweet Angela is cooking up a storm in the kitchen, which smells like meatballs.

"How's my beautiful wife doing? It's like an Italian kitchen." I take a ladle spoon and dip it into the sauce, nice and thick with a bit of spice.

My hands are shaking, but she can't see them, thinking what to say to Angela. I hate to lie to my wife, and she's pretty good about keeping secrets, so I think I'll tell her what Pete told me.

"Angela, honey, I have something important to tell you, but lips sealed, you promise?"

"Of course, Tommy, you look so pale and shaky. What's up?"

I pause for a few seconds getting up my courage to tell her she's kinda weak and I don't want to scare her. I clear my throat.

"Well, I heard from Pete earlier today when you were cooking." I feel a bit nauseous.

"What, what? Tell me."

"Well, Pete got a call from Boss Johnnie, and Robbie is alive!!"

"Thank the Lord," says Angela with a wide smile on her face. "I'm so happy, can we call Sylvia? She'll be ecstatic, I know. Tell me more details."

"Well, he's alive but with injuries, and we don't know what they are, according to Pete."

"Oh, that's horrible, scary," says Angela, with a fearsome look on her face. "What could they do to him?"

"Oh, many things, they're so sickening I don't even want to mention it."

"Should we call Sylvia right away?"

"I guess we should go over there because she will need support, and so will Simone."

"Well, it's around five pm now, maybe after we eat; we'll leave the boys here. Billy is old enough to take care of the rest, I think."

"Of course, he is, don't be silly. He's very responsible."

"Really? I'm just kidding. He really is a good kid."

We clean up the kitchen, make sure the kids aren't fighting, and jump in the taxi to take off for Sylvia's place, a short drive. My stomach is very jittery, and I don't know what to expect from Sylvia. We Park right in front of her row house and ring the bell.

Simone opens the door, sort of shocked to see us but greets us with a half-smile. "Hi Uncle Tommy, what's up?"

"Hello, you pretty girl, where's your mom?"

"In the kitchen cooking and drinking red wine, as usual.

"How's my sis-in-law doing today?"

"What are you doing here so suddenly? Without calling, you're scaring me."

"Simone, come in the kitchen, please," says Sylvia with a nervous-sounding voice.

"Okay, I'm coming."

We sit down at the kitchen table. I'm thinking, how should I begin? A few seconds of silence.

"Sylvia and Simone, I have some good news for you."

Sylvia jumps up from her chair and starts to hug me. Simone is quiet and listening.

"Wait, wait, wait, let me tell you what it is first. Pete got word from boss Johnnie that Robbie is alive, but nothing else, no details and hangs up."

"Oh, but that's wonderful news, Tommy!" Sylvia starts crying for joy.

Simone goes to hug Sylvia.

"See," Sylvia says while wiping her tears, "I told you, Simone, that dad was not dead, that you have to keep hoping all the time that he is still alive. Do you know when they will release him?" Sylvia asks with a croaky voice while Simone weeps.

"No word from Pete, my dear, but maybe more

information tomorrow. Let's all have a glass of wine to celebrate that Robbie is alive. Sylvia, will you do the honors? We'll even give Simone a small glass."

Simone has a quizzical look on her face like she doesn't believe a word I said. I bet that she still thinks he's dead, and they are telling lies to keep us quiet. We toast to the good news, drink our wine, and leave.

On our way home, me and Angela talk about the discussion we had with Sylvia and Simone.

"So, how do you think I handled myself?"

"I think you did a great job, Tommy. The only thing you left out is that they maimed Robbie in some way."

"I know, that will have to come later."

"It's like we're lying to her, Tommy."

"No, we're just not telling her everything yet; she's still in distress, and we need to do things slowly."

"Let's go home and have a stiff drink."

9

MARGARET

TWO DAYS LATER

The phone has been dead. Two days ago, we heard that Robbie was alive and now, silence. So, we're all nervous and jerky and can hardly mention Robbie's name without tears in our eyes.

We're all asking questions, especially to Pete and Sylvia, but no answers yet. You would think by now that we'd have some concrete information because Pete has the most ties to the Boss, and they owe him a favor, as I understand it. Oh well, we all have to be patient, even though we aren't, and I'm probably the most anxious next to Sylvia and Simone.

Guess what? I live in Brooklyn, too, along with my hubby Ted. We have three kids in middle school, only one year apart. Boy, we worked hard those three years, and even now, they're triple trouble, but we love them to death. Ken is the oldest, about to go to high school next year. Then, there's Mary in seventh grade (a genius), and finally, Chris in sixth grade, who is most handsome.

We live near the school so the kids can walk there, though sometimes my sweet Ted will drive them cause they can be lazy. Sometimes the kids stop at a drug store/soda fountain after school and don't get home until almost dinner. I think they sit and chat and maybe go to the park two blocks away. I hope they are behaving!

Ted owns a pawn shop in Brooklyn. It's been in his family for many years; he got ownership after his father passed away. He sells all kinds of junk (well, I call it junk!) We sell guns and gold and jewelry and stuff.

We have a sliding gate that Ted puts up at the closing time because it is not the best neighborhood, and the crazies tend to steal from pawn shops.

Sometimes if it's real busy, I will help sell stuff, but real weirdos come in, and they scare me. Sometimes, a policeman will stop by and ask if everything is okay, making me feel safer.

It's a Friday afternoon, and I'm at the store with Ted, as it's bustling. Mostly, people are looking and testing guns. I don't mean they're shooting them, just touching them. I help a guy looking for a used piece of jewelry for his wife. I show him several rings, bracelets, and necklaces, and he tends to dawdle handling every piece.

Finally, after what seems like an hour, he chooses a cheap bracelet, not real gold and I wrap it up, and he pays cash. That's all we take here, no credit cards and definitely no personal checks. We've been burned before, never again.

"So, what do you think, we should wrap it up for the day?" says Ted in a cheerful voice.

I look at my watch, and it's five-thirty pm.

"Yes, my dear, I think it's time to hit the road."

We put valuable stuff away from the window facing the street, grab our personal things, put up the "closed" sign, and swing the gate shut. We walk home hand in hand, glad the day is over. It's stressful working in a pawn shop with too many strange characters.

"We're home, kids," Ted says, happy to see his three adorable nuts.

I'll start dinner. You check on the kids and make sure they're doing their homework."

As I'm making a meatloaf for dinner, I get a call from Pete.

"Hi Pete, I was just going to make my daily call to you, but you beat me to it. What's up?"

"Well, I got a quick call from Boss Johnnie, and he told me that they don't think Robbie is the suspect, but here's the bad part, they smashed in all of his teeth before they knew for sure. He's in pretty bad shape physically and mentally. They told me that my favor is I could go see him, but they're not ready to let him go for a few more days."

Silence.

"Are you still there, Margaret?"

I feel as if I'm going to throw up.

"Yeah, geez, I can't believe it. That's like torture, it's horrible, Pete, and that's the big favor that you can go see your beaten-up brother?"

"Yup, that's it. I didn't want to cross these guys; you want me alive, right?"

"Of course, I do, but I can't believe these guys. They're so cruel."

I'm thinking of what Robbie looks like, poor brother.

"Pete? When are you going to see him?" My voice is shaky, and I have a tear in my eye.

"Probably tomorrow if I can get off work; Johnnie said to be there at ten am sharp."

"Do you think I can come with you?" I feel dizzy and afraid they may do something else to Robbie.

"Well, you could escort me for sure, but whether they will let you see him is something else. We can try, so meet me at work, and we'll go together. Don't tell anyone else, or Sylvia will have a freak-out, okay?"

"Of course, I understand."

My meat loaf is still cooking. I check on it and go to the den where Ted is watching TV. I'm scared to talk about Robbie, but Ted should know.

I sit next to him on the loveseat, curl my head in his neck. Silence. "Ted?"

"What is it? You look so pale and feel clammy."

"I just got off the phone with Pete, and he told me that Boss Johnnie told him that Robbie got his teeth smashed in and they won't bring him home for a few more days. Pete is allowed to see him tomorrow, and I'm going to try to get in with Pete."

"Oh, my goodness, that's horrific, those dirty crooks, they'll do almost anything to get you to talk. I'm sick of this whole thing," says Ted with an angry-looking face. "Does Sylvia know?"

"No, nobody, except Pete, you and me. We made a pact not to say anything yet."

"I think it's a good idea for you to go and support Pete."

I'm so glad he said that. He's so understanding. I just love that man.

The next day, I make breakfast for the family, and my hands shake as I turn the eggs. I hope nobody notices; I mean the kids.

"Mom, you're shaking. What's wrong with you?" says Ken, the oldest, with a questioning look on his face.

"Nothing, I just didn't get enough sleep last night, that's all, so a bit shaky. Did you guys get your homework done and backpacks stuffed?"

They all said yes, mom, and ate their breakfast. After they left for school, Ted and I talked about Robbie.

"I hope you have the stomach for this, Margaret. It's pretty nasty, you know?"

"Yeah, I know, maybe they won't let me in, but I

really want to see him. He's my brother! Well, I've got to get ready to meet Pete at his office, so I'll see you later. Wish me good luck, honey, because I need it."

I'm feeling squeamish as I head toward Ted to plant a kiss on his forehead.

"Goodbye, my sweet Ted. I'll keep you posted, okay?"

"Yes, darling, and be very careful. Those guys are nuts."

I leave the house and take the rail to Pete's office. I'm sweating like a pig, and it's fifty degrees out! Pete is waiting for me in the lobby. I guess he sees my pale face.

"Calm down, Margaret, we have to act civil, not all teary and freaked out."

We arrive at the Boss' brownstone row house in Brooklyn. His house looks like a mansion compared to any of ours. He's been known to have some kind of dungeon in the basement where he interrogates his "subjects." I feel like my hands are all clammy, and my throat is closing up. Pete takes my clammy hand and tells me not to worry.

Pete rings the bell, and we wait about a minute. A well-dressed butler-type man greets us. Pete does all the talking, and I kind of hide behind him.

"We have an appointment with Boss Johnnie at ten am," Pete says.

"And who are you?"

"I am an acquaintance, sir, and this is my sister," Pete says.

"Step in. I'll let the boss know you're here."

We wait in a dark hallway with no seats for about ten minutes, then finally we are asked to follow this gentleman. The place is a maze with antique furniture and walls covered in wallpaper. Finally, we get to Boss Johnnie's office, a sprawling room with more antique furniture and paintings of the clan.

"What can I do for you, Pete?" as he smokes his cigar.

"Well, sir, this is my sister, Margaret, and we got permission from you to visit our brother Robbie who has been here a long time."

"I see," says the Boss with smoke rings coming from his mouth, puffing away. "Yeah, you might not recognize him too well, kinda beat up, you know?"

"That's quite alright," says Pete. "We're ready," as I'm trembling like crazy standing there, feeling like I have to pee.

"Okay then," says the Boss. "You asked for it," as he puffs away and smiles.

"Take them to see Mr. Robbie."

The butler-type gentleman takes us through more mazes, then downstairs, where it gets darker and darker. Finally, he opens a door, and our brother is sitting on a wooden chair.

I get dizzy and fall into Pete's arms. As he pulls me up, I begin to scream.

10

DANNY

I could practically hear those screams at my house because I live near Margaret. She went with Pete to see Robbie; now I feel it was wrong for her to do. Pete dropped her off at home, and boy was she a mess. Ted (her hubby) told me he could hardly understand her words.

She goes running to him, muttering, holding on real tight. He just lets her bawl before Ted opens his mouth, or she gets over her crying. Minutes go by, and she finally calms down, sits on Ted's lap. Whew, what a scene that must be.

I heard all this from Pete, who was with Margaret, my sister. Yeah, Pete calls me after he drops off Margaret. Poor thing, she had to actually witness this mess. Thank God Pete was with her. Pete and I discussed how to break these awful details to Sylvia.

So, here is the gruesome news: the bosses smash Robbie's teeth out, then they break his nose, punch him in the eye and smash his ears. That's, of course, according to what Pete saw and heard from Johnnie, finally.

When I hear what Pete says, now I feel weak and dizzy, have to sit down and pour some bourbon for myself. I work at home for a business, kind of keep the books. I'm the only bachelor in the family. I make a good living and try to help my family. We're all very close, you know.

The phone rings.

"Hey, Pete, still standing?"

"Barely," says Pete with a tired voice. "It really is a mess, and I'm trying to think of the best way to tell Sylvia and Simone."

"I'm willing to go with you, being that I'm still a lonely bachelor with few obligations, ha- ha."

"I'd like that, and I know that Sylvia would appreciate your presence. Let's see. It's about four-thirty pm now. We could meet at Joe's bar at five-thirty pm, get a table and figure out the scheme, yes?"

"Yeah, that sounds fine. I should be able to leave my office by then."

"Okay then," says Pete, "see you at Joe's."

I hang up. I'm thinking, how the heck are we going to tell Sylvia all the gory details? She'll faint, but she's fainted before, so I guess she can handle it, even if she faints again.

I take the rail to meet Pete at Joe's bar in Brooklyn. It's an old raunchy place but has some character, peanut shells on the floor, tables with uncomfortable wooden chairs, and a large bar that runs the length of the place.

People tend to stand at the bar, those heavy drinkers, but we'll sit at a table like gentlemen. I arrive before Pete and order Bourbon and soda, my favorite drink, and tip the barmaid before Pete arrives. I let her know another person should be here shortly. Probably got stuck in traffic.

Here comes Pete, now ambling with a kind of frown on his face. He doesn't look happy.

"HI there, brother, how are ya, kid"?

"Tired and worried, I guess," says Pete as he looks around the place, trying to find a barmaid. "Guess I'll just wait 'til she comes around. In the meantime, we can chat."

The barmaid comes along just as we begin our conversation.

"Can I help you guys?"

Pete says, "I'd like a drink, please, and another one for my buddy here."

"That would be Bourbon and soda, right?"

Pete nods, and she waddles away, thinking, boy does she have a big ass on her.

"Well, let's think about our scheme," says Pete, seemingly ready to fly.

"I think Robbie will be home in three days, so we have to prepare Sylvia and Simone, not surprise them. They already know that the boss had his teeth smashed in, but they don't know about the broken nose, the blackened eye, and the smashed ears, which could be a bigger injury than we think, and his emotional status too."

"Okay, so when should we tell them? I don't think Margaret should go. She's too emotional and weak. Come to think of it, maybe just you and I go, leave the girls out of it, and we can't have too many people mixing the broth, you know?"

The barmaid comes with the drinks.

After a little more conversation, Pete and I develop a plan.

According to boss Johnnie, Pete will call the boss after our visit to make sure of the release date, but he's pretty sure it will be in three days. Then we'll tell the rest of our sibs that we think only two people should go to Sylvia's place.

Then, sometime tomorrow, around five pm, we will go with a large bottle of red wine. She needs some advance notice and has to learn the gory details so she's prepared for the worst and may need to make doc and dentist appointments, or even a hospital visit, who knows. Robbie is in pretty bad shape.

THE NEXT DAY

I call Pete around four-thirty pm to make sure we're still on for Sylvia's house, which he confirms. I decide to take a taxi, and we're going to meet outside the house and go in together.

I see Pete coming now, and we're both a little

nervous about doing this job. I ring the bell, wait a few seconds, then ring again. Sylvia opens the door.

"Oh, my goodness, what are you two bros' doing here? Want to stay for dinner? I'm making pot roast, plenty for everybody." I'm thinking, when do we tell her, but I'll let Pete take the lead.

"We were in the neighborhood, so we went to a liquor store and bought some red wine, your favorite," says Pete.

"That's lovely," says Sylvia with a half-smile on her face. "Is there something else that you came to tell me?"

"Let's sit down and open the wine. By the way, where is Simone?" says Pete

"She's upstairs. I call for her. Simone! Please come down. Your two uncles are here."

Simone comes running down the stairs, gives each uncle a peck on the cheek.

"Sit down with us, honey. We're having a discussion."

"What discussion?" says Simone with a worried look on her face. "You mean about Dad?"

"Yes," says Pete in a very soft voice. I feel awful to have to break this news

I open the wine bottle and pour four glasses, one half for Simone.

"Don't tell me he died," says Simone, as her cheeks begin to flush. "I always knew it."

She sits with us with her head bowed. I'm glad Pete is doing this, not me. I'm a wimp.

Sylvia looks pale and very drawn.

Pete clears his throat. "The good news is that Robbie is alive! The not-so-good news is that he is injured."

Sylvia gasps, and Simone covers her eyes with her hands.

"It's so painful to hear this and to wait all this time," Sylvia starts weeping softly.

Simone goes over to comfort her, puts her arms around her mother.

Pete continues. "I know it's really hard, Sylvia. Do you want me to say more?"

Sniffling, with tissues in hand, Sylvia agrees to hear Pete out.

"The not-so-good news is more than what you were told at first. They knocked out all of Robbie's teeth, broke his nose, and gave him a black eye. From my vantage point, that's all I could see. They didn't allow me to speak with him, and it was a short visit. But they did tell me they would release him in three days from yesterday, so really two more days, but I will confirm that with the boss. They will most likely clean him up, so you won't see blood, but you will see a battered husband."

I feel like bawling myself, but I'm trying to be strong. I'm looking at Sylvia's face as she hears the brutal details, it's droopy and sad, and it looks like she is going to cry any minute.

"Is he in terrible pain? Poor thing, he'll need a lot of care and rest when he comes home," says Sylvia, wiping tears from her cheeks.

"I know," says Pete, "and we're all here to help you in any way we can; don't forget we're all sibs, and we care about our brother Robbie. And don't think about the money; I still have an outstanding loan with the Boss, and it's not due for three months, so I can help financially."

Simone is quiet and softly weeping, not uttering a word, then:

"How will dad talk and eat without any teeth?"

Pete explains that he can get dentures for a while, you know, the kind you take in and out.

Simone makes a cynical-looking face. Sylvia needs another glass of wine.

"How about another glass of wine, Syl?" says Pete

"I can't even think right now, I'm so upset, but okay, I'll take another glass."

We all sit quietly for a while, thinking to ourselves, anxiously awaiting Robbie's return.

Pete says, "Just think, in two more days, you'll have your hubby home alive, although battered, but it could have been worse; these guys have hitmen who will kill you for their own gain."

"Can I go with you to pick Robbie up, Pete?"

"I think it's best if you prepare the house, bedroom, etc., and call Dr. Carramato to prepare him for what's to come. I think Danny and I can handle it. Oh, and by the way, he may have some mental problems we have to deal with because who knows what they said to him, how they really treated him; did they tie him to a chair? (Sylvia gasps) or who knows what else?"

"Is that what they do to a human being? Tie him up and beat him?" Sylvia's face is all contorted and angry-looking.

"Look. Syl, that's what these guys do. Period. It's their way of revenge or a payoff, in a way. I'm going to call all the sibs and explain everything. Then I'm going to confirm with Boss Johnnie the exact time of pick up. Lastly, I'll call you and finalize his homecoming, okay? Now should we clink our glasses to Robbie's return?"

We all clink glasses, except Simone, who runs upstairs and slams the door.

11

FRANKIE

ONE WEEK LATER

I got word from Pete that Robbie's release is tomorrow! Wow, that is so great! I know he's battered, but hey, he's alive, and he's a strong guy and will heal, especially with Sylvia's tender care, and, of course, all of us will help. He'll need the company. I just hope he's okay mentally cause those guys can be really tough on anyone, no-nonsense mobsters.

With all that's happened in our family, we haven't told our kids yet. We were about to, but the news here is that Anna and me, we're arguing more and more about everything. It's grating on me and her, and I think it's goin' to come down to me movin' out soon.

With all when we got a hysterical call from Sylvia that Simone was havin' a nervous breakdown. So, life goes on, but not too peacefully, and we're sleepin' in separate rooms. She gets the "Queen's" room, and I sleep in the den on the couch. I guess we're gonna have to tell the kids tonight.

Here comes Anna to let me know dinner is almost ready.

"Hey, Frankie, I know you're tired from work, but can you raise yourself up to come to dinner in ten minutes?"

"Sure, my dear Anna, but are we tellin' the kids tonight, barring any unusual phone calls?"

"Yes. My dear Frankie, so we need to chat for a minute while they're still doing their homework."

"Okay, shoot. What do we say?"

"I think we should sit them down and say we have something to talk about, okay?"

I think Anna wants to get this over already and me out of the house.

"Yeah, okay, you do most of the talkin', then I'll put in my two cents."

We are now at the kitchen table with Frankie, Jr., and Gracie. Anna brings in ice water, then goes back and gets the salad. She gives each of us our plate and sits down.

"Kids?" says Anna with a kind of squeaky voice, "Dad and I have some things to discuss with you. Is this a good time?"

"As good as ever," says Frankie Jr.

"Fine," says little Gracie with a coy look on her face.

"I'll start," says Anna, "and then Dad will speak too."

"Well, you see, kids, me and Dad are not getting along these days. We're not as happy together as we used to be. Now, you know it's not your fault at all. We both love you very much, and we respect each other too. So, we're going to separate for a while, sort of like a trial."

I'm startin' to sweat and feel so bad for them; I can see a tiny teardrop on Gracie's face.

"The plan is that Dad is going to move out, but close by," says Anna very directly.

"But? Says Frankie Jr, a questioning look. Will we see Dad a lot? I mean, sleep at his new place?"

"Of course, you will, like almost every day," says I. "I can even pick you up at school sometimes, and we can go to Coney Island and have lots of fun together. Don't worry, I still love you both very much, and I'll be around the corner."

"But Dad? Can you still tell me scary stories at night?" says Gracie, trying to be brave.

"Sure thing, sweetie pie, that will never change," Now, Grace has a smile on her face.

I'm not sure Gracie understands everything that's going on: she's only eight.

Anna chimes in, "Are you kids okay with this arrangement? Just for a trial period, then we'll see how things go."

"But who is going to take care of you, Mom?"

"You, Frankie, you're going to take care of me."

"Can I take care of you too?" says Gracie, with a cheerier face.

"Dad, did you find an apartment yet?" Say Frankie Jr, inquisitively.

"Not yet, but I'm lookin'."

I'm thinkin' to tell them that Robbie is coming home tomorrow.

"Hey, you both need some sleep, cause guess what? Uncle Robbie is comin' home tomorrow!"

We keep discussing plans for a while, and then it's time for the kids to finish their homework and get to bed. Anna says she is going up to "her room" and she will see me in the morning.

I'm still hoppin', not tired, so I think I'll give Pete a call, see what's up.

"Hello, Pete, how ya doing, buddy? Checkin' in to get the final plan. Hey, can I join you and Danny for the pick-up?"

I'm listenin' carefully as he's murmuring. Maybe he's tired.

"Oh, I see, so two is the maximum from the Boss, okay then give me a call after you pick up Robbie, can't wait. Okay, then, bro, good luck, and I'll hear from you tomorrow. By the way, what time are you pickin' him up? Ah ha, ten am? Great, I'll be glued to the phone, even at work."

Now I'm pretty tired and nervous about Robbie. I think he's in horrible shape, so upsetting.

I go upstairs to see the kids before they go to bed. I'm ready to tell Gracie a scary story which she loves, even before sleep. I give them each a kiss, close their doors. The "queen's" door is closed. I go downstairs and flop on the sofa bed, say my prayers for Robbie and snore myself to sleep.

The next mornin', I wake up before everyone, Robbie on my mind, and got to go check out a new construction to see how much cement we need. I take my jalopy to work cause it's a messy, dirty business. Sometimes it starts up, sometimes not. I am lucky today. I left Anna and the kids a note that I had to leave early for work.

My boss, Gerry, tells me that the cement is of poor quality, and they had to mix it with something to get it to stick. He says that I should make sure the trucks have the proper cement before leaving the plant. I apologize and tell the boss that it won't happen again.

So, I walk around the worksite to make sure the mixers are doing the right thing, schmooze with them for a few minutes, and walk to my car. Just as I'm about to get into my car, I get a call from Pete.

"Hi bud, it's Pete. Danny and me are on our way to pick up Robbie. You want to meet us there?"

"Sure, I'd love to. Give me the address, and I'll wait outside for you." I hear him givin' me numbers and street names, and then he says be quiet and don't talk to anyone. Now I'm a little frightened.

So now I'm outside this huge brownstone mansion, where Pete told me to go, and I'm pacin' back and forth with my hat on and my head down; Oh, I see Pete and Danny comin', (I cross myself).

"Hey guys, this is quite a place, very swanky, but I bet all of them live like this, right?"

Pete says, "Hush, we have to act like gentlemen and follow orders, okay?"

We both nod and follow Pete. Knock on the door. Butler answers the door and takes us to the waiting room. Now I'm sweating and feeling very anxious. I have a sad heart right now for some reason.

After about twenty minutes, the butler says to follow him. He takes us into the Boss' office and says to sit down, and he pulls up another chair. Soon, the boss comes in and takes us into a dark chamber. It's empty, no Robbie! We are all stunned...more than stunned...

Pete asks the boss where Robbie is, and he leads us back to his office, complete silence. By now, we're all sweatin' and horrified. We prefer to stand and listen.

"Uh hem, I'm going to be straight with you," says the Boss. "Robbie is dead! He lied to us, and we do not tolerate that kind of behavior."

All three of us put our hands over our faces and gasp. Pete starts to weep.

"Where is his body?" Danny says with an angry voice, "I demand to know."

"We don't give out that information. It's private for us. Just know he's dead.'

Pete gathers his thoughts, "You told us the other day that he would be released! What happened between then and now."

"I'm not at liberty to say, it's against our code. Now, if you would please let me get back to my work, I would appreciate it."

The three of us walk out cryin' like babies cause we don't understand, and we are devastated.

We hug each other in a circle, just shocked and disbelievin'. Danny says we should go to a bar and get drunk. We decide not to call anyone at the moment, and Pete says, "If Sylvia calls, please do not answer it."

We stop crying for now, but we're all angry and vengeful. Pete says, "If it's the last thing I do, I'm going to find my brother."

12

PETE

We stand outside the Boss's house, sniffling and talking very quietly. The shocking news of Robbie's death is hard to believe, and we're deciding how to handle this.

Is he really dead? Or is this one of the boss's pranks? Should I go back in and talk to him? Or just wait it out for a few days to see if anything pops up?

"Well, bros, so you want to tell Sylvia while Simone is at school?"

"Yeah," says Frankie, "maybe that's the best way cause she needs to get over the shock first before Simone comes home, and we have a few hours."

We all agree that we should go over to Sylvia's and tell it the way it is

"Okay," says Danny, "so let's go."

We all hop in Frankie's old jalopy car and drive over to Sylvia's house, not too far away.

"I just hope Sylvia doesn't collapse. She's very fragile these days," says Frankie.

"We all hope that, bros, and if we do it the right way, she may understand. Now listen, we got to act strong but sympathetic. We tell her that maybe his death was for the best since he was so beaten up, more than she thinks. This is not an easy job, and I am still thinking of what to say. I'm also still thinking about where they may have buried him."

We arrive at Sylvia's house, and I see her peeking out of the curtains in the living room. She must hear Frankie's car pull up; her face looks sad, so let's be gentle now. The door is open before we reach the last step. We walk in very silent. Sylvia looks pale, and she may know what we're going to say.

"Greetings, Syl."

"Don't tell me, please don't tell me!"

We each give her a hug, and then I say, "Let's all sit down in the living room."

Her hands are already covering her face, and she is weeping quietly.

"He's dead, right? They slaughtered him, right? Those lousy pigs. I need a gun. I'm going to kill that boss!"

I go over to Sylvia and put my arms around her, and she screams with anger, shaking all the while.

"Where is my baby? Did they shoot him or strangle him to death? I want to know, and I want to know where his body is right now," she yells and cries at the same time, and it doesn't stop for minutes.

I put my arms around her and stroke her back. It seems she's inconsolable.

After her crying stops, she stares into space, like she is in shock. About three minutes later, she comes back to reality.

"Pete," she says in a weak tone of voice, "we've got to find out about Robbie's body; how can we have a proper funeral if we don't have his body? And do you swear on your life that he's really dead?"

"Sylvia, I can't swear on my life for anything with these crooks. They live on lies, demands, revenge, and death. When we went to pick him up, he wasn't there for sure. The Boss, Johnnie, told us he was dead, and that's all he would say, so we left, thinking that was the truth. But is that hundred percent correct? Who knows? Maybe I can contact some underlings to snoop around, find some dirt."

"Who might know something?"

"I have a few names, and also Frankie knows a few people, right, Frankie?"

"Right, at least I can try to talk to some guys."

"No guarantee, though," as Pete looks Sylvia straight in the eye. She nods her head.

I'm thinking, boy, is this going to be a problem!

"Syl, you look skinny. Can I make you something to eat?"

"No, Pete, I'm really not hungry; I'm nervous about how I should break it to Simone?"

"Do you want me to hang around until she gets

home from school? My kids have soccer practice, and Viv will be fine."

"Thanks, Pete, for the offer, but I think I want to be alone until Simone comes home, and that won't be until about four pm."

"Okay then, is there anything I can do for you now?"

"Yes." says Sylvia in a firm voice, "Find my Robbie!"

"We'll try. I'll make a few calls back at the docks and talk to a few people who are around."

I get back to the docks kinda late, but Eddie happens to be there, and I think he maybe knows someone who knows someone. You know how it goes. I see him walking towards me now. He probably wants to know what I'm up to.

"Yo, Pete, what's up, buddy?"

"Nothing much, just had to take care of some business this morning, that's why I'm late getting here."

"What kinda business pal?"

"I guess the Boss didn't tell you, but it's really bad news."

"Tell me, please."

"Well, About two weeks ago, some of the "boys" shoved Robbie out of his home, in a car, then to Big Johnnie's house. Sylvia and Simone are a mess. Anyways, until a few days ago, no word from Robbie, until I went to see him, boss's permission, of course. He was accused of stealing from the business; still don't know if that's the real reason; Robbie was a mess, bashed in teeth, broken nose, black eye, smashed ears; Boss wouldn't say a word, we left. A few days later, told to pick him up, gone! No Robbie, Boss silent! So, that's the story. Got any thoughts?"

"Let me see," says Eddie, massaging his chin. "Owe anything, Pete? How about the other bros?"

"I mean, they have loans with the Boss, but they haven't been threatened for a while, so cool there. I'm trying to think; was it revenge?"

"No, I don't think so; he said he owed me a favor, so that's how I got to see smashed-up Robbie. Do you know where they bury the bodies, Eddie?"

"Well, I may have an idea. Sometimes they dump them in the river in a weighted body bag; sometimes, they dig a grave, sometimes they chop them in a garbage truck. And sometimes they put them in cement. That's all I know right now. I could probably think of more places, but not offhand."

I'm thinking about what Eddie says, and since Frankie is in the cement business, maybe that's where they hid the body; hmm, just thinking. I gotta call Frankie right now cause he knows all those guys there that mix cement.

"Hey, Frankie!"

"Yeah, bud, just got home and takin' my coat off. What's up?"

"I'm tryin' to find out what they did with Robbie's body, and I have an idea. Want to hear it?"

"You bet I do. Spill it out."

"Well, it could be a lot of things, but I think we should investigate the cement business, and since you're involved in the biggest cement company, maybe you can help us."

"You mean you think that Robbie is in one of my many buildings that use cement? Where would we even start to look?"

"Do you know some insiders who mix the cement and know where it's still dryin'? Cause once it's hard like a rock, it's kaput," says Frankie in an almost laughable tone.

"I know it's hard, Frankie, but this is your brother, and Sylvia is so distraught that she might buy a gun and shoot someone."

LATER THAT DAY

I call Sylvia around five pm to see how Simone is doing since she's been so angry and depressed, and Sylvia is going to talk to Simone about Robbie's death; I would like to keep her in the loop too.

The phone keeps ringing, ringing, no one answers. I try again at six and seven pm; even Simone isn't home. Now I start to get nervous. Where could she be at this hour on a weeknight? Simone always has homework, and Sylvia goes to bed early

I decide to go over to Sylvia's place to check on things. When I get there, I can't believe my eyes: I think she did buy a gun, that little sneak, and probably shot the bodyguard on duty in front of her house.

I guess she thinks he didn't protect her from Robbie's ordeal. I check his pulse, dead. But where is Sylvia? I scour the house, and it is empty.

I call all the sibs, but they have no idea of what just happened, no witnesses, no nothing, just blood oozing from the guy's body. I explain it to them, and obviously, they are utterly shocked at this deadly event.

Sylvia with a gun? She must be out of her mind. I don't think she ever owned a gun before.

I call the police. Shortly after, I hear the sirens coming my way. They stop near me, but I have a good alibi just in case. Cops check the body, take it away and bid me goodbye, but with a strange look on their faces.

Sylvia's probable motive? The new bodyguard didn't protect Robbie from being kicked out of the house by the Boss' hitmen. Now, where the heck did Sylvia and Simone go? There must be something else going on. I'll find out soon enough.

13

DANNY

LATER THAT NIGHT

Oh my God, I got so much stuff in my head. It's spinning! I just got frantic calls from Pete and Frankie. Now we got problems all over the place. I'm crossing myself, and I have a freakin' headache. I have to calm down and think this through. And to top it off, I had a date last night; she seems to be crazy about me, but I don't think she's that great. Whew!

So, Robbie is dead, we pretty much know, not one hundred percent, but we don't know where the body is. So, we gotta do some digging and pushing. I mean pushing those we think might be responsible. We all got some leads, but we really gotta use them.

Assuming Robbie is dead, where is the most likely place they would dispose of him? Then, I just heard a few hours ago that Sylvia might have shot her bodyguard and then disappeared. I'm gonna call Pete to discuss all this.

"Hello Pete, it's Danny; I'm freaking out about all this terrible news, buddy."

"I know," says Pete in a nervous voice. "I'm trying to deal with Robbie and Sylvia and Simone's disappearance too. I believe Sylvia may have bought a gun, not only because she threatened to, but I found her bodyguard shot to death in front of her house. Police took his body away, searched the house, no evidence anywhere, and no Sylvia, so I have some digging to do with the boss about a few matters."

"Does the whole family know by now?"

"Yes," says Pete in a quiet voice, "everyone knows as much as we know."

"How about you dig for evidence on Sylvia and Simone, cause you got good relations with some of those bosses, and I'll call Frankie about Robbie's body, sound like a decent idea? Okay then."

I hang up the phone, not knowing where to begin.

I call Frankie, though it's getting kinda late.

"Hey, Frankie, it's Danny," I could hear him yawning loud like he's ready for the sack. "What's up?"

"What's up? A hell of a lot, don't ya think?" says Frankie, "I mean, we have a murdered brother, a dead bodyguard, and the disappearance of Sylvia and Simone; isn't that enough?"

"Calm down," I say, "we'll get it all sorted out."

Frankie replies, "I'm gonna take care of Robbie's body, I hope, cause I expect to see one of the bosses tomorrow at my work. I think I know who to talk to, so hopefully, we'll have some information soon. Listen, I got my own problems too, you know. Anna is driving me crazy to get out of the house and find another place already. So, I got plenty of aggravation. I think I have a place nearby, so I can see the kids pretty often. It isn't the most beautiful, but the kids have their own room, and we have to share a bath, not so terrible. Anyways, I gotta get some sleep. Big day tomorrow. I'm thinkin', geez, why doesn't Anna give me some rope? I mean, I'm gettin' out but hey, give the old man a break."

THE NEXT DAY

I'm up early cause it was hard to sleep, too much on my mind. The phone rings, I think it's Pete or Frankie or Tommy or..., but it is Anita, that lovely girl I met once, who is crazy for me. She always seems to call at the wrong time.

"Hello?"

"Hello, Danny, this is Anita, just calling to see if you've calmed down a little."

"Well, Anita, the whole family is crazy right now with so many bad things going on, but I'd love to meet you for a drink sometime soon, but not now. Let me get things straightened out family-wise, you know, and then I'll call you back, and we'll meet for a drink. I have a nice place in mind."

"Okay, Danny, sounds good, looking forward to it, oh, by the way, good luck with everything."

"Yeah, it's going be tough, and sad but we'll all get through it. We're strong."

The next thing I know, the phone rings again.

"Hello"

"Hey, it's Pete, Danny; listen, are you free in about an hour to come with me and Frankie to the cement plant? We're going to talk to a few of the managers there, connected to Johnnie."

"Sure, I can meet you, Pete. What time?"

"How about eleven am? Meet us at the gate entrance."

I find my way to the entrance of Panelli's Cement. I wait for Pete and Frankie, pacing back and forth, then I light up a cigarette, bad habit, but hey, I'm alone, so it's something to do.

Now I see Pete and Frankie walking towards me, traveling at a good pace.

"Hey guys, great to see you, hope we get some answers here."

"I think we will," says Frankie, "let's be positive."

All three of us walk in the gates, and this guy walks towards us. Maybe he's the one.

"Hey, Alex," says Frankie, "Meet my two brothers, Danny and Pete; so, what's the deal here?"

"Well, I'm the top manager here as you know Frankie; and after I spoke to you, I told you that only Johnnie knows about things; So, like a good family member, I got a tip-off that perhaps Mr. Robbie's body is buried in one of three new buildings under construction. He wouldn't exactly tell me which one, but I can go with you to show you the buildings, then you could hunt for yourself, understand?"

Pete replies, "We understand, but we don't know the motive for this vicious act, so somebody has to some explaining to do."

"Well, that's up to Johnnie, not me. My instructions are to take you to the three places, that's it; if you want to know more, call the Boss."

"How far apart are these buildings?" Asks Pete with a harsh voice.

"Three blocks each about, I think," says Alex. "You guys can go in one car and follow me."

We decide to use Frankie's jalopy and follow Alex to the first building. It's in Brooklyn, and it's about five stories high, looks like a skeleton at the moment. We follow Alex around to one of the construction men, Freddie.

"Hey, Freddie," says Alex, "show these men where you poured the undried concrete.

He leads us to where he pours the stuff and has just finished smoothing it out.

"Hey," says Frankie, "You notice any dead bodies stuck in here while you've been pouring and smoothing?"

"Nope, but feel free to see for yourself, walk around, talk to some of the other cement people."

So, we walk around, inspecting different parts of the building, and no sign of a body, or even a body part sticking out. We talk to several guys here, and they say they haven't seen anything like this.

We're frustrated, to say the least. Alex leads us to the next building. We do the same thing here, talk to mixing guys and others involved in construction, and even inspect it more carefully, just looking for more clues, anything, but no luck.

When we get to the third building, we're tired of walking, tired of seeing nothing, and Pete is getting more frustrated by the minute, I can tell, like he's almost giving up but doesn't say it yet.

"I think the Boss is trying hard to mislead us," says Pete, head down, really depressed, I think.

"What should we do now?" asks Frankie, in a desperate tone of voice. Pete says nothing, but I know he's thinking hard. After a minute or two, Pete looks up, and a tear runs down his face.

"We need to speak to the Boss now," he says as he tries to compose himself.

"I'll use the pay phone," says Frankie, "let's call Johnnie now, okay?"

Pete nods, takes the phone, and tries to remember the number.

"I got it, Pete, no worries," so Pete dials and gets the butler (associate) on the phone.

"Yes? Mr. Valenti, what can I do for you?"

Pete says, "How did you know my last name?"

"Ah, the Boss knows everything."

After the conversation, the boss invites us to his residence. After waiting quite a while, we're told to go into his office, as I said before, a palatial place with old mobsters' photos on the wall.

"Ah, my dear family, what can I do for you today?"

"Boss Johnnie, we've come to ask you some questions," says Pete. "Where is my brother Robbie's body buried? Are you taking us on a wild goose chase?"

"No such thing," replies the Boss.

"We were led to believe that he was buried in cement in one of your buildings."

"Nonsense," says Johnnie. "if you do me a big favor, I will tell you."

"What?" says Pete excitedly.

"Don't look for his wife, or there will be trouble."

"What do you mean?" asks Pete, "don't tell me she's dead too."

"Just what I said. Now, Robbie's body is chopped up and lays in a garbage dump.; you'll never find him, so don't look. Remember the favor, or else. You may go now."

There is complete silence as we leave the Boss' office. We are dumb-founded, broken-hearted, so we lean on each other and pray.

14

MARIA

Oh my God, we are all mourning Robbie's death. A ghastly way to die, it's really hard to believe. Then, we learn that Sylvia may have shot the new bodyguard and escaped with Simone and is nowhere to be found.

As I believe it, Boss Johnnie has it out for Pete, meaning that he's been ordered (they call it a favor), to not try to find her, or else, and we know what that means. To sum it up, it's a mess, and I don't know what Pete has in mind. I wonder why Pete is not allowed to look for her? I think there is something else going on.

Poor Pete, I feel for him and his wife, Viv, who never really talks about it. She's shy and doesn't particularly like the life Pete lives, so Viv kinda stays in the background, doing her artwork, which she loves, and has talent. Viv doesn't yap like the rest of us, so it's almost like having a ghost around, but Pete's happy, so, there you go.

Pete said that me and Jim should meet at his house tonight with the rest of the family to discuss funeral arrangements for Robbie, even though his body hasn't been found.

I guess most of us will be there, but I just can't imagine how ugly things have turned out. We'll all try to agree on what to do about Robbie, Sylvia, and Simone.

Me and Jim arrive at Pete's house about seven pm and the only ones missing are Frankie and Anna. But I think she's out of the picture now since she basically kicked Frankie out of the house.

"Are we still waiting for Frankie? And, is Anna coming?"

Pete gets up from his couch and comes to give me a hug. Viv is not with him. She must be in her studio.

"We're still waiting for Frankie," Pete says with a bit of annoyance; "He's dropping the kids back at Anna's place, so he'll be here any moment now. How about some nice Italian wedding cookies, anyone?"

"I'll have one or two or maybe more," says Tommy with a big smile on his face. Angela takes one, too.

"I'll have one, too," says Margaret, "they look delicious. Who made them?"

"I picked them up at the bakery around the corner, all homemade."

Just as he says that, Frankie enters the house.

"Well, look whose here," we all say.

"Welcome, bro," says Pete, "I'll give you some wedding cookies and, I know, a Bourbon on the rocks for the old man, right?"

"You got it," says Frankie.

We all have our booze and munchies, and now we talk.

Pete stands up and begins, "It's so good to see many family members here, though it's a very sad occasion. We have two tragedies to deal with, and I need your help in solving both. As we all have learned in the last day or so, Robbie is dead, though I haven't seen his body yet. So, we have to decide on our next step. I have seen the Boss, and he has told me, after a merry-go-round visit to the cement factory with Frankie and Danny yesterday, that Robbie is not disposed of there. He told us, as you probably know that he was dismembered and put in a garbage truck and taken to the dump, and he didn't say which one. Now, one thing we could do is go to the manager of the garbage company that Robbie worked for and dig for some information there. I think the big guy is Rudy Garcia. He may know something. Or, if we think this is a lost cause, and we just want to have a nice ceremony for Robbie, we can do that too. Does anyone want to say something about Robbie, other than we miss and love him, and we hope his soul goes to heaven? May he rest in peace."

"I know we're talking about what to do about Robbie now," says Tommy, "so don't you think it might be good to confirm with this guy Garcia that, in fact, he was disposed of there?"

"I think that makes sense. I mean, why close the book now when we still have some leads," says Margaret.

"I agree," says Frankie, "I think we should see this guy Garcia and hopefully get some answers."

"How about the rest of you? Maria and Ted, you cool with it?" asks Pete.

"I think you, Pete, should be the one to go since you seem to have more clout with these turkeys," says Danny.

"I don't mind doing this, but maybe Frankie should come with me. Now I'm not favoring any of my sibs. I just think Frankie might be a good companion and knows how to talk to these guys. Does everyone else agree? Show of hands? Okay then, I'll set up the appointment, maybe for tomorrow afternoon; would that work for you, Frankie?"

"Yeah, if it's not my turn to take the kids. I'll call Anna (if she'll talk to me) and check; in fact, I'll give her a buzz now. Excuse me, folks, we never know how this conversation will go, so I think I'll call on the phone in the kitchen."

"Hello, Anna? It's me, listen'. I'm callin' to find out the schedule with the kids for tomorrow cause I got an important appointment."

"Well, if you really want to know, tomorrow is your day with the kids, but I'll be a good egg, and we can switch so you can go to your very important date."

"It's not a date, Anna, like with a woman, (boy is she nosy). It has to do with finding Robbie's body, geez!"

"Well, sorry about that, but remember you're taking them the next day, and don't be late."

"I got it, bye."

"All set, so, Pete, if you can call and get an appointment with this Garcia guy, that works for me."

"I think it might be too late to call him now; if I can even find the number, so why don't we all retire for the night, and I'll let all of you know in the morning."

So, one by one, or two by two, we all leave and go home. Finally, I ask Ted what he thinks, and he says that he believes it's a run-around, but he'll go along with it, same for me.

THE NEXT MORNING

Ted and I are up early, awaiting Pete's call for clearance to go see Garcia at the garbage dump. A few minutes later, as we're drinking our usual strong coffee, we get a phone call, probably Pete.

"Hello, yes, Pete; oh, you got an appointment? Great, what time? Is there any chance I could join my brothers? I'll just listen, is that okay?"

"Not really," says Pete with a sigh, "but I'll say yes this time, but not Ted, too many people."

"Ted has to work anyway, so no problem there."

"Okay then," says Pete, "We'll pick you up in an hour. Can you be ready?"

"Of course, bro, just knock on the door."

So, I'm the lucky sib. I hope it's not another runaround. I go back to the kitchen to tell Ted the good news.

"Honey, Pete is allowing me to go with him to the garbage company office."

"That's great, Maria. Pete is such a cool guy, isn't he?"

"Yup, that's my oldest brother. He's the one who has the most contacts and speaks so eloquently, just kidding."

"Well, I'm going to fix my face and get ready to go, so I'll kiss you goodbye now, and I'll be in touch; have a great day, my love.

"You too, but be careful, just listen."

"Okay, I will."

A while later, Pete knocks on the door. Frankie is in the car waiting. The ride to the Waste Management office isn't too far. They have their own parking lot, so very easy.

We walk to the entrance and ring the bell. A tall brunette meets us and takes us to Garcia's office.

"What can I do for you lovely people?"

"Let's not joke around," says Pete with a forceful tone.

"I'm not joking. What do you really want?"

"I want to know if my brother Robbie's body is in your junk pile?"

"I can't say for sure," says Garcia, "but I can drive you there if you want to rummage through garbage."

"You have ties to Boss Johnnie. You must know more than you're telling us," says Pete.

"Well, to be honest, the boss did tell me to dispose of him there, but exactly where I can't tell you; I don't go up there, I'm in the office, a manager."

"Can you lead us to the dump?" queries Pete.

"Sure, just follow me. It's about a ten-minute drive; it smells pretty bad there, so just warning you."

So, we follow Garcia to the dump. He drives quite a way up 'cause it's like a big mountain.

We get out, and Garcia tells us it might be around this part. We start looking for body parts, ugh, what a horror, and boy does it stink, of course, it's a garbage dump.

Pete and Frankie are looking very carefully, but to me, it's like looking for a needle in a haystack. We spend about an hour there, nothing resembling a leg, an arm, nothing. Pete decides he's going to call the Boss.

"Hello, It's Pete, is the Boss around?"

Pete waits, fidgeting with his cross necklace, then takes out a cigarette and lights it. It's taking a long time to get the Boss on the phone. Finally.

"Hey, Pete, what's up?" says Johnnie

"You know what's up, chief!"

"Ah, still looking for Robbie?"

"You know it," says Pete in a frustrating voice.

"Listen, Pete, Robbie was dumped in the East River in a weighted bag, so now pal, he's at the bottom, don't bother looking for him."

"You lied to me and sent me on a wild goose chase."

"Don't fool with me, Pete," says Johnnie.

Pete hangs up, furious, goes to Garcia, who is waiting in his car, and says, "You'll get yours!"

15

TOMMY

Boy, I just got a call from Pete, and he is fuming because he got tricked once more by the Boss. From the sounds of it, he'd like to break Garcia's neck for giving him the run-around at the garbage dump. Now we know where dear Robbie lays, at the bottom of the East River, at least that's what we were told.

We're mentally exhausted from all of this trauma and chaos. I'd like to help Pete out from under this horror, but I'm not that well connected to the Boss or even Eddie. Now that we know where our dear brother lies, I think we need to plan a memorial for him.

Then we gotta deal with Sylvia and Simone's disappearance. We think Sylvia took revenge by killing Robbie's bodyguard. I wouldn't blame her and Simone for escaping; they're probably in Arizona by now at some sweet resort. I think we need another pow-wow to plan Robbie's service and then deal with Sylvia's safety.

I am going to ring Pete right now.

"Hi, Pete, it's your bro Tommy here. Listen, I don't know if anything has been planned, but we need to think of Robbie's memorial service, right?"

"Yes, we do, Tom, and that means another pow-wow with the family. I'll call everyone and try to set it up for tomorrow evening, again at my place, okay for you?"

"I'm sure it is, but I'll check with my beautiful Angela. I'm sure she can make it too, and the kids can take care of themselves; I don't know why I just said that, but I guess they can. So seven pm tomorrow?"

"Sounds good. If anything changes, I'll give you a buzz," says Pete with a broad smile on his face.

THE NEXT EVENING

"Okay, everybody, slurp down your beers, and let's get down to business. It actually was Tommy's idea to have this meeting sooner than later, so we could say our goodbyes to dear Robbie, who departed this world way too young. May he rest in peace. In fact, let's all say our prayers to Robbie in silence."

"Now that we've taken care of that, I think we need to talk about the details of the memorial service," says Pete. Do any of you have some ideas?"

"Well, I think we should have something outside, since it's summer, maybe at ma and dad's graveside," says Danny. "I think that would be very special, right?"

"Wait a second," declares Maria, "how about having it in our church. Wouldn't that be more appropriate?"

"Not necessarily," says Margaret; "I kind of agree with Danny that outside near our parent's gravesite would be great."

"I think maybe we should have It at one of our houses, then it would be very personal," says Margaret, sort of defiantly.

"I have an idea," declares Maria. "How about we each write our choice on a piece of paper, put them in a basket, mix them up and let Pete pick one out."

"I think that's a great idea," says Frankie, "it's the fairest way to do it."

"Okay, kids," says Pete, "without looking, I will pick one of them; remember, only one choice per person."

"Ah-ha," he says with a funny laugh, "and the winner is (drum roll) Margaret!!!!"

Everybody claps, and Margaret gets up and takes a bow.

"That means," says Pete, "that we will have the memorial service at the gravesite of ma and dad!!" That's what I really wanted anyway, but I stayed out of it.

"Now that everyone who wants to has spoken. I will pick the date and time," declares Pete. "I think that it would be nice if each of our women in this family lays a bouquet on or near the graves of our parents to commemorate them and Robbie. I will order a small stone for Robbie to put next to them. Does everybody agree on this plan?"

We all say yes at the same time, which delights Pete.

"How about one week from today at noon, does that work for everyone?"

They shout, "YES!"

"I can get the stone engraved quickly. How about the words on the stone?"

Frankie says, "WE MISS YOU, ROBBIE, REST IN PEACE?"

Everybody nods and agrees on these words. After another brief conversation, we go home.

On our way home, Angela and I discuss the ideas, and we are happy that we could all agree because that's not always the case. We get home, and our five kids are eating popcorn and watching and playing games. Angela yells at them to brush their teeth and go to sleep.

ONE WEEK LATER

We're up early to give the kids breakfast and to get ready for the memorial service. They have school and then sports after, so they are taken care of. Angela has a beautiful bouquet of different colored daisies to put on or near the gravesite. Then, we taxi over to meet the rest of the family.

We see some of them standing over ma and dad's graves, looking very solemn. A few stragglers arrive, like my sister Margaret and Maria, who are sniffling and carrying tissues; Pete and Viv aren't far behind. A few moments later, everybody is here. Pete starts the service.

"We're all gathered here as a family to honor our beloved brother who died before his time, who endured a horrific dismemberment and death (at least we think he's dead). We remember him as a loving husband to Sylvia and a warm and sweet father to Simone. We also remember him as a faithful and kind brother to all of us. We will miss his funny jokes, his roaring laugh, his generosity, and much more. May he rest in peace."

We all cross ourselves. Many of us weep quietly, using tissues to wipe our tears. Then each person per family lays a bouquet in front of the small stone that Pete had made with the inscription. We bow our heads and say silent prayers. We kiss each other goodbye and get on our way to Danny's place for some food and drink.

The aftermath of the funeral is calm, no yelling, but chatting quietly, eating some food that Danny ordered, and drinking some beers or wine. The conversation is mostly about how nice the service was and that we put Robbie to rest. (Or, did we?)

We toast to our health and pray for Sylvia and Simone's safe return, a real mystery to me and most of us. We're all in shock and don't understand this whole incident.

"Speaking of Sylvia," Frankie asks, "Does anyone know exactly why she disappeared?"

There is complete silence for a few seconds until Pete stands up as if to say something.

"My dear family, I have something important to share with you. The last time I saw the Boss was a very distressing event. I was so upset that I kept it to myself, unable to speak about it. That's when he told me that Robbie was not thrown into wet cement, nor was he chopped up in a garbage truck and taken to a dump. Rather, he was bagged and weighted and thrown into the East River. Do I believe all this? I'm not sure. Anyways, the Boss threatened me not to look for Sylvia, or else! I suspect Sylvia ran before me, and the police arrived. Why did she run? I have my suspicions, but I won't say a word until I have more information."

I don't know what suspicions Pete has cause we're not that involved with the Boss. I'm sure we'll find out soon enough. This family needs some peaceful, quiet time. I'm not a big churchgoer, but I think me and Angela should go and pray for Sylvia and Simone. This family needs some peace and quiet.

16

PETE

TWO DAYS LATER

I have suffered from excruciating headaches for the last week or two; a lot on my mind, and not everything is resolved by far. Viv gives me this special tea to drink and some aspirin, but they still go on and on, from the stress, I believe.

I have nightmares about Robbie and Sylvia. The other night I had a dream about Robbie; he was able to break out of his weighted bag and swim to the surface and call me. I go to pick him up, damaged but not dead. Wow, that really scares me.

Then last night, I dreamt about Sylvia and Simone; they are fine and just enjoying their time away from the house; there was no dead body in front of her house. I don't believe that dream for a minute.

I don't know what to do about the boss' threat to me, not to go searching for Sylvia. I can't just walk away from this, but I don't want to jeopardize my family either by getting too involved.

I don't even know if the boss killed the bodyguard and her, although it could be a clean job, silencers, and blood cleaned up in the house, who knows? But I have to save Sylvia, find her, or else I'll go mad.

Viv comes into the kitchen to get her morning coffee. I sit there staring out the window, my head spins, trying to think of my next step. Boy, is this going to be hard.

"What are you staring at, hon?" He looks like he's really out of it. "Where is your mind?"

"Oh, I'm just thinking about poor Sylvia and Simone, what their situation is and how we can help without getting too involved with the Boss, etc."

"I know it's got to be grilling on your mind, dear, but let's enjoy a cup of coffee together before you go to work. The boys already left for school, so it's nice and quiet at the moment."

"Okay, I'll try to focus on you for a minute, I haven't really been fair to you, with so much going on in the family, and that's not right."

"I understand, and you know I support almost everything you do for me and the kids."

"Well, my new job is going well at J.C. Penney," says Viv, "and I was lucky to be in the cosmetic department because you know how much I like to mess with my face and body. The standing for eight hours is tough, but they give me ten-minute breaks, a half-hour for lunch, and I get a ten percent discount on all of their clothes, furniture, sheets, perfumes, and whatnot."

"That's great, hon, and did you get a raise in salary?"

"Yup, a five percent raise, that's all they're giving to salespersons now, not bad."

"Not bad at all. Every little bit counts in our situation. Now, can I tell you what's on my mind?"

"I know," says Viv in an expectant voice. "You don't know what to do about Sylvia and Simone, so okay, spill it out."

And, just when she says that, the phone rings.

"Hello? (voice crackles for a few seconds), Sylvia? Is it really you? Are you okay, and Simone? I can't believe it, I've been, or we've been so worried about you for days now, even thought you might be dead; why did I say that? I don't know where to begin, Syl..."

"It's a long story, Pete," she says, "and I'm calling from a payphone, so I can't be tracked, and there are some things I can tell you and some not."

"I'm listening with all ears," hard, and I hear Simone whispering to her. But shaking and sweating at the same time. I hear her breathing

"Where are you, Syl?"

"That I can't tell you, or else I'm in big trouble. In fact, we all may be in big trouble. Who knows?"

"Syl, tell me what you can, okay?"

"Well, first of all, I was getting some strange phone calls from the Boss and others."

CLICK. The phone went dead, just as I was about to get some information from her. Damn! I wonder if she'll call back. Maybe her money ran out.

I go back into the kitchen to tell Viv what happened.

"Viv, you're not going to believe this, but Sylvia tried to call me from a payphone, and we got cut off, damn if I know where she is, and most of the time, you can't track phone booth calls. Let's stay off the phone for a few minutes, and she'll probably call back."

"What did she say, Pete?"

"She just said that if she tells us everything, we all may be in big trouble." My hands are sweaty, and I have another headache.

"Do you want some tea? That always helps."

"Nothing will help now until I hear from Sylvia again."

"Maybe we should listen to some music to get your mind off of this."

"No, I can't concentrate; I'll just pace the floor until she calls."

"Well, that's silly," says Viv, "But each to his own."

So, I pace the floor back and forth in the hall while my mind is spinning, thinking of all possible angles. I light up a cigarette, and as soon as I take my first puff, the phone rings again.

I dash to pick it up.

(Crackle), "Hello, Syl, is it you?"

"I'm sorry, Pete, but my money ran out, and we're in nowheresville, so I have to talk fast. So, as I said, strange phone calls, threatening me if I rat on Boss Johnnie for the death of Robbie, I'll be dead soon, and maybe some revenge on you too. There's more..." (voice fading...)

"Syl, can you hear me?"

"Yeah, now I can. What were you asking?"

"Syl, who killed the bodyguard?".

"I'm sure it was the Boss' henchmen, but ordered by him. Then I believed I was next cause he didn't want me alive, or I might get the gang in trouble. So, when I heard this news, I ran with Simone to an undesignated place. Oh, I can tell you a little more. After I ran, calmed myself and Simone down, I called the police."

"You did what?" I say in an astonished voice. "Why didn't you call me first, Syl? You were really smart to run, though, before the bodyguard was shot. You could have died too. I couldn't get you on the phone; I try and try, then I go over to your place to check on you, and find a dead body on the street, blood all over the place. After that, I searched the house for you, but you and Simone were gone, and the house was totally clean. Whew, what luck! Syl, are you still there?"

"Yes, I'm here, but not for long. So, as I said, I call the police while I'm driving and they say to go to the nearest town where there is a police station. So, that's where I'm heading. But, Pete, I would love to tell you where I am but I can't right now; do you understand? I'll be dead, and you too. After I talk to the police, they may bring in the F.B.I. since this is a mob murder that we know about, at least I'm pretty sure, and the F.B.I. might get involved."

"How far are you from the nearest big town?"

"Oh, I'd say about twenty-thirty miles, not too far. After I talk to the police, I'll find a phone booth and call you."

"About what time will that be, Syl?"

"I don't know, in fact, I don't even know what time zone I'm in, but I can ask."

"Oh, Syl," says I, "I just can't imagine what you're going through. It must be frightening."

"Yes, both Simone and I are quivering, fearful, on the run, and who knows what's in store for us in the end. But we're holding up, saying our prayers, and hoping nobody in the family gets hurt because of me."

"Don't say things like that, Syl. We love you, and we will do anything to protect you."

"I don't want you to get in trouble, Pete, so please do not get mixed up in this mess; they'll maim or kill you like they did to Robbie, you know their power."

"Okay, but I don't want anyone following you or finding you after you speak to the police."

Please call me, promise?

"Yes, of course, Pete, but it may take a while until

they finish interrogating me, so don't go into a funk if you don't hear from me for a while. It's only five miles now to the next big town, so keep cool, and I'll be in touch, promise."

She hangs up the phone, and I start to cry. I'm devastated and can't even think at the moment. My mind wanders to all these horrible possibilities; we may never see her again, the mob network is big, and if they find out she got involved with the police, etc., they could still kill her or us.

I don't even have the strength to call any of my siblings, just worn out.

"Hey Viv, do we have any anxiety medicine around?"

"Why, what happened on the call with Sylvia?"

"You don't even want to know. All I can mutter at the moment is bad, very bad."

"Okay, I'll see what we have in the arsenal, but you have to tell me what happened."

"I will as soon as I calm down."

17

FRANKIE

ONE DAY LATER

Oh my God, I just got a call from Pete. I didn't get every detail, and I am sick to my stomach about Sylvia and Simone. I'm almost sure it was the Boss buggin' and threatenin' her, poor thing; what choice does she have? She has to run; those dummies don't fool around, you know.

And, another thing that pisses me off is that the other family members may be in trouble. Of course, if she rats on Johnnie by going to the police, that could be trouble, but I understand her reasons for all of this.

After all, she lost her wonderful husband in the most awful way and put us all on a freaking goose chase to find out he was killed. I'm thinkin' that we better have alibis in case the police or worse, the

F.B.I., get in touch with any of us. Oh God, I can't believe this. My family could be devastated.

And, on top of all this, Anna is buggin' me for more child support. I'm givin' her as much as I can afford, but she wants more. I'm thinkin' that I'm not gonna deal with another loan shark. She'll have to make do.

The kids are adjustin' to their new life pretty well. I see them most weekends and once or twice for a nice Italian dinner out. Don't get me wrong, Anna is talkin' to me, just in the wrong way. If she'd be a little more understandin' of my situation, that would be great. Anyways, me and the kids are doing just fine.

I'll be right back; the phone is ringing, and it's probably Pete.

"Hello?"

"Oh, Pete, I was just talkin' about you and the fiasco with Sylvia and Simone. What? You'd like me to come over later to talk? Let's see, it's Tuesday, okay, cause I don't have the kids tonight. What time? Okay, eight pm sounds good. I'll be there."

I'm getting ready to go to Pete's house, and the phone rings again.

"Hello? Oh, it's Margaret. How are you, my dear sis?"

"Not So good, Frankie; I just spoke with Pete, so I know most of what's going on with Sylvia and Simone. I'm so scared for them, but also for us, 'cause we're part of the family, and the Boss may come after us."

"That's definitely a possibility, but we can handle it, so don't worry."

"What do you mean a possibility? That's awful," says Margaret.

"Listen, sis. I know these guys. They play games, get you all riled up, and do nothin'; on the other hand, they can be vicious. So, just cool it until I can give you more information, okay? Hey listen, sweetheart, I know you're afraid, we all are, but we have to remain calm. I'll keep you posted; I promise."

"Well, I'm still shaking, but I'll have a glass of wine, think of poor Sylvia and try to calm down," says Margaret.

"Okay, love, get some sleep too. Goodbye." I hang up and try to take a deep breath, thinkin' of what Pete may tell me when I get there.

I arrive at Pete's place, and strangely enough, Vivian is there to greet me.

"Come on in, Frankie. What would you like to drink?"

"Same old thing, Bourbon and soda will be fine. By the way, I've missed you at the last couple of family pow-wows. Where you been?"

"Trying to stay out of the foray and stick to my artwork on the side; I have a show coming up."

"Really? That's wonderful, Viv; I know you have talent, but a show? Wow!" I don't really like her work, but would never say anything.

Pete walks into the living room with a glass of

red wine. He looks a little tired, probably been on the phone for hours.

"Hey, bro, how are you?"

"I could be better, but I'm hanging in," says Pete.

"Well, let's make a toast to us and the safe return of Sylvia and Simone."

Me and Pete sit on the couch with glasses in hand. He looks awful, bags under his eyes. It looks like he aged in a week.

"Okay, Frankie, I think it's better if we talk face to face. I'll try to fill you in as much as I can. And, by the way, I'm expecting a call from Sylvia, and I wanted you to be here to listen in, and then we'll talk some more. In the meantime, I told Vivian, of course, and called all the sibs, and they're scared to death that they could be pulled into this mess."

"Of course, I understand very well," I say.

"So, I guess you're pretty much up to date as to Sylvia's predicament, and, even if you aren't, I'll talk. You know that there was a dead body at Sylvia's place, and she takes off even before the dead body cause she gets threatening calls from the Boss, and she has every right to run. She calls me twice from a phone booth, doesn't tell where she is, probably instructions from the Boss, who knows. At any rate, she says she's going to call me after she speaks to the police, but that was last night, and I never heard from her."

"It's possible that the police station is understaffed, and she and Simone stay overnight at a motel nearby, who knows," says I.

"Yeah, I guess that's the reason, but we should be hearing from her very soon," says Pete.

He seems very nervous; his eye is twitching, and his hand is anything but steady. He has too much pressure on him; the others have to step up a little and take some of that off; it's not fair to put the burden on Pete.

"So, you think she's finished with the police by now?"

The phone rings. Pete almost stumbles over a small statue of Jesus as he runs to pick up the phone.

"Hello?" (crackle). He waits seconds, and then he hears a voice on the other end.

"Hello, Sylvia, can you hear me?"

"Yes, I can hear you pretty well."

"Did you speak with the police? What did they say? Where are you now?"

"Take it easy, Pete, we're staying in a motel; we got to this place too late to speak to the police, and they were swamped, and I'm really worn out, and so is Simone; you want to say hi to her?"

"I'd love to," says Pete with a half-smile.

"Hi Uncle Pete, we're managing, though I'm so scared of everything, the police, my mom, my other family; I feel like this is a bad dream." We could hear her weeping in the background.

"Can I speak to mom again?"

"Sure, Uncle Pete, bye." She hands the phone to Sylvia.

"So, what do the police say to you the next day?" asks Pete

"They talk to me for about an hour, two investigators and me and Simone in the room. I tell them everything, the threatening calls, the dead body (as I know from the gang), and the fact that I had to run to save my life and Simone's. I can't tell if they believe me or not. But they did say that they are getting the F.B.I. involved because they know this crime family and their behaviors. The detectives at the police station asked me all kinds of questions about my past life, what my dead husband did for a living, and then about my family."

"What did you tell them about your family?"

"I told them we have a big family and that we are all very close."

"Is that all, Sylvia?"

"Pete, as I said before, there are certain things they told me not to tell anyone, even you!"

"Why is that? We're family and concerned about you and Simone. Are they treating you with respect?"

"Yes, kind of, I mean, they are very straightforward and hardly smile, but they don't beat us; we're okay, I guess. The next thing will probably be interviews with the F.B.I. 'cause that's what we were told. I'm running out of money, so I have to get off the phone in a minute. Any more questions?"

"Can you talk to me about your location? I mean, it's like you're a complete stranger who's been told to say nothing, not your whereabouts when you'll be home, nothing."

"I'm really sorry, Pete, but again, if I break my promise, I'll be dead, and so will Simone. So, hang tight for now, my dear brother-in-law, and I'll keep you as posted as I am able to. After I speak with the F.B.I., I will call you, okay? We're both keeping our cool as much as possible. I have to go, bye."

And she slams down the phone.

"What do you think, Pete?"

"I think it looks bad, Frankie."

"Well, maybe we can negotiate with the Boss."

"Frankie, you must be mad, though I would like to give him a piece of my mind. He's playing games with Sylvia."

"What games, Pete?"

"We may never see her again."

18

SYLVIA

TWO DAYS LATER

Well, now I feel I can finally talk; here we are in Topeka, Kansas, in the middle of nowhere, cornfields, barns, a lot of dirt roads, smelly cows, paved roads in the city (which is nothing like New York City) some boutique shops, a Walmart, a police station and courthouse.

Oh, and I forgot a hotel where me and Simone will stay for a few days. The room has twin beds, a bit raunchy could be cleaned better, but we'll survive. Listen, we're not paying for this, so we can't complain (don't ask me who is paying for it).

I spoke to Pete last night, but it is late, and we have instructions to keep moving to this place in Kansas. He seems frantic, and frankly, I don't blame him. I mean, we're out of sight but not out of his mind, nor are we out of the family's minds.

I feel terrible that I'm not allowed to talk to my family. At night I say prayers for me and Simone and for them too, hoping someday we'll be back in Brooklyn. Although the way this is going, it doesn't look good, we'll see.

If I talk to my family, as I said before, I'm meat. Believe me, it's very lonely, and thank God for Simone's company, although she's pretty sad at the moment.

"Mom? This room really smells, and the bed is like an air mattress. It's killing my back."

"I have an idea, darling. Why don't we take my perfume and spray all over, including the bathroom."

"Great idea, then it will be on us too, and we'll all smell delicious. You know I really miss school and my friends."

"I know, dear, and it must be an awful feeling, but hang in there until we talk to the F.B.I."

"It's hard. I feel so out of it," says Simone, "no homework, missing my classwork, socializing, and having fun. I'm still a kid and shouldn't be in this predicament, right?"

Poor kid, I feel terrible for her. On the other hand, maybe I can convince the authorities to leave her out of this and send her to Uncle Pete. Who knows?

"Mom? When is our appointment with the F.B.I?"

"They should be calling any minute with our appointment time. I think tomorrow morning."

"It's five pm, and I'm starving," says Simone, walking to get her coat and smiling at her mom.

"That's fine with me. How about this diner down the street? They have burgers and other stuff. It looks pretty clean."

"Sounds good," remarks Simone, "I'm up for it and famished too."

Just as we are about halfway out of the door, the phone rings. I have to answer it.

"Hello?"

"Mrs. Valenti? This is the local F.B.I. office in Topeka, calling to let you know that we scheduled an appointment for you tomorrow at nine am; does that work for you?"

"Absolutely, that would be fine. I have your address, and we have a car, so we'll see you tomorrow."

"Is that okay, mom?"

"Well, dear, we really don't have a choice. It's their call, so we go. Problem with that, okay?"

"No, mom, it's just that I don't like getting up that early! But I guess it's okay."

We drive to downtown Topeka, about ten minutes from our hotel. The city isn't much, mostly old buildings, maybe one or two modern ones, and the F.B.I. office is in one of these.

It's easy to park. They have their own lot. We take the elevator to the ninth floor and look for the F.B.I. sign. It says Mr. Alan Parker and some other names below.

The doors open, and a gray-hair gentleman

greets us with a strange accent. I guess kind of country.

"Hello, you must be Mrs. Valenti," and looking at Simone, asks her name. "And you are?"

"Simone Valenti, nice to meet you, Mr..."

"Parker, Alan Parker, come in, please and follow me to my office, and please have a seat."

"Now, Mrs. Valenti..."

"Please call me Sylvia, sir."

"Right, Sylvia, a very pretty name. Now, Sylvia, do you know why you are here today?"

"Well, I think so, but not totally sure."

"Well then, Sylvia, I will begin. When we hear from any police, no matter what town or city, and it involves the Mafia. Usually, we, the F.B.I., get involved. The reason we get involved is that these mobsters do terrible things to innocent people, many illegal activities, killings, and sometimes the police cover-up for them; in other words, they don't necessarily protect you. Not all police, but it seems that in New York, Chicago, Miami, and other big cities where the Mafia dwell, they pay off the police, so they won't get into trouble. Now I hear that some of your families are involved with some Bosses in New York City. Is that correct, Sylvia?"

"Yes, some of my family is involved with the Bosses, but some are not, and mostly involved with loan sharks, theft, for which my dear Robbie was wrongly accused and killed; perhaps some bookies involved, but this is the first time that there has been a death in the family."

"Does your family borrow money from these loan sharks?"

"Yes, I believe so, sir. My late husband took out loans from them. In fact, he was in the cement business, which I believe is owned by a Boss."

It hurts when I say these things.

"Did your husband deal with laundered money?"

"I really don't know; he didn't talk much about his business to us."

"Sylvia, do you know why your husband was killed by the Mob?"

"I know very little since weeks ago when two unidentified men drag him out of the house early morning when we are having breakfast. I only get two calls from him; my brother-in-law, Pete, who knows one of the Bosses in New York, speaks with him a few times. Then he is given permission to see him, only once, and my husband is wounded."

"Sylvia, can you explain these wounds?"

I have to collect myself first, take a deep breath.

"Not perfectly, sir, because I personally never got to see my husband before he is brutally murdered, to everyone's surprise. I learn all the details from my brother-in-law, Pete. I think they break his nose, punch him in the eye and smash his ears at least; they may have done more, but I didn't see it." I am told that he is coming home in a few days but never did come home. The boss tells Pete that he is dead and not to come looking for his body, or me or else."

Simone starts to weep quietly, a tissue in her hand.

"Why did you run from the house with your daughter, Sylvia?"

"I get threatening phone calls that I might be next if I tell anyone about Robbie."

Simone has her head down and hands clasped.

"I see, Sylvia. So, you run to protect yourself after the death of your husband because you are afraid the Boss will kill you and Simone. Did you have a bodyguard?"

"Yes, but he is always taking breaks and disappears for a time."

"Sylvia, did anyone in the family know your plan to leave?"

"No, sir. I am scared and pack up quickly with Simone and sneak out when the bodyguard is on a break."

Simone starts to make weird faces, blinking, probably scared.

"Do you have a vehicle, Sylvia?"

"Yes, I do, and I drive out of the city, heading west, not really knowing our destination."

"What is your goal here, Sylvia, now that you are on the run?"

I guess I'll have to think one up quickly.

"My goal is to drive until I come to a decent size city and call the police and tell them everything. While driving, I did call Pete and only Pete, and it was from a phone booth; I think I called him twice, but I say I will not call again until after I speak with you. I never tell him where we are or where we're going."

"So, let me get this straight," says Mr. Parker with a straight face. "The reason you leave in a hurry is because you fear for your and your daughter's life."

My hands are sweaty, and I'm nervous. Simone keeps looking from me to him.

"Yes, that's correct, sir. Then, after I leave and call Pete, I find out that my bodyguard is shot and killed in front of my house; Pete finds him and calls the police. According to him, they give him a dirty look, and then they take the body away. Pete searches the house after calling me for at least three days, day and night; he thinks I might be dead too; the house has nobody in it, and it is clean, with no blood anywhere. He decides that I fly the coop and have no notes to give him any clues. He contacts the rest of my family and, as you can imagine, they are all panicked, not only for me and Simone but for themselves, who also have connections to the Boss. I don't tell all the specifics."

"So, Sylvia, you believe that the Mafia, your so-to-speak Boss, killed Robbie, your husband, and then has it out for you via the bodyguard, so you run before his attempt to kill you, so the Boss doesn't take the hit."

"Yes, sir, I believe that is the intention here and our reason for the run."

"Okay then, that makes sense to me. Now, is Pete pretty honest?"

"Yes, very much so, sir."

"Well, I still don't think it's a good idea for you to notify anyone in the family regarding your whereabouts. The Mafia is all over the place, and they communicate."

I wonder what is coming now.

"Sylvia, after thinking about what you are telling me, it seems as though you are still frightened to return home, is that right?"

I would like to, but I'm freaking scared for both of us.

"Yes, Mr. Parker, I'm frightened that the boss will find me."

"Well then," says Mr. Parker" with a definitive-looking face, "We, meaning the F.B.I., has something called a Witness Protection Program. This means that the F.B.I will send you far away to Arizona, get you a new home, and you will live your nice, quiet life out there, of course, with your daughter. But here is the stipulation."

Uh oh, what is he going to say? I'm shaking.

"You both have to make a complete change of identification."

I feel like I'm going to pass out.

"What do you mean, Mr. Parker?"

"I mean that you will have to change both your names, get a new driver's license, a new social security card, a new passport, etc. In other words, you won't be Sylvia Valenti anymore. You might be Amanda Smith or something like that. You will be living in a new place."

I'm sick to my stomach. Simone is staring out the window.

Mr. Parker pauses for a moment when he sees the look on our faces. He takes out a cigarette and lights it, and breathes out a circle of smoke. I'm sure he knows we're terrified. He's trying to give us a chance to take it all in.

"I forgot to emphasize that there will always be an F.B.I. agent checking on you from the local office, which communicates with us, so no need to be afraid."

Yeah, that's what he thinks.

"Are we clear on this, Sylvia? Any questions?"

"When do we move? And will we get help changing all of our identification?"

"Absolutely; we will take care of everything, and no one, including your family or the mob, will ever know you again as Sylvia and Simone Valenti.

Me and Simone look at each other dumfounded.

"To my mind, that's the best protection you can get and be completely safe, never have to worry about being afraid or hurt, in you next life. We do this for many people in this situation. You're not the first. Are you ready to have a nice, peaceful life?"

We gaze at each other intensely, pause for a moment, smile and nod.

"Mr. Parker?"

"Yes, Sylvia"

"I have one question; can I call my brother-in-law Pete and say goodbye?"

"Of course, you can, from our office where it cannot be traced."

Me and Simone hug each other with a half-smile.

19

PETE

I knew it, that bastard Boss; he sets up the whole thing, scares Sylvia and Simone to death, threatens their lives, kills the bodyguard, and is after them so that he will wipe his hands clean and will not have to face authorities, possibly prison; unless she rats on him which he knows nothing about, we hope.

He does have his special contacts so that he might know something, but the F.B.I. is involved now, so he'll back off for a while. However, to cover his ass, he may be after me. I miss them already; happy they didn't get killed.

In the meantime, I get my last phone call from Sylvia. God bless her. She did the right thing. She calls me from the F.B.I., which can't be traced, to let me know they're safe, but with sweeping changes in their lives.

All she is allowed to tell me, as the F.B.I. listens

in, is that she will be a new person in an undisclosed place. We both cry on the phone; I will miss my family so much I can't hang up. She hands the phone to Simone, and strangely enough, she is calm, probably in shock; she speaks in weird phrases, not making a lot of sense.

Then Sylvia gets back on the phone to say her last goodbye, and she hangs up. I feel so empty now, like a chunk of our family is gone forever. I'm thinking of retribution before the Boss men kill me.

It's going to be tough, but my soul tells me to do something. I mean, there have been two murders and two attempted murders, enough! If I'm gonna do something, it's got to be right.

"Hey, Viv, how about pouring the old man a drink; I just got off the phone with Sylvia for the very last time, and I'm feeling sad, angry, and scared."

"Oh, Pete, of course, I'll make you a drink, honey, the same concoction?"

"That's fine. I gotta take a load off, so I'll be sitting in the living room."

I'm thinking of different plans, thoughts swirling around my head.

"You look like you're in a trance," says Viv as she walks towards me with a glass of red wine.

"You need to relax, Pete. You're all rolled up into a tight ball after these horrible ordeals."

"I know, Viv, but I can't help it; if I don't get some revenge, I'll never sleep another night. So, I'm sort of thinking in my head what to do."

"Pete, with this mob family, well known to police and the F.B.I., you'll never get to the Boss. I mean, you'll never put him down, right? So why are you obsessing over this?"

"I'm not going after the Boss, Viv, but I might go after someone else, easier to get to, you know what I mean?"

"But who?" says Viv in an inquisitive voice.

"I've got two in mind, but I don't want to say the names just yet; first, I want to talk to Frankie and Tommy, maybe Ted too. I want to bounce some ideas off their thick heads, just kidding."

"You mean I'm not worthy of knowing?"

"Of course, you are worthy, my dear, but my bros would be offended if I didn't discuss it with them first, you know kind of men's talk, but then you're next, my sweet."

"Okay, okay, I get it."

My wife is so understanding. It just makes me smile.

"How about we go out to eat tonight? Maybe that will calm me down a bit and a treat for you, Viv."

"Sounds wonderful, my sweet. I'm delighted. Where should dine?"

"Are you up for fish?"

"Anytime, my dear."

"How about Monty's Fishery?"

It's a short walk to Monty's, and we both order bourbon and soda. After my third drink, I'm relaxed until tomorrow when I gotta make some important plans.

THE NEXT DAY

I didn't sleep that well last night, tossing and turning, my head spinning, but I'm awake, and it's six am. I try to go back to sleep but can't. So, I make a strong cup of coffee, search the fridge for some stale doughnuts that Viv bought last week. While I'm eating, I get a call from Frankie.

"How ya doing, pal?" says Frankie in a cheerful voice; top of the mornin' to you. "I thought you might be awake and just wanted to know how your last goodbye to Sylvia went?"

"Very sad and tearful, buddy; we'll never see them again." Tears form in my eyes. "I'm glad you called, Frankie, we need to talk about some kind of revenge on the Family, not Johnnie, but I have a few ideas."

"Shoot," says Frankie, "I'd love to hear them."

"I can't; it's not fair; we need to have Tommy, Danny, and even Ted around too."

"I got it; so, why don't we meet at THE BAR? We've all been there before, so we know the place. How about tonight, after work; I don't have the kids, so all is good. Do you want me to call the bros?" says Frankie

"No, it's okay, I'll do it."

We meet up at THE BAR at five-thirty pm, order our drinks and some nibbles.

"Okay, bros, we got a big problem on our hands."

"Oh yeah? What's that?" says Danny smiling.

"Listen, you know damn well what it is," says

Tommy with a smirk. "Tell him, Pete, he's just joking around."

"Okay, guys, get serious now. We gotta make a plan to get revenge on the Boss; we're losing too much family. Now, we can't knock off Johnnie, that's for sure, but we can knock off Alex at the cement plant or Garcia at the dump. They are in cahoots with Johnnie to get these murders done and send our dear Sylvia and Simone away forever. We gotta think carefully about who to kill first or maybe both, and what are the consequences? Any thoughts from you guys?"

"Geez," says Danny, "If we knock off one or both, we are putting our families at great risk, right?"

"Right," says Frankie, "but they have to pay in some way for what they did, you know."

"Maybe we should hire a killer," says Ted in a quiet voice. "I may know someone who is a friend of one of my helpers at the pawnshop."

"Really, Ted, that would be amazin'," says Frankie. "But first we gotta check out this guy and plan with him how we do this so that Johnnie doesn't come for us."

"Ted, tell us about this hitman; this is serious business."

"Okay, guys, this fella that helps me out sometimes; he has a record of drug possession, vehicular homicide, and driving without a license. But I hire him because he has served his prison time, goes to drug rehab, and manages to get back his driver's license. He belongs to a small gang, not associated with Johnnie's large clan. This guy, Mark Estes, knows the game, you know what I mean. He's very sneaky, and his friend, Mike Lopez, takes care of people and has a good record, as far as I know. We first have to talk to Mark, my guy, who will then put us in touch with Lopez."

"Will your guy talk to us?" asks Danny.

"I think he will, and I think his buddy may too if we present the facts the right way," says Ted.

"Pete, what do you think?" asks Tommy, with a curious face.

"I think we should go for it. My feeling is we just can't let the mob get away with knock-offs every time, and it's our family that got killed and taken away. Why don't we let Ted take the lead, that is, if he agrees? Is this job too heavy for you, Ted?"

"No, I think I can pull it off, but let me talk to my guy first and see where it goes. If he agrees to work with us, great!"

"Thank you, Ted, for helping us get our revenge. When you contact this guy Mark, please give me a buzz."

"Sure, will do, Pete."

"Is everyone ready for a second round?"

"Yeah, let's do it; I agree with Pete, we just gotta get our revenge. And, if this Ted thing works out, we may even save our asses," says Frankie. The last thing we want to do, though, is hurt our families. And, to tell you the truth, I'm still a little scared."

"Frankie, I think we're all scared, but it's on our conscience, and if we don't act, we'll never erase it from our minds. I'll admit, it's a gamble, and we all have to agree."

"You're right, Pete, and I think we all agree, though with some fear in our hearts," says Tommy as he takes a deep breath.

"Okay then, let's agree to let Ted do his thing, and we'll hear back soon enough, right, Ted?"

"Yes, I'll get on it right away. Tomorrow I'll speak with Mark and get the ball rolling."

"Then let's have a toast to our new plan. I hope this works, or else we'll all be knocked off."

We clink our glasses and guzzle down our bourbons. Ugly thoughts are spinning around my head, but I don't say a word to them.

"I wonder how Sylvia is doing in witness protection?" asks Tommy.

"At least she's safe and away from Johnnie and his gang," says Danny.

"I'm getting a call. I guess I should take it.

"Hello?"

"Hello, Pete, this is Eddie, remember me?"

"Of course, Eddie, how are you?"

"Well, not so good, aches and pains, and the boss has me very busy collectin' money."

"What does that mean?"

"Well, Pete, remember that loan on your house? That's due at the end of this week. Time flies, doesn't it, Pete?"

"I got it on my calendar Eddie, so no worries, you'll get it."

"The Boss is angry, and he wants his money."

I hang up the phone, take two aspirins for a headache and head home to talk to Viv. With all that's been going on, it doesn't enter my mind. I walk head down, worried to death about the future. I don't know where to begin. It's going to be a long night.

20

TED

I get home late, and I'm a bit tipsy after a few bourbons at THE BAR. Margaret is still awake because I can see the light peeking through the bottom of the door. I walk in, she startles and puts her book down on the nightstand. I must look like what the cat dragged in.

"So, my dear, you're finally home; it's almost ten pm. Did you get a lot accomplished at THE BAR, other than drinking?"

"Oh yes, at least I think so. We are all revved up to do something, make a plan. We talk about what we want to carry out and who should be involved."

"And? Who should be involved?"

"Guess who, my darling wife?"

"You, my dear husband. I know you have good contacts, more than the rest of them."

"Well, me sort of indirectly. You know Mark at the shop, right?"

"Yes, I do. What are you getting at?"

"He has some friends who belong to a small gang. Basically, they knock off people, for money, of course."

"Hmm, I have no idea that Mark is in that business," says Margaret with an inquisitive look on her face.

"He's not a hitman. He knows someone who is, this guy, Mike Lopez. I'm the designated contact to see what we can do about the murders and attempted murders."

I don't really like being in the middle of all this, but it's my family too.

"But isn't there a great risk to all of us? I mean, we could all get killed," says Margaret.

"I believe if we do this carefully using an unknown gang, we may be okay, but there's always a risk, and I don't know how big."

"If I didn't think you are so adorable, I would knock your head off, just kidding. So, when does the action start?"

"Tomorrow! I will feel out Mark and see if he picks up on the plan. From there, it goes to Lopez. It's not going to happen right away, there have to be negotiations, and we have to split the cost."

"But aren't we still paying off loans, cars, houses, etc.?"

"Yeah, but I still have some cash stashed away for emergencies. Actually, I don't know what's there, but I know it's for a good cause.

"Honey," says Margaret, "I don't know how much we have for emergencies and other bills, but do we have to spend all our money on revenge, with perhaps a lot of risk?"

"No, my dear, you're right. I promise you we'll have a few pennies left! Just kidding. Now, it's after eleven pm, and I think we should both turn in for the night. You ready?"

"You bet!"

I hope I can sleep and get this revenge thing out of my mind for a while.

THE NEXT DAY

I did not have a great night's sleep, but a good cup of cappuccino does the trick every time, and my wife makes the best. I usually get to the shop around ten am, and Mark follows me at eleven am because he has his rehab group on certain mornings.

"I'm off to work, Margaret. I'll see you later." I hope it's not another late night. I kiss the kids before they go to school, each one eager to learn, thank God! I think I'll walk to work on this bright day. It's not that far.

As I'm walking, who do I meet in the street but Eddie, one of the Boss's cronies.

"Hey, Eddie, how are you doing? What are you doing in my neighborhood?"

"Ah, pretty good, just making some rounds to

pick up some dough for loan pay-offs. By the way, you up to date?"

"I believe I am, Eddie, but feel free to check on it."

"Oh, I forgot to ask. Do you know where Sylvia disappears to?"

"Honestly, Eddie, I really don't. And, since the family is quite upset about it, I would rather we don't talk about it anymore."

"Okay, just wonderin'."

"Are you sure you're just wondering, Eddie? Or do you know more than nothing?"

"Just that the Boss is curious and keeps askin' me, that's all."

"Well, you can tell Boss Johnnie, he's caused enough problems, so lay off."

"Whatever you say, old pal, nice meetin' you, take good care."

"Goodbye, Eddie."

The one person I didn't want to see today. Why do I have such bad luck?

I know he knows about Sylvia; he was in on the murder and the threats and the attempted murders and Sylvia's disappearance, too. He's a cover-up for Johnnie.

I keep walking, but a bit faster until I reach the office. I unlock the gates and open the door. I'm a little paranoid, so I quietly creep in and look around and listen for noises. The coast is clear, and I check to ensure my gun inventory is intact and the other stuff I sell.

Shortly after I open up and take care of some customers, Mark walks in and gets set to help me.

"Hi, Mark, how is your group going?"

"Oh, just fine, I actually like the people there, very friendly, and we all contribute."

"Mark, when this customer who is looking around leaves, I need to talk to you in private."

"Did I do something wrong?"

"No, not at all. It's something important for me and my family."

The store is empty now, and it is lunch hour, so I think this is a good time to approach Mark on the plan. I'm a little nervous, but I'm going for it.

"So, Mark, let's talk for a minute, okay?"

"Sure, Ted, good time for me."

"Okay. I'm going to make it short and quick. We've had two murders and two attempted ones in the last few weeks. Three are family members. One is a personal bodyguard. We know who the perp is, the Bellini Family, Boss Johnnie, and his cronies. Pete and our family desperately want revenge, but none of us know a killer. However, you, Mark, may associate with one. We understand the risks involved. The only killer we are aware of is Mike Lopez and his cronies, a lesser-known gang. They may be able to knock off two people close to the Boss, who constantly give us a run-around after my brother-in-law is killed and his wife and kid run for their lives and are now in the witness protection program, somewhere in the U.S. We don't know their whereabouts, and we will probably never see them again. We know these two guys are connected to the murders. So, if you talk to Mike, we would be most appreciative. We have no idea of price or if he's willing and able."

"Well, first of all, I'd be happy to talk to Mike, second of all, I think he still works, third of all he'd love the dough, so putting all of this together, I'm pretty sure he'll take it. Do you want to be around Ted when I speak with him?"

"Not especially, Mark; I think it's better if you describe the situation and get an answer, then we could all get together and discuss how, when, where, and who."

"I'll be happy to do that for you, Ted. You've been so kind to me, got me this job, knowing my background and all."

"Oh, Mark, you are doing everything you can to rehab yourself, and I like to help people who try to succeed."

"Okay, Ted, you got a deal. I'll work on it and call you as soon as I know something."

We shake hands and smile at each other, knowing that we're both trying to accomplish something of importance and is risky as well. I do admire Mark for being a hard worker and his interest in learning the business.

Someday me and Margaret are going to retire. That is when the kids leave the house and move somewhere like Florida, where we can just sit under a palm tree and drink pina coladas. Oh, to be old and lazy, not to be connected to anyone, except my family.

"Well, kiddo, is it okay if I leave a little early today and spend some time with my wife and kids?"

"Sure, Ted, you've been under a lot of stress lately. Don't worry. I can close up and lock the gates."

"I appreciate that kid, don't forget to call Mike. See ya."

As I walk away, maybe three hundred feet from the store, I hear a couple of gunshots. I run back fast, then stop for a second, out of breath, praying that it's not my store and Mark.

I wait until I don't hear any more shots, then I see two guys running down the street, ducking into an alley, out of sight. I continue my run towards the store. Oh my God!

21

MARGARET

Oh my God, I just got a frantic call from Ted, telling me that Mark is shot in the leg. I'm shaking and crying and need a glass of wine. He's still on the scene with the police. An ambulance comes and takes Mark to the emergency room.

Ted says he never saw the shooters because they ducked out of sight. But I'm sure the police will find them. What happens, I think, is that the shooters see Ted leave, and then as Mark is closing up, they move in.

I think they are looking to steal some guns; I'm sure Mark did his best to protect himself against the robbers, but they still got him good. I'm waiting for another call from Ted, so I learn more about what happened and about Mark's condition.

I think he'll be taken to Richmond University Medical Center on Staten Island, and that's where my kids were born, so I'm pleased about that.

"Excuse me for a moment. My phone is ringing, and I think it's Ted."

"Hello, oh, Pete. I guess you know about the disaster this afternoon; I'm very upset, and of course, Ted is frantic. Do I need what? Oh, your help now? Well, let me speak to Ted, he should be calling me any minute, and then I will call you back. Goodbye, Pete."

I'm feeling dizzy. Maybe it's from the red wine. I think I'll sit down and pray for Mark, poor soul, he is such a nice man, and I think he's lonely.

The phone is ringing again.

"Hello, oh thank God, it's you, Ted. I feel so terrible about Mark, any news?

"The police will do a thorough investigation of the crime scene and will get an experienced detective. Right now, I'm wrapping things up at the store; there is yellow police tape around the premises, so we're not allowed in at this time."

"What about Mark's condition?"

"I'm not sure. I will be heading over there when the police say I can leave. He is at the emergency room at Richmond Hospital."

What should I tell the kids?"

"Nothing yet, Margaret. I'll call you when I find out a bit more, okay?"

"Yes, darling, oh, and I have to call Pete back; he called, very worried and wants to know more."

"Well, then, just tell him Mark got shot in the leg with a .45 semi-automatic handgun, and that's all I know right now."

"Okay, Ted, be safe and call me from the hospital. I'm worried too."

I hang up the phone and collect myself, pour a glass of water, and sit at the kitchen table. I'm thinking about what just occurred and wondering if it was just a random armed burglary. Or was this somehow connected to Boss Johnnie?

I shouldn't even be thinking things like that, should I? Anyway, I'll continue drinking my water and finishing my crossword puzzle. Oh, I forgot to call Pete back.

"Hello, Pete, hi, it's Margaret. Sorry I had to hang up on you. Ted says to tell that his employee Mark, you know the guy who's is supposed to connect with Lopez, got shot in the leg as he was closing up the store. I don't know anything more, and Ted is on his way to Richmond Hospital. I will probably meet him there."

"Was Ted there when it happened?"

"No, he just left to come home when a few minutes later, he hears gunshots and goes running back to the store. But by the time he gets there, the burglars are gone, and Mark is shot. Hey Pete, do you think Boss Johnnie has anything to do with this?"

"You never know, but it's probably just random violence, which is rampant in this city, especially with the Bellini Family here and other mobs. Should I call Ted?"

Tonight or in the morning would be best, Pete, but thanks for always trying to help out. We really appreciate it."

"Okay, maybe I'll call back later; how late do you guys stay up?"

"We usually hit the sack around eleven pm, so yeah, we might connect tonight."

"Ah, Margaret, I don't want to be pushy but do you think Ted can take care of the Lopez business by himself?"

"I really don't know, Pete. I guess it depends on Mark's recovery or if Mark tells Ted to go ahead with meeting this guy alone or maybe even at the hospital with Mark. Nothing is clear at this moment, Pete, so sit tight, and we'll talk later."

"That's fine with me, Margaret. Are you okay? Kids too?"

"I haven't told the kids yet, Ted told me not to, but yes, they are doing fine, thanks for asking."

"Okay then, I'll speak to you later tonight."

"Good, Pete, thanks for thinking of us."

I keep thinking this shooting is too much of a coincidence, and my mind wanders a lot.

Phone rings.

"Hello, oh Ted, so happy you called. I'm so worried; are you at the hospital?"

"Yes, and Mark is being operated on to get the bullet out of his thigh; He should be in recovery soon and then in a room."

"I'm coming over to keep you company. I've left the kids some chicken from last night and some salad and pops in the freezer. I'll tell them I'm going to the store to help you and that often we stay open until nine on Thursdays.

"Are you sure that's okay for you, honey?"

"I'm sure dear, I'll see you over at Richmond in the waiting room. Goodbye."

I hang up, a bit shaky, and get the kids' dinner ready for them on the table.

"Ken, Mary, Chris. Please wash your hands and come down here. I need to speak with you."

They all scurry down the stairs and ask me all kinds of questions.

"SSH…not all at once, please. I need to tell you something. Mom has to leave for a couple of hours to stop at a friend's house and then help dad at the store; it's very busy there. We should be home about nine, and I want you all in your pajamas by then. Please put the dishes in the dishwasher, but don't start it, okay, everything clear?"

I kiss each one on the forehead and leave for the hospital.

I see Ted sitting in the waiting room reading something.

He sees me and rises to hug me.

"What's happening?"

"Sit down first, dear, calm yourself. Mark is out of surgery. They got the bullet out, but a fair amount of blood loss. He should be back in a room shortly. Lucky guy, it could be much worse. Those bastards, the doc says Mark is in good spirits and should be in the hospital about three to four days to make sure no infection, and by the way, he is on pain pills and antibiotics."

"Thank the Lord. I was praying all the way here.

Oh, by the way, the kids are fine. Set dinner out for them and told them to clean up and pajamas on."

"You're a taskmaster, I'll say," says Ted, "those kids are great and even listen sometimes."

We read, talk, pray until the doc comes out in scrubs.

"Good news, folks..."

"Oh doc, by the way, this is my wife Margaret, she helps out in the store sometimes, meet Dr. Ramos. He is the surgeon."

"Nice to meet you, Doctor. How is Mark doing?"

"For a pretty deep wound, he is doing well. He needs some rest, which means short visits for the next forty-eight hours; he has a lot of trauma. They are moving him up to room 461. Give them a few minutes, and then you may have a short visit."

"Thank you, Doc, for all of your great skills and care. We appreciate it."

We sit down and wait, it seems like hours, and I'm getting hungry.

"Are you Mr. and Mrs. Esposito?"

"Yes, we are," says Ted, eager to stand up and move.

"Well, sir, follow me, and I'll take you up to your friend's room."

We follow the gentleman as he takes us to Mark's room.

Ted knocks on the door and slowly pushes it open. We enter quietly and smile at Mark, and he returns the smile with some effort.

"Hey, buddy, you're looking good. You sure took a good one and are lucky to be alive. I feel so bad leaving you at the store to close up. That was stupid of me to do. We should have done it together, or I should have let you go home first. That will never happen again, Mark."

Mark smiles, but you can see he's in pain. I put the flowers I bought at the gift shop near him on his nightstand. He begins to talk, though with effort.

"It's crazy, Ted, just out of the blue. They were after some guns to steal. They pointed at me, then shot me, nothing I could do at that point. I think they stole some 9MM handguns, but then everything becomes a blur; the next thing I know is an ambulance comes and also the cops. I am bleeding pretty heavy; I feel so bad."

Ted goes over to Mark and holds his hand. Mark has tears rolling down his cheek.

"You're not going to get rid of me, are you?"

"Never, and don't worry about Lopez, you're right. We'll do it together."

22

PETE

FOUR DAYS LATER

I'm shocked and saddened by Mark's incident and because it may stall our negotiations with Lopez. Mark is out of the hospital and is recuperating at his small apartment on Staten Island. I spoke with Ted a couple of times, and it seems like things are going the right way. Ted is supposed to call me any minute to meet at Mark's apartment sometime today. I just hope Mark's head is clear enough to talk about our plan. I'm still in the revenge mode, and the sooner, the better, no matter the risks. I think I'll call Viv and tell her I might be late, so I don't get the "where have you been" routine.

"Hello, Viv, it's me, honey; just wanted to let you know that I may be late tonight, not real late, but don't wait for me for dinner. I think Ted and me are going to meet at Mark's apartment to talk with him about Lopez and the plan."

"How is Mark doing, by the way?"

"He's recovering at home, and I think it's probably okay to see him now."

"Well, hon, I really don't know, but I think she's the girlfriend who goes to rehab with him. Anyway, Ted has seen him and says he looks well, some pain, but he can handle it."

"Oh, I'm so pleased with that news; I got really scared that he might die from his wounds."

"I doubt that, honey. The store remains closed, with police tape around it, so Ted can't go to work until the cops and the detective tell him it's okay. According to Ted, they're doing a good investigation, fingerprints, hidden cameras, and more. They don't have the suspects yet, but they will soon enough. These guys know what they're doing."

"So, I should feed the kids, and you'll be home around ten?"

"I hope so, but I'm already beat, so yes, it won't be too late." Please, God, I need some time with my wife.

"Okay then, Pete, say hi to Ted and Mark, and I'll see you later. I'll wait up for you."

I'm doing some paperwork in my cubbyhole office at the docks. Usually, I'm loading and unloading, but I also have to keep track of certain things. It's nearing five, so my boss makes us clock in and out, but I'm still waiting for Ted's call. Somebody taps me on the shoulder.

"Hey, Pete, how ya doin'?"

"Hey, Monty, I'm fine, getting ready to go for the day?"

"Yeah, just thought I'd stop by to say hey; family okay?"

"Yes, everyone is fine at the moment."

"So sorry, man, I mean about your brother gettin' killed by the Boss. We gotta be careful around here. You cross someone, and bam, you're out. Anyways, nice talking to ya, Pete. See ya around sometime."

"Okay, Monty, thanks for stopping by." Wonder why he's so friendly all of a sudden.

My phone rings: "Hey Ted, everything cool? Do you think it's okay if we meet at Mark's place in like half-hour or so?"

"Yes, I think it would be fine," says Ted; "I already spoke to him about Lopez, and he's ready to chat about it."

"Great, so how about we meet there at around five-thirty pm? I'm almost ready to clock out. I take it you're home now, Ted?"

"Yes, Margaret and I are chatting and drinking a bit of bourbon, and the kids are fighting upstairs. That's why we need the bourbon."

"Got it, okay, so I'll see you at Mark's place. I have the address."

I clock out a little past five pm and hop on a ferry

to get to Mark's place. I hope Mark is feeling well and that we make some small talk first, but then we get into the gritty stuff. There are so many "ifs" about this plan. I pray that it plays out.

I arrive at Mark's apartment, which is thankfully on the first floor of a four-flight walk up in a brownstone. I can see the door is slightly open, so he doesn't have to get up and use his leg. I knock and walk in slowly. Mark is on a couch propped up with many pillows under his leg. He looks a bit pale but otherwise okay. His leg is bandaged up.

"Hey there, buddy, you look great. I hope I'm not disturbing you."

"Oh no, nice to see you, Pete, you're looking pretty fine yourself. Can I get you something to drink?"

"No, you can't get up, Mark, but if it's okay, I'll help myself to bourbon and water."

"I have crutches right here, so yes, I can move around. My girlfriend has been helping me cook and clean a bit, so that's been good, and I'm feeling better each day. Ted called and said he'd be here in a few. Do you want to order some pizza? They'll deliver pretty fast. I hear somebody walking in the hall. It's most likely Ted."

"Hey, Ted, come on in, we're shootin' the bull. There's beer in the fridge, and Pete's drinking bourbon, so what can I get you?"

"Well, I guess another bourbon won't kill me, but I can get it myself. You just lay there and rest. Can I get you something?"

"Nay, I'm on antibiotics, so the doc told me to stay dry a few more days."

How many stitches do you have?" says Ted, while making his bourbon concoction.

"Actually, I have staples, and I don't count them. So, should we order a pizza? What kind do you two like? How about an "everything" pizza?"

"Sounds great. I'll call for it. Should we get a large?"

"Absolutely," says Mark. "All I can tell you is that the hospital food is poison. Maybe I lost a couple of pounds, but I'll make it up tonight."

Ted gives me a nod, and I nod back to have Ted start talking while we're waiting for the pizza delivery.

"So, we're blessed to see Mark in such good shape. He's strong and willing and will keep healing as the days go by. We're gathered here tonight for a short meeting about our plan of revenge for the murders and disappearance of our family members. As Mark and I talked earlier, before he was shot, he agreed to talk with Mike Lopez about hiring a killer and how much it is going to cost us. Mark tells me that Mike is still in the business and is willing to have a meeting with us. Mark, do you want to add to this discussion?"

"Sure; well, Lopez is a small operation compared to the Bellini Family. He has three or four guys that scout things out and one or two snipers. He tells me that he's very busy now, but he'll fit us into his schedule. He says there are a lot of snaggers and killers around the city competing for money and loyalty, and power. Anyways, I think we're good to go as soon as I hear back from him."

The phone rings.

"Oh, that might be him."

"Hello?"

"Hi, Mark, this is Mike Lopez speaking.

"Hi, Mike, how's it going?"

"Pretty damn busy, but can't complain; the money's coming in, and we're able to take care of our families. So sorry, Mark, to hear about the shooting. Catch them yet? I know it takes time, but you got a good detective on the case. Them pawn shops get hit a lot. Everybody needs a gun in my crowd."

"Yeah, I know what you mean, Mike; you still got time for us?"

"For you, Mark, and your special friends, I'll find the time."

"When can we meet in person and get the dates, cost, and other stuff settled?"

"Wait, let me look at my calendar book, let's see, um, maybe tomorrow after I speak to my guys, probably around six pm cause they do a lot of work on night shift starting around nine pm."

I'm getting nervous that he's giving us a lot of small talk.

"Great, Mike. I got my boss Ted here and his brother-in-law Pete, who works at the docks.

We'll set it up with you after they check with another family member."

"Right on, Mark, so I'll hear from you later on tonight, right?"

"You got it, talk to you later, bye now."

We stare at each other, not knowing quite what to expect from this call.

I ask" "How well do you know this guy, Mark?"

"He's been an acquaintance of mine for years; we used to play basketball together, and also we play poker with some other guys. He's not my best friend, but I think he's genuine."

"You think he'll give us a discount because we know you?"

"I doubt it, but you never know; we'll negotiate, like with everything else."

The pizza arrives piping hot, and we all chomp it down in a hurry.

"Ted and Mark, thank you very much for putting us in touch with Lopez. I appreciate it. So, I guess we're finished for the moment. I'll call my brother, Danny. He has a big place, then call Mark to set up the time. Is that okay, Ted?"

"Sure, is, buddy; looking forward to what's ahead."

"Let's pray for success." Amen, then I think of all the bad that could happen to our families.

That makes me very nervous, but we have to do this for our future sanity. Please, God, help us in this effort. We need you to guide us.

23

TED

After we leave Mark's apartment last night, I call Danny to see if we can use his place to meet with Lopez tomorrow at six pm. He says it is fine and he even offered to barbecue some hamburgers and hotdogs for us, for whoever shows up.

The phone call went well with Lopez. From what I can tell, he seems nice enough and willing to meet and work with us on his busy schedule. Now, the hard part comes, we don't know Lopez, have never seen him, and can we trust him? My mind is so jumbled with thoughts. I can't think clearly anymore. I just hope we don't get taken.

I call the rest of the family to see who wants to come, and it looks like Pete, Margaret, Frankie, Tommy, and Maria, so far. I want to keep this meeting orderly without Frankie shouting out of place.

The main goal here is to scout out Lopez and

his men to see if we get along together, get the job done, and what the price will be. Then, as a family, we have to decide if we want to knock off Alex and Garcia or just one of them. My soul tells me both are very close to the Boss and need to be knocked off if it's possible.

"Hello, oh darling, what? Yes, you can come tonight. I'm at the pawnshop, cleaning up a bit. The tape is still around, but the police and the detective have done their work inside the store so I can get in and put things away. I'll come home and pick you up around four-thirty pm, so get a pizza for the kids, and tell them I said to behave, or else!"

"Okay, dear, what about our dinner?"

"Danny has offered to barbecue some burgers, so we're taken care of."

"Alright, I'll see you later, bye."

No sooner do I hang up the phone than detective Walter walks into the store.

"Hey, Walter, how are things going with the investigation?"

"I can't really talk about it yet, Ted. We're looking at a couple of guys, suspicious with records and all, but nothing concrete. We'll get this police tape off pretty soon. In the meantime, you probably have some paperwork to do and cleaning up a bit."

"Yes, I'm keeping myself busy; by the way, Mark is coming in tomorrow just for a short time to get the hell out of his tiny apartment. He's a brave guy and didn't let the burglars get much; the worst is he got shot. We've lost some money, of course, because the business has been closed, but I think we'll make it up in the next couple of weeks. Funny, I've never had a problem with a robbery or a shooting in fifteen years. In that sense, I'm lucky. Good thing my wife wasn't working at the time of the shooting; sometimes, she helps in the store. When do you think we'll have a person or persons of interest?"

"Maybe a week or so, it takes time, Ted, we don't want to charge the wrong ones.

Well, I better get my ass moving. I have a lot of other cases. You take care, Ted, and I'll keep you posted. Bye now."

Boy, I had such an urge to ask Walter if he could nab Garcia and Alex, but I know that would give the whole thing away, our plan, I mean.

I think I'll call Danny and see what's happening over there for the barbecue and meeting with Lopez.

"Hello, Danny?

"Oh, hi, Ted, we're expecting a crowd tonight, some family members plus the Lopez guys at around six pm, so come at five pm, and we'll chow down."

"Okay, see you there."

I close the store, lock the gate and drive home to pick up Margaret.

"It's pizza night, dad. Mom says you guys are going out. YAY, we have the house to ourselves."

"Yeah, but you behave, no messing around and clean up the kitchen; mom will have a cat fit. By the way, where is mom?"

"She's upstairs prettying herself," says Mary with a coy look on her face.

"Margaret, are you almost ready to go?"

"Yes, dear, I'll be down in a minute."

I pace the floor as I'm a bit anxious about this meeting; I don't know what to expect.

We arrive on time, and I see Danny chatting with family members and slugging down some beer; he notices us.

"Hey. Welcome, Ted and Margaret, the crowd is almost here, still waiting for Frankie, but he called and said he's on his way. We're trying to stick to beer tonight. If you don't mind, I bought a keg, thought it might be easy. Just help yourself over there where the cups are; I'm about to start cooking some dogs and burgers. That's my repertoire. Being a bachelor, I eat out or pick up a lot."

"Yeah, I get it. How's business going?"

"Just fine, working hard, that's all. How's the store coming along?"

"Well, the police tape will come down soon; I did speak briefly with Detective Walter today, and he's got some suspects but won't say a word.

I see Mark sitting in a corner drinking his beer. I give him a nod; we smile at each other.

"Hey buddy, you enjoying the food?"

"Delicious," says Mark, as he chomps down a burger.

"You ready for the meeting? You nervous?

"Na, not at all. I think it's going to be very smooth, no worries, Ted."

We mingle with the family, talking niceties and chowing down our food until about five-forty-five pm. Then I ring a bell that Danny gives me, and everyone quiets down to near silence.

"Good evening, dear family members and my buddy Mark. We are gathered tonight to meet Mike Lopez and his assistants to discuss the ins and outs of our revenge for the murder of Robbie, the bodyguard, and the disappearance of Sylvia and Simone. We hope to find out how they do this, when, and what it costs. Before we meet them, we have to decide whether we want to knock off Alex or Garcia or both. To keep from arguing, I think we should take a vote. Does everybody agree on this?"

I hear yes, so I assume we will vote.

"Okay, raise your hand if you vote to knock off Alex from the cement plant."

All hands go up.

"Okay, now who wants to knock off Garcia from the garbage company?"

All hands go up again.

"Okay, lastly, who wants to knock off both Alex and Garcia?"

All hands go up, and all say yea and clap

"Well, I take that as a definite YES on both. Please understand that Lopez may not be able to do both, and it may cost us too much. Let's hear him out and ask questions after he talks."

I cross myself and pray to God that this is a success.

At six pm, the doorbell rings. You could hear a pin drop.

24

PETE

While we are all clapping together to declare our enthusiasm for killing both Alex and Garcia, I have a sudden panic attack, realizing the probable cost of this venture and that I still have a mortgage to pay off.

That call from Eddie the other day to remind me of this is making me very nervous, and then to pay off these guys may be too much for all of us, not just me. We all have a lot of debt. I'm anxious to hear what Lopez has to say.

Ted opens the door, and a tall thin man with a ball cap comes in first, followed by two short men, also with ball caps. Ted shakes hands with the guys and invites them to have a drink. The tall guy, which I assume is Lopez, asks for a beer.

The two short guys ask to have cold water, as they explain that they'll be back on the job soon, later tonight, and are not allowed to drink before an important job. I get it and am proud of them for staying clean.

While Ted and Margaret help get the drinks, I introduce myself as one of the family.

"Good evening guys, make yourself comfortable," as Danny and Tommy get extra chairs for them. "So, you're Mike Lopez, I assume."

"Yes, I am, and these are my best sharp shooters, Lonny and Sam. They work weird hours. As you know, the trade calls for that. They mostly work from midnight to eight am, but sometimes it starts around nine pm, depending on the demand. It's gonna be pretty busy tonight, I can tell ya."

The short men remain quiet.

Mark goes over to greet them.

"Hey Mark," says Lopez, "how's your injury? You're lookin' pretty good."

"I'm doing much better. Close call though, Mike, I'll tell you. So glad Ted wasn't there."

"Yeah, I know what you mean, could've been much worse."

The short men remain silent, with no smirks on their faces.

Ted introduces the team to family members and says that we all agree on them doing the work, provided we agree on the price. Then Ted lets them have the stage, so to speak. No microphone, just loud voices.

"Thank you for inviting me to come and speak to you guys about our work," says Mike in a friendly voice. "We are a team, like a family, who provides a service for our special customers. We don't do this kinda work for everybody. It has to come as a recommendation. And, you guys are recommended to me through my buddy Mark here." He looks very embarrassed, and his face is red.

All family members stand up and applaud as Mark turns red.

Mike continues. "So, as I said, we are very happy to provide you with the best and most clean service you will ever know. Now, I understand there are possibly two guys you want to knock off, is that right?"

All the family members shout, "YES!"

"Okay then," Mike continues, "So what we do is we get the names, business, and home addresses of these two, and then we'll quickly scout them out and take them off of you guy's hands. We never tell our customers when we do our work. That's secretive for many reasons, but mostly our protection. Now, the cost is twenty thousand per person, so that forty thousand total, all cash. We ask for all the dough up front cause this is dangerous work, and we really don't know you all. Any questions?"

"Would it be possible to give you half down and the rest when the job is done?" asks Danny with a curious look on his face.

"Absolutely not," replies Lopez, "we need cash up front or no deal. Hey guys, we're giving you a bargain price, no messin' around."

"Will you keep us informed of what's going on?" asks Tommy.

"No," says Mike, "this is a secretive operation as I said before; you will only know when it's done."

What if you only kill off one of them?" asks Margaret. "Will we get half our money back?"

"This is a nonrefundable operation, ma'am, and don't worry, you asked for two. You get two."

"If you guys all agree, and I'll be generous and give you a week to decide, then we sign a piece of paper and collect the money at that time. Pass your agreement on to Mark here, and he'll let us know your final decision and the exact date. Remember, we need exact names, addresses, business, and home, telephone numbers too."

"Okay, says Ted, "We'll digest everything you told us, and we'll be in touch with Mark and give him a date at which time we seal the deal."

Me, Ted, and Mark shake hands with Lopez and his silent men. Ted walks them to the front door. We all remain silent for a few seconds. Then I stand up amid some murmurs from family members.

"I think it's best for all of us to quickly digest what we heard tonight from Lopez. I'm going to turn it over to Mark for a few questions, and then we'll make a decision to go for it or not. In the meantime, be thinking about things like money, loans, revenge, family fears, and so on. Okay, Mark, I give the questions to you."

"Thank you, Pete, Ted, and others. I am happy to

speak to your family. First, let me say a little about Mike and his team. They have like a ninety-eight percent good record. That's why they can ask for all the money up front. Now I'm sure this sounds weird to you, as most of the time we are used to putting down a deposit. However, these guys are doing dirty work, as you know; very difficult and risky work, like they could get themselves killed. Any questions?"

Tommy raises his hand: "This may seem dumb, but what if they take all our money and run with it? We really don't know these guys from a hole in the wall, so to speak, except for Mark's recommendation.

"That's completely up to you as a family," says Mark. "These hit men and their teams are very well trained. Mike's group has been doing this work for ten years. I can't tell you exactly how many they've knocked off, but it's plenty, and they have very satisfied customers, repeat ones too. Next question."

Frankie raises his hand, "What is the fallout for us? I mean, is this is very risky if some "family" or boss finds out about this and traces it back to us, we are now a target!"

The family members begin to talk among themselves showing curious looks. I decide to let them chat and get out their emotions, which are running high at this moment. Ted comes over to me, scratching his forehead.

"I think money and fear are the big potential stumbling blocks."

"We'll make a go of it if I have to steal to get the money."

Ted and I shake hands in the midst of family members doing their math.

25

TED

LATER THAT NIGHT

After Pete and I shake hands, I sit down next to Margaret amongst the talking family. I'm exhausted, drained, and unsure of the immediate future. We sit silently for a few minutes, and then I get up to pour two bourbons for us.

We both need it. I'm thinking about what Mike said, and my mind splits in two. One half says, absolutely do it. We'll figure out the money somehow. The other says, what are you crazy? You'll get yourself killed in the end; somehow, the Boss will get the word, and then it's all over.

"You made a strong drink, honey," says Margaret,

"Thank you, dear. What did you think of Mike's speech tonight"?

"Well, frankly, I was a bit surprised at the price

and the fact that it's non-refundable, even if he only gets one of them, but look, as you and especially Pete are always saying, we have to do this for our own conscience. So, I'm for it. Jesus, Lord, let this be a success, or we'll all be shaking in our boots."

"You're right, Margaret, my doubtful side is coming around to the definite side, and we just have to do it."

"Are we going to quiet everybody so we can come to a decision and get a date for next week?"

"Yes, dear, I will get them all to shut up, and we'll do just that."

The family members are still chatting away and have been for a while now, so I think it's time we make a family decision. I can hear Frankie speaking loudly, and I don't know what that means. Maybe he's complaining about money as he usually does.

"Okay, everybody, let's stop talking now and get down to business. By now, you have been able to discuss among yourselves all the details that Mike proposed to us. I'm assuming you are doing your math and know what the number for each family will be. We have six families left, which makes it $6,666, or we can round it off to $6,700 a family. Now, when you think of it, it's really not that much money. Most of us have that stashed under our mattresses."

"Who has the full names and addresses of Alex and Garcia?" asks Danny.

"I think that between Mark and Lopez, they have a way of getting those details. We should let them do their work and not interfere. What we must decide now is how many of you, knowing the details are on board? Please raise your hands so I can count. Well, it seems like we're all on board, even Frankie. Thar's good to see, folks; now we have to pick a date for Mark to hand over the money and get a signed receipt."

"First of all, do we all have the cash on hand?" asks Tommy with a curious look.

"I have," says Frankie.

"I have it too," says Maria.

And then the rest chime in with a YES!

"Okay, so the money is no problem. What about the trustworthiness of this guy Lopez?"

"Well, I guess we have to take Mark's word that Lopez is an experienced contract killer and has qualified sharp shooters on his team. And he presumably knows how to scout them out and knock them off."

"What about the danger to our families?" asks Frankie, "this whole revenge thing that Pete is so determined to do?"

"Wait a minute there, Frankie. Didn't we just all decide to knock these two punks off?"

"Yeah, we did, but you were the one that said you couldn't live with yourself if we didn't do it."

"Look, Frankie, don't put the blame on me. That was just my position. Everyone is entitled to their own opinion, right?"

"Yeah, I guess so. It's just that in my heart, I'm a little scared."

"Well," says Pete, I think we all have some fear in doing this plan, but the good outweighs the bad, and I hope we'll all feel better about it after it's done."

"But what if it fails and he can't get to them at the right moment?" asks Tommy, with a serious look on his face.

"Look, as the contact person, I feel that Mark is an honest guy who's trying to help us. He's had his problems, but now he's a clean guy, a hard worker, and I don't think he would offer us scumbags to take care of our issue. So, we must have some faith in his recommendation, and on Lopez's record," I reply with a consistent tone of voice.

"I say the sooner, the better, in case anyone changes his mind," says Tommy.

"Mark, can we move up the date with Lopez?"

"I don't know, but I can try to reach him now."

"That would be great."

While Mark telephones Lopez, we keep talking about the pros and cons even though we've decided. I think it makes our group feel better by chatting and convincing ourselves that this is the right thing to do. Pray to God it works

"Well, folks," says Mark, "Lopez says that he can start doing the background stuff in the next couple of days, once he has the money and the signature, if you all can give me the cash tomorrow and sign up, then we're good. I suggest that Ted and Pete sign off on this cause he needs two signatures. So, why don't we meet here at Danny's place (if you don't mind

Danny) at five pm and do the transaction; I will have Lopez review it before we meet. Then I will bring him the cash and the receipt. You will all get a copy too."

"So, the receipt will be our assurance that he got the money and all is well, right?" says Maria.

"Yes," says Mark, "you got it."

"Thank you, Mark, for speeding up the process. No point in waiting if he's willing and able."

I feel a little sigh of relief from my family, now that they know this is real. We're all yawning because it's getting late and time to go home. I grab Margaret's coat, and off we go.

"What do you think, Margaret? I mean about the meeting and the comments?"

"I think everybody is tired of this already and eager to get it over with. I don't even think they care that much about the possible fallout to the family."

THE NEXT EVENING

Pete, Mark and I meet at Danny's place as planned. Mark has a paper in hand with all kinds of clauses on it. First, Pete looks at it carefully and gives a nod, and then he passes it to me to read.

"What do you think, Pete?"

"I think it looks pretty legit. I mean, we don't have a lawyer on this, but I would say it's okay."

"Mark? Did you read this too?"

"Yes, I did, and it looks fine to me. I've seen his agreements before, and this is standard."

"Okay then," says Mark, "I believe it's time to hand over the money, right?"

"Yes," says Pete, "and I have it in this envelope. I would like to count it if you don't mind."

"That's fine with me."

Pete takes his time counting the money, not once but twice. It almost seems like he's hesitating to give it up.

"I counted it twice, and it's exactly $40,000 bucks. I just hope he keeps his word."

"Thanks, Pete," says Mark, "I can pretty much vouch for this guy and his team; you won't be disappointed, Pete and Ted."

"So, what happens now?" I ask inquisitively. I mean, what is the next step?"

Mark answers, "Well, you can see that Lopez has already signed the agreement, so now that we have the money, I will deliver it to him immediately, and, of course, I will let you know when that part is done."

"What next?" asks Pete as he sips another bourbon and soda.

"After that, Lopez and his hit men get to work, background checks, where to do the job, and more. Don't forget they have to do everything very secretively."

"When will we know something?" Asks Pete.

"When the job is done?" says Mark.

"How long will that be?" says I.

"It depends on a lot of things, but I can't really

give you any more information; but to keep you guys calm, I would say about a week."

Pete and I shake hands with Mark. I must say our hands are pretty sweaty, but hey, this is a big deal, not just the money, but just the mystery of it...and the danger.

We both cross ourselves and have another bourbon. Danny joins us for the toast to a successful job. Amen.

26

FRANKIE

FOUR DAYS LATER

It's hard to swallow, even sixty-seven hundred bucks, because we still have a loan on our house, and I have rent on my apartment; remember I moved out from angry Anna several months ago, and I'm payin' her some child support; geez, can't I get a break?

And then, on top of all of this, I get a call from Eddie that the Boss wants his money! Of course, I'm in agreement with the family about knocking off Alex and Garcia, but to tell you the truth, I'm scared to death (excuse the pun). I guess I shouldn't complain.

I mean, after all, I got great kids who like to visit with me at my place and an excellent job at the cement company; I could use a promotion and get some extra dough; come to think of it, I may ask my boss (not the big Boss) about a raise.

I would say nothing about our plan. Just let him know I'm supportin' two homes. I'm countin' the days, even hours, to hear from Mark or Lopez as to whether the job was a success. I'm stoppin' at church every morning now to pray before Jesus that my wish will come true.

Lately, I've been thinkin' of my family members who have passed or disappeared; I guess I'm nervous and anxious about Lopez's ability to pull this off, and it reminds me of death.

The phone is ringin'.

"Hello, oh it's you, Eddie; listen, I got the picture, the Boss wants his money, well tell him to shove it, cause at the moment I ain't got it, and he'll have to keep his pants on."

"Whoa, wait a minute now, when the Boss speaks, we get movin', understand? Cause if I don't bring it, I get shit."

"Well, I'm sorry for you, Eddie, and I didn't mean those words. It's just that I'm strapped right now with family obligations. Can I have another two weeks, and I'll scrape up some dough for you, okay?"

"Hello, hello?"

I guess Eddie hung up on me; boy, did I get rowdy! I'm in that kinda mood, you know; you can't be nice, and ass kiss all the time. Anyways, they don't know nothin' about our secretive plan; they can't possibly know cause the Lopez gang has nothin' to do with the Bellini Family."

Wait, I'm getting another call.

"Hello, oh Anna, it's you; now what do you want?"

"You're late with your child support this month, Frankie."

"Okay, Anna, you're right. But you also know that I had to lay out $6700 bucks for the plans, which you are aware of, my dear."

"Where did you get the money for that, may I ask?"

"You are well aware that it's my money stashed in my underwear drawer, safe from you and the kids, though I trust them at least. Next time they come to me, I'll buy them some clothes at a consignment shop 'cause I'm pretty broke now, and I owe money on your house and mine."

She hangs up on me. What are you going to do with a pesty ex-wife? Ah, I think I'll have a drink after two aggravating phone calls. I hope we hear from Lopez sooner than later 'cause I might drive myself crazy.

Ah, this bourbon tastes good. I'll turn on the radio and listen to a little baseball. Maybe that will comfort my mind, along with the bourbon. No sooner do I sit down than the phone rings again; I'm pretty popular today, nothin' great so far. We'll see what this one brings.

"Hello, oh Pete, thank God it's you!"

"Why?" says Pete with a questioning tone. "Is everything okay?"

"Yeah, I guess, except Eddie calling me a minute ago, demandin' me to pay off my loans. I sort of told him to piss off, which probably angers him, and that's not good for me; I've been in a bad mood phone call which should come soon. So, no apologies. I called to tell you that I also got a call from Eddie; it must be his day to collect the loan money; I suspect the Boss is after him to get the dough. Don't you think it's a bit weird for Eddie to call us this week, the one when Lopez is doing his work? It's today, I'm anxious about the killer job, and Anna calls me for more money, damn her! Sorry for bein' so crabby."

"I completely understand Frankie, we all are moody at times, and especially now that we're waiting for some news, a little suspicious, don't you think?"

"Yes, I think it's a bit eerie, and I don't quite get it, but maybe cause it's the end of the month, who knows? How should we act when they're at our throats like this?" asks Pete.

"Hey, I already spoke my mind to Eddie in a very direct way; now he may have me talk to the Boss, but I can't help it; I am not expectin' any calls now except from Mark, Mike, or anyone in the family."

"Do you want me to contact the Boss and try to calm him down until our plan is complete?" asks Pete.

"I wouldn't touch that guy with a ten-foot pole

right now, but he likes you, Pete, better than me; If you feel comfortable, absolutely, give him a lie, anythin' to get him off our backs, Pete."

"Okay, I'll see what I can do; remember, if you hear from Mark, call me, or I'll call you."

"I certainly will, and please take care Pete, we know the Boss is not trustworthy, to say the least; in fact, he's cagey and mean and lies all the time, so go lie to him. He deserves it. Bye now."

Whew, what a day so far! And I haven't even got some work done. I have to check the cement to see if it's good quality or if they have to add somethin' to make it good.

I'm takin' a short break now and thinkin' about this Eddie thing, all of a sudden out of the blue; he hasn't been botherin' us for months. I'm chewin' that maybe Lopez would give me a loan. Nah, probably not, but hey, he's makin' some dough with his big job.

We'll see after all is done.

"Hello, oh hi, Ted, just the right person to call; I'm in a bad mood, and I know you'll lighten it up, right?"

"Well, Frankie, I do have some good news; just got a call from Mark. He says all the background stuff has been done, so now it's a question of the exact timing; that's all he says to me. I tried to get more information, but it's secretive, so nothing, just waiting. But he says it won't be long now, so everybody relax and let them do their job."

"I get it Ted, thank you for keepin' us informed; we're all very nervous."

"I can imagine," says Ted, "but don't be because I know this guy, and he's one of the best."

"Okay then, talk later, bye now."

TWO DAYS LATER

I'm sittin' with my kids at breakfast, so glad it's my turn for a visit. They like comin' here too. I make them eggs, toast, and juice, then pack up their lunches and off to school.

Then I gotta get myself ready for work. So I go upstairs and look in the mirror to shave. Oh boy, have I aged in the last couple of months, more gray hair, a few more wrinkles; it's been a tough time, and I think we all took it hard.

Uh oh, the phone's ringing. "I'm comin' whoever you are."

"Hello Frankie, it's Pete; guess what?

"You talked to the Boss?"

"No, much better than that!"

"OH YAY, the job is successful?"

"OH, yeah, man, we did it!! Our revenge is complete. I just got word from Mark, who got word from Lopez, so it's real!"

"How do we know that? What proof do we have?"

"Frankie, remember all the discussions we had and Mark's word that Lopez is a good guy, well that's all the proof we'll ever get; we won't see their dead bodies, just like we never saw Robbie's body; that's how they do their jobs."

"Yeah, you're right. We have to trust him. Well, if that's the case, then let's celebrate!"

"Absolutely, I'll make some calls, and we'll celebrate at my house; how about tomorrow night, a barbecue!"

"Sounds great Pete, will you gather everyone?"

"Yes, of course, about five pm, drinks on the house!"

"Okay, Pete, thanks for all you do for the family. Sometimes we aren't grateful enough to you, but all of us should be. You're our big brother, and we really think you are our leader."

I hang up the phone, finding it hard to believe that Alex and Garcia are gone. In a flash, it's all over, and so much plannin' goes into this, hours of talkin' and votin' and givin' up our hard-earned dough.

But now it happened. I wish I could clear my mind of Eddie, the one person (or maybe two includin' the Boss) we don't need pesterin' us now.

I'm a happier man, at least for the moment. I look forward to the celebration and will hide my fear. We got what we wanted, damn that's so great. I'm on my way home to tell my kids the good news. I might even call Anna, that is if she'll speak to me.

"Hi kids, job is done!"

"What do you mean, dad?"

"Remember when I told you a few days ago that

we are gonna knock off two bad guys cause they hurt our family?"

"Oh yeah, we remember!"

"Well, we accomplished that, and we're having a cookout at Pete's house tomorrow night. How about that, kids? We won!"

27

PETE

I am pinching my cheeks today because we are celebrating the success of our mission. My only concerns, Eddie and the Boss bothering us with calls and threats, maybe somehow finding out that two of their employees are missing.

But we'll figure that one out at the right time. God willing, I'll get the loan paid someway.

"Hey, Viv, how are things going in the kitchen, my love?"

"I'm making some potato salad and coleslaw and pounding those hamburger patties."

"Looks good, Viv, and thanks for pitching in and hosting the family; I really appreciate you."

"By the way, where are the boys?"

"They're riding bikes in the neighborhood. Pete, I'm getting a little nervous about our loans."

"I know Viv, but I promise to take care of it, so please don't worry."

"I'll try not to, but I don't want you to get on the wrong side of Eddie and the Boss."

"I will talk to my immediate manager to try to get a raise and maybe a bonus, Viv. I'm keeping my distance for a little while, but I have a plan to pay off these damn loans, praise to God. Frankie's in the same position, and probably the rest of the family. So, please, Viv, let's enjoy our celebration."

"I plan to, Pete."

She kisses me on the cheek and goes back to work making patties. I feel so lucky to have such an understanding wife; she accepts my explanations without too much questioning.

"Hello, oh hi, Frankie, what's up?"

"I just got another call from Eddie; the Boss is pressuring him."

"Look, Frankie, ignore it for today, and let's have the celebration we deserve. By the way, did someone invite Mark?"

"Yeah, I think Ted did, and he's coming."

"Alright then, we'll toast to our success."

"You got it, man. See ya there, bye now."

The family arrives between five and five-thirty pm. Viv and I make them drinks. There is much chatting going on, and I let them continue until about six; then, I decide to make a toast.

Just as I am about to raise my glass, I hear gun shots outside my house or nearby. The family members' faces turn white, and there is dead silence. I try to calm their fears.

"Listen up, all of you; I know you heard the gun shots, but let's not panic immediately. I am going to check it out with my gun in my pants, and I'll be right back."

I quietly walk towards the front door, open it, and stick my head out. I see a black sedan racing down the street; it is going so fast I can't make out who it is or the license plate. I don't want them to panic, but I think it's either Eddie, the Boss, or one of his henchmen.

Before I go back inside, I think about what I want to tell them. I guess I'll let them know that it is a bunch of kids setting off firecrackers, nothing to worry about.

I walk back inside and out to the backyard, where we're about to have our celebration. There is still dead silence with the same white faces and wide-open eyes. Nobody has stirred; it's like a ghost town.

I'm sticking to my tale until I know more about what's going on. Viv comes running when she sees me and whispers something about the Boss in my ear. I whisper back not to worry; I'm going to explain to everyone.

"My dear family, you can relax now, I went to check outside, and all I could see were a bunch of kids setting off firecrackers. So, there is no need to worry, and I will continue with my toast.

"We all have been working very hard to get our revenge against the death or disappearance of members of our family (I cross myself). We all had to put up hard-earned money, and some of us suffered financially because of this mission. But it is in our blood not to let these terrible events go unnoticed. We were successful in getting the job done, thanks to Ted and Mark. There could be consequences for doing this job, but right now, we're celebrating. So, let's toast to happiness and our success."

Everybody raises their glasses, and we all say hoorah!

As you can probably imagine, my head is spinning at the thought of those gun shots. I'm not that surprised because, in my heart, I know there will be some consequences. Eddie and the others will most likely realize their missing employees by the end of the week.

And who will they suspect but me and probably Frankie because he opened his big mouth and told Eddie off, and I still owe them for the mortgage; I paid off some by laundering some money, but I don't know if I can keep doing that.

I have people watching me from all sides. I wouldn't be surprised if Frankie is laundering too. I sometimes see him carrying a weird bag of something that looks like a cloth grocery bag, but I know what's in it. So, he's making some money to pay off his loans, maybe.

I return to the cookout, and now everyone is chowing down and seemingly more relaxed at my lie. I walk over to Viv, who is talking to Margaret, and place a kiss on her cheek.

"What about me? Don't I get a kiss from my dear brother?"

"Of course, you do, and in fact, I'll kiss each cheek, an extra for good luck."

"Gee, thanks, bro; you gave a hell of a speech there; we all hope we're safe now," says Margaret.

"You will be, and besides, each family is going to have a bodyguard with a gun outside the homes."

"Yeah, but Sylvia's bodyguard was killed, so how are we going to be protected?"

"You will be, trust me; these are sharp shooters, and they have eyes in the backs of their heads. But, remember, they cost money; we'll figure it out how to pay them."

"Well, I think I can trust your intuition, bro, but I'm more scared for you, Pete, because the Boss may know who is up to this when they see missing men."

"Not to worry, sis, I'll be fine. I have my tough wife to protect me, just kidding."

Frankie comes over to me to congratulate me on my toast. He looks a bit pale; I'm sure he's had a few drinks. His kids come tagging behind him.

"Hey man, did you have enough to eat?"

"Yes, I'm stuffed, and the honor goes to Viv, who I know did all of this, not you, right?"

"Right, she's a good cook and a superb hostess."

Frankie tells his kids to go play.

"So, bro, where did those kids get the firecrackers from?"

"I don't know, maybe across the state line, not sure."

"Those were very loud crackers, more like gun shots, Pete."

"I know they were gun shots, Frankie, but I didn't want to scare the family."

"Did you get to see the car?"

"Not really, it was dark, and it literally screeched away."

"Do you think it is the henchmen?"

"I really don't know, Frankie, but it could be anyone of the gang. It's only been a few days since the knockoff, so maybe they haven't missed them yet, or maybe they have noticed."

"Ah damn it, I think we're in big trouble, Pete, I mean big trouble. Did you get those well-trained bodyguards for us cause we'll need those guys? Should we train our wives how to shoot, just in case they bypass the body guard? And, should we tell our families, not the kids, but our wives?"

"Listen, Frankie. I would keep them thinking firecrackers for the time being until I get some information. Otherwise, they'll be frightened. Now, about the guns, I think it might be a good idea to train them, but not right now. The body guards will cost us, so we have to figure out how to make more money."

"Are we really expectin' a revenge blowout from the Boss?"

"I really don't know what they're up to and what

they know, but missing employees from their businesses could be of some concern. I think we'll be okay; remember, Frankie, nothing said to the family yet."

"What if Ted calls, smellin' somethin' fishy, should we talk to him?"

"I would try to keep it loose, no details, which we really don't have anyway, but nobody else."

"Well, it was a great celebration for as long as it lasts," says Frankie. "I got to gather my kids cause they have school tomorrow. As soon as you find out anything Pete, let me know."

"You'll be the first one to know. Speak to you later. Thanks for coming and bringing the kids."

Some family members come up to me and ask whether firecrackers went off right before my toast. I tell each of them it was, and I found a piece of evidence to show them. They all file out with a kiss and a wave goodbye.

Viv has a strange look on her face.

"What's the matter, darling?"

"I have a funny feeling you're not telling the truth about the loud bangs."

"Viv, I didn't see any car, didn't smell gun smoke, and I know what that smells like."

"Yeah, but you know there's a potential problem lingering, right?"

"Yes, I do, but I don't want you to worry about this now. I'll tell you when to worry, okay?"

I hug my wife for comfort and think that another

war is on the horizon and I must find out details from my sources. We can't afford to lose any more family members.

We both decide a glass of sherry might be nice. We clink glasses and bow our heads in prayer.

28

FRANKIE

THE NEXT DAY

Boy, am I freakin out! Between the gun shots, the phone calls, and the extra money for protection, I'm gonna have to think of a black money scheme, Pete too, and maybe Ted and Mark.

I'm glad we didn't tell the rest of the family, though they may find out from somebody's big mouth. It's possible that Lopez can help us earn extra money; we'll probably be in touch with him soon. Gotta talk to Pete first.

This turned out to be such a mess, with the Boss demanding his money, and Eddie, of course, gets a piece of it, and who knows who else. Lately, I've been goin' to church at night and just sittin' there staring at Jesus and Mary. I'm not prayin', but it makes me feel good to be there like someone is watchin' me.

Sometimes I think I'm in the wrong business; the Boss owns, or has his hands in, a lot of businesses around New York. God help me find some other way to make money.

Pete's calling me. "Hello, oh hi, Pete, just left church, didn't really pray, just sat there and stared; it made me feel better. How about you? You doin' okay?"

"Not really. Viv keeps bugging me about the firecrackers; she's smart and doesn't believe me, but I have been able to keep her quiet for a few hours now. I've been thinking about how to pay off our loans and also money for specially trained bodyguards."

"Oh yeah? Tell me please, cause I've been thinkin' too."

"Why don't we meet after work at Tony's Bar at six pm, and we'll compare notes?"

"Great Idea," says I with a broad smile on my face; "I'll see you there, gladly."

"Okay, kid, see you there; we'll figure something out."

We meet at Tony's; the place is packed with young people sittin' at the bar and smokin'. We move to the rear, where it's a bit quieter.

"What are you ordering?" says Pete, "wait, don't tell me, bourbon and soda, right?"

"Actually, I think I'll have just straight bourbon this time. I need it like hell!"

We order the drinks, and then we settle into an important conversation. I don't want to mention this to Pete, but I'm pretty damn scared at this moment. We have to find ways to make money, even if it's not legal; we're not so clean anyway, so that it wouldn't matter.

"Well, Pete, what are you thinking?"

"I'm thinking we should all pack up our stuff and disappear, just kidding, of course. We know we can't work with the Bellini Family to make money; we owe them too much already. I think we should get in touch with Lopez, who might have a smaller operation, but may have some ties and suggestions for us. I'm not even sure if he launders money or does protection work, is into drug trafficking, or isn't into anything except knocking off people. But we should definitely contact him. I'll call Mark to get his contact information."

"Hey, Mark, it's me, Frankie, remember me? Well, Pete and I would like to be in touch with Lopez again, but for another reason. Maybe you could join in too, cause we need a lot of us doin' different things, ya know?"

"Actually," says Mark, "Lopez is big into black money as a side business, so he will likely give you lots of information 'cause now you're a customer. Actually, here in New York, there's lots of black money in different businesses."

"That sounds awesome, Mark; can you give us Lopez's number, and we'll call and tell him you sent us; that way, you get a piece of the action, whatever action that is."

"Sure thing, let me know how it goes."

"Wow, that's just the person we might need, and now we have the number, great!" says Pete with a big smile on his face. "It's about six pm. You think we should phone Lopez now?"

"Why not? At least we'll get a yes or a no."

"I'll call him," says Pete, "he might know me better than you; actually, he knows Ted pretty well too. If we have any specific meetings, we'll include Danny and Tommy but not our sisters or sisters-in-law. They're too emotional and will automatically start questioning everything, can't say that I blame them. Okay, I'll try Lopez now. The line is busy; I'll keep trying. Come on, Lopez, pick up the phone!"

"Hello, Mike, sorry to bother you, this is Pete, a friend of Ted and Mark, remember me?"

"Oh yeah, how ya doin'?"

"I'm doing fine, Mike; I want to thank you again personally for the amazing job you did for us."

"Aw, that's a small job for us, though I'm glad you are happy."

"Mike, I have some things I want to discuss with you, not about knocking people off, but something pretty important."

"Well, Pete, do you want to meet in private with me?"

"That would be perfect. Would you be okay with my brothers joining me because it pertains to all of us?"

"No, I wouldn't mind at all. Let's set up a date to

get together. How about Thursday at six pm? Where would you like to meet?"

"That's really kind of you, Mike; I'll call my brothers and let them know it's this Thursday at six pm at my place."

"Sounds good to me. I hope I can help," says Mike.

"Well, Frankie, we got a start. Mike is willing to meet with us here at my place on Thursday at six pm."

"Yeah, I hope he can help us cause he doesn't know yet what we want."

"Frankie, you always jump to conclusions. Just relax, will you? You'll know soon enough!"

We part ways, and I go to my little apartment. All the way home, I'm thinkin' that Mike won't have any jobs for us; I cross myself and hope that we'll get money somehow. After all, we have to support our loved ones.

As I return home and put the key in my lock, I hear gun shots outside, but it's pitch black, and I can't see clearly. I open the door and slowly go to my gun case, which is under the bed. I open it and take out my .45 semi-automatic hand gun.

I shove it in my pants, look around my apartment first, and then stick my head out of the door. The shots stop, so I go back inside and sit on my couch. Then, I get up and pour myself some bourbon.

I pace the floor, a bit flustered, all the while drinking my booze. It's too late to call anyone, and the kids are with Anna, thank God. As I drink my bourbon, I think that those shots are warnings from the Boss, I'm sure.

This is the second time, we gotta get these sharp shooters to protect us, but we gotta earn some money first. Hopefully, Lopez will have some good ideas.

As I'm about to enter my bedroom to undress, the phone rings in the kitchen.

"Hello, Pete? How come you're still up? I've been drinkin' bourbon and thinking for the past hour or so. What's up?"

"Frankie, the Bosses are definitely warning us of bad things to come. I heard gun shots outside, but they seemed to be pretty close to the house. Even Viv heard them and freaked out. I keep telling her it's the kids down the block shooting off firecrackers, but now she really doesn't believe me."

"Slow down, Pete; I just heard them in my neighborhood too. I check outside but can't see anything; I did smell gun powder, though, and that shakes me good. We know who it is, but there is nothin' we can do about it, 'cause we can't find them. This is really gettin' creepy."

"Yea, it sure is," says Pete, "Thursday is still three days away; by then, we could be dead; you think Lopez can push up the date to tomorrow night?"

"I don't know his schedule. You know he's a busy man, knockin' people off, and God knows what else he does."

"Should we call him in the morning to see if he

can meet us earlier? We can tell him about the gun shots, and maybe he'll feel sorry for us," says Pete.

"I think you have his number. Maybe check with Ted or Mark to make sure it's okay. We don't know this guy that well, but Mark does."

"Okay," says Pete, "I'll call Mark in the morning and get him to change the date."

"Sounds good to me, Pete; look, when we decided to knock off Alex and Garcia, we knew at that time the boss would eventually miss them at work, even though they're not the higher-ups. So, now we're gettin' his revenge; we're tryin' our best to protect our families, but we're all broke from owing more money than we thought. Mark tells us that he has other businesses, so let's see what comes up."

"How about we speak in the morning after the phone calls; we're both exhausted, and a bit scared at this point," says Pete.

"Okay then, bro, just relax and try to get some sleep, okay?"

"Yeah, man, have a good one. Bye now."

Now, I'm perturbed. The boss seems to be pickin' on me and Pete, maybe because he knows it was our idea to knock them off. Well, I think I'll turn in for the night. My bourbon is startin' to calm me down.

I'm gettin' in my pajamas, and BOOM, another gunshot. I'm sleepin' tonight with my gun by my side.

29

TED

I just heard about the gun shots from Frankie late last night. They scared him, but again it was dark, and he couldn't see anything but could smell the gun smoke. Geez, what's going on here? I didn't think the Boss' revenge would start this early, but I guess he got word that two of his employees are missing, and he's got it out for us.

I'm hoping that Mike Lopez can help us earn more money so we can hire the right bodyguards. I have this sinking feeling that somebody will get hit in the crossfires if it comes to this.

"Hello, Pete? Great to hear your voice this morning. What's happening, buddy?"

"Well, I just spoke to Lopez and literally begged him to move the meeting up to tonight. I want all the men in the family there because this pertains to all of us; we all need the protection."

"I got it, buddy; are you going to let them know the time and where?"

"Yes, I will," says Pete, and again we can have it at my place at six pm. The only problem is that I don't want Viv to know what we're discussing, so I'll have to get her out of the house somehow. Have any ideas?"

"You could suggest to her that you're having a business meeting with your men from the dock and no women allowed. Maybe she could come over to visit Margaret, and they can sit and drink wine, or she could go to Angela's place and sit and drink wine. Will she go for that, Pete?"

"I'll work on it," says Pete.

"Okay, do you have in mind your pitch to Lopez? Or do you want me to do it?"

"Actually, Ted, I think you should do it; me and Frankie are getting too crazy after hearing the gun shots; we might not be in our right minds. I mean to be clear enough as to what we're asking for."

"Sure, no problem, Pete, I'll be happy to talk for all of us. You just convince Viv to leave the house; I don't think it will be a problem."

"Okay, thanks for heading up the meeting tonight Ted, I'll make sure to let everybody know," says Pete.

"Hey, got an idea; I'll tell Margaret to call Viv and invite her over for a "girls" night, just the two of them to chat and drink wine."

"Sounds good to me; she'll be happy to get rid

of me and these meetings anyway. Well, I'll see you later, Ted, take care."

I have to think about what we need from Lopez. We know he has some side businesses. They all do. We all need to make more money. Even before we laid out the dough for Lopez, we were in debt, more so now because of the money we paid him.

I have to tell Margaret where I'm going tonight. I'll be fairly honest and tell her that I'm meeting the family men to try to help us financially, but I won't mention Lopez and his possible ideas.

I get home around five pm from the office, and I see Margaret in the kitchen fiddling with something. "Hi, hon, I'm home. How's my beautiful wife? What are you trying to do?"

"Open a can of string beans for dinner, but this damn opener is the worst!"

"Here, let me help you; there it's done, no need to whine about it. By the way, honey, I have a family men's meeting tonight at Pete's house. We want to limit this meeting to a few people, so we thought we would just have the brothers and in-laws, not any wives. So, I thought you could invite Viv over to be with you and sit and chat "girl talk" and maybe even have a bite and drink some nice Italian wine. How does that sound? The meeting shouldn't take long."

"Not a bad idea; will you eat there?"

"Probably will have some munchies, but mostly talk."

"Talk about what?"

"Well, we all need more money to pay off our loans, so we're trying to figure out how we can earn a bit more, maybe ask our bosses for raises and other stuff."

"You're not going to do something crazy, are you?"

"No, honey, just honest money. Why don't you go ahead and call Viv and see if she's free to come over? I know that Pete already spoke to her about it."

Don't worry. I'll get Viv out of the house; I'll call her now. What time are you leaving?"

"In about forty-five minutes."

Margaret is able to coax Viv into coming to our place. Perfect!

At five-forty-five pm, I head over to Pete's house; everyone is there, all the men, except Lopez.

"Hey, Pete, good evening. Where is the most important person?"

"He called and is running a few minutes late. No worries, he'll be here. Can I fix you a Bourbon?"

"You certainly may, my bro, and I take it that the girls worked something out 'cause I don't see Viv around."

"Yes, it is working out perfectly; in fact, they are going to have dinner at the diner near your house."

"Great, I'm glad they have a chance to visit together."

I grab my bourbon and greet my other brothers. We chat for a while, then Frankie gets nervous that

Lopez won't show up. I tell him to calm down and stay calm during the meeting. He seems agitated. We keep chatting for a few more minutes, then finally, the doorbell rings.

I open the door, and Lopez greets me with a big smile; he is alone, I guess because his men are doing their "jobs."

"Come on in, Mike, you know all these people from our last meeting... we're all related, and we only have the men in the families attend tonight. Mike, can I get you a drink?" says Pete with a grin on his face.

"I'll just have a beer, thank you."

I notice that Lopez is dressed well in khaki pants, a long-sleeve blue shirt, no tie, but very clean looking. I get a beer for him, and he takes a big swig. I speak quietly to him, almost like a whisper, and tell him to explain his ideas slowly and carefully, as some of our family is very scared. He smiles and agrees to be very clear. Everybody takes a seat; there is silence.

"Good evening, folks. I think you know me by now. I want to just assure you that your job has been taken care of, so you can rest easy on that one. Now, I have spoken with a few of you about some kind of financial help needed, is that right?"

Everybody says yes.

"Well then, let me start with a few ideas for you. First, I know you guys need protection, as Pete tells me; I can get it for you, but it's expensive; we can discuss this at a later time when you have earned some cash. I do have a few side businesses goin' on at the moment. They involve black money, which means it's not good in the banks. Any questions so far?"

"I think we all realize this, Mike; we don't deal with banks anyway," says Frankie.

"These transactions don't leave this room; anything we talk about here, stays here, no shoutin' to friends, your wives, etc. Any profit we make goes to me, and you each get a cut. So, basically, I'm the new Boss. One business is buying and selling cocaine, right here in Brooklyn; I have my sources. Another business is a cash-only jewelry shop on Long Island; I give my customers a discount, but we're still makin' profits the government doesn't know nothin' about. I have a night guard business; this is where you would go and stand guard on small businesses in shady neighborhoods that need them 'cause they get broken into. I also have my sharp shooter business; you all know about that one, but we can always use extra hands and guns. I also have an interest in a gas station here in Brooklyn, where I get oil cheaper off the docks and keep the profits. Does everybody understand these ideas?"

I can see that each person's eyes bulge, mouths open and frozen in their seats. It's like a silent movie going on, but hey, these are pretty big ideas, and we want to make sure that all of us are clear on this.

"Any questions from the peanut gallery?"

"Yes," says Frankie. "If we're interested in your ideas, do we get to choose our added profession? And, what is the pay?"

"It depends on what you choose and if I have room for you; it also depends which jobs, the risks, the hours, etc., but I have varied interests, as you can see. So, I suggest that you think about the different ways you can make more money to pay off Boss Bellini. So, just let me know who wants to do which job, and I'll try to make it happen. Any more questions?"

"Yes, Tommy here; what kind of risk are we talking with these ideas?"

"Well, I've been in these various businesses almost since I was a teenager. My dad started most of them, and I'm still alive and kickin', so I'd say if you're careful and you work quietly and don't do any blabbing, you'll be fine, and you'll have money which you can stash away any way you want. Any other questions?"

"Mike, when would you want us to begin?" asks Pete.

"Whenever you all decide on your new side jobs, just ring me up, and we'll get you started. Remember, all of this talk stays right here, or all hell will break loose."

I ask Mike, "Do you think Boss Bellini will catch on to what we're doing?"

"We stay close to each other in our own families, and we don't mix with the Bellini's."

"But Frankie and me have heard gunshots near our houses the past night or so," says Pete. "Is that some kind of revenge warning?"

"Who can say?" says Mike with a grimace.

30

FRANKIE

After Mike Lopez gives his schpeel, my eyes still bulge, and my head spins. My opinion is that all of these side jobs are risky, though Pete might not think so. But what are the other things we can do, mow lawns, never?

We all need the money to get the protection, 'cause Boss Bellini is on the run; yes, I guess we could work in the real world, but nobody would hire us with our backgrounds. So, we're stuck where we are, for better or worse.

So, we all have to think about which job we like the best. Pete wants to call another meetin', so we know what each family member will be doin' and the pay, of course, is the most important thing.

From what I know, Pete has the list of jobs and the pay. Lopez told him the pay might not be the same each week, dependin' on what we bring in or how well we do our work. So, we'll have to wait and see. I know this much; we all need the money because we're all in debt.

I'm thinkin' that there is a real possibility that we may get caught 'cause those gun shots are not firecrackers...and we heard them more than once. If anythin' happens to my kids, I'll feel so guilty the rest of my life; I can't even say what I would do. I cross myself and pray that all goes well. I think I'll go to church tonight.

"Hello, Pete?"

"Yeah, it's me, just wanted to let you know we called another meetin' tonight at my place. I know this is getting crazy, but we have to know the details of these side jobs; I got a paper from Lopez which tells us about the pay and the hours, his take on how much money we bring to him. Can you make it, Frankie?"

"I think it's my night with the kids, but maybe I can convince good old Anna to keep them until the meeting is over."

"Well, do your best cause we'll miss you, and you will miss an important part of these offers."

"I'll do my best to be there, Pete. By the way, what time tonight?"

"Six pm at my place."

"You got it, Pete. Bye now."

This is part I hate, havin' to deal with Anna and the kids. It hasn't been easy. I just pray that she's free tonight and can take the kids for a few hours. Now, I have to call and argue with her.

"Hello, Anna? It's me, Frankie, how ya doin'?"

"Fine, Frankie; what favor do you need now?"

"Well, Anna, we're havin' a meetin' at Pete's place tonight, and I gotta be there at six pm. I know it's my night to be with the kids, but could we switch? And maybe you could take them tonight, and I'll do you a favor too."

"Well, I do have a date with my girlfriend, but maybe I can have her come over instead of going out. But, Frankie, let me warn you; don't pull this shit on me too many more times, or I'll start saying no to you, understand?"

"Yes, I do, Anna, and boy do I appreciate your kindness (I feel like I'm going to throw up)."

"Okay, Anna, I'll drop them off before I go to Pete's place. Thank you from the bottom of my heart."

"Oh, shut up, Frankie."

And she hangs up

Boy, what a lovely woman! Sometimes I feel like stranglin' her, she's so damn angry all the time; and what did I do? She kicked me out of the house; she probably didn't like my line of work either. Oh well, at least I can see my kids

I drop my kids off at Anna's place, and I'm greeted with a scowl. The kids kiss me goodbye, and I tell them that I'll be back later to pick them up, and if they get tired to sleep, I'll carry them to the car. They're pretty heavy, but we'll figure it out.

"Hey, Pete, it seems like we see each other almost every day now, not that it's bad, it's great!"

"Always good to see you, bro; go help yourself at the bar; we're still waiting for Danny, but he should be here soon."

I help myself to a bourbon on the rocks and schmooze with my brothers. I can tell we're all nervous (except for Pete) about these new jobs and the risks we're takin'. But hey, that's life in the underworld, right?

Danny arrives, Pete calls us to order, and we all take a chair or the couch. He has some papers in his hand, and I'm guessin' we'll each get a copy tonight.

"My dear brothers," says Pete with a smile, not looking nervous at all.

"I know we've been meeting a lot lately, but for good reasons, right? We're all in the same boat here, to make extra money to pay off our loans and to get good protection for our families, so we don't live in constant fear of Boss Bellini, whom I believe knows a lot by now, and he may be after us. That's the reason for this meeting; to give us side jobs so we can make extra money. Remember what Lopez says; no talking to anyone, even our wives, about what we're doing; just make up some kind of story that you have to leave the house. If this leaks in any way, we're in trouble not only with Boss Bellini but with our new Boss Lopez. Does everybody understand the consequences of this? Okay, then, I have some papers here that list the jobs and the pay or the cut. Like for instance, the jewelry store, it's a cash cow, and it's doing very well; so, if you work there and you sell a piece, then you get forty percent of the profit, and the Boss gets sixty percent. It's just math, but you have to document on a certain form which I have, exactly what the cost and profit are, and then every week the Boss will collect his money, and you will keep yours. Next, if you decide to work in the drug trade, the more dangerous, I will say, you can make lots of money if you're smart about it. But it's also the trickiest because the cops and the under-cover detectives are all over the place, so be extra careful with this one. Next, if you want to help small businesses from being broken into or destroyed, you can be a night guard in poor and edgy neighborhoods. This means you watch mom and pop stores to make sure there's no trouble; you'll definitely need your gun for this job. This is a bit risky cause there are also gangs in these neighborhoods, but I think the pay is pretty good. The last, and maybe the most dangerous, is to join Lopez's sharp shooter team, where you go out at night as a team, and you kill the people the Boss wants knocked off. You where you might get hit in the crossfire, but it pays well. Are there any questions?"

"I have one or a few," says Tommy. "Which one do you think is the least risky?"

"Well, in my opinion, the jewelry shop is the least risky because you're just selling and keeping some of the profits, little risk there unless some jerk robs the store and ties you up or worse."

"Other questions?" repeats Pete.

"Yes," says Danny. "Which one do you think will make the most money?"

"In my opinion, I think either the drug or the sharp shooter business, but again they are the riskiest."

"Frankie? I see you're very quiet tonight; you must have some questions, right?"

"Well, Pete, I'm just takin' it all in and doin' my thinkin', that's it. Oh, I forgot, do we get a copy of the sheets you have with the different jobs and the pay?"

"Yes, you all get a copy of the job descriptions and the pay. Now, Lopez told me the pay might vary according to how much you sell or kill, like the jewelry shop, the drugs, the sharp shooters. The guard business is a steady pay per week and depending upon how many signs up, we can do shifts; but remember, some of that money always goes to the boss.

"Should we just hide the cash in our houses?" asks Tommy.

"Well, it's dirty money, so you can put it in a safe deposit box in a bank, or get a heavy safe at home, or hide it in a secret place."

"Any other questions? Yes, Danny, go ahead."

"Well, I have another idea, so listen carefully. In order to get protection, which is a big goal for us and it's expensive, we could do an exchange with Lopez. We work for him, and in exchange, he provides protection for us. Now it doesn't make us cash, but we get most of what we want."

Frankie blurts out: "Yeah, but it doesn't give enough cash to pay our debts."

"It's just a suggestion," says Danny; "think about it; we could get killed by the Boss because of what we did to his men. Maybe we should get raises at work to make more money for the loans."

"Ha-ha," says Frankie, "I wouldn't count on it."

"Okay then," says Pete. "I think Danny's idea is not bad at all, and I think we should mull it over in our minds."

"I will pass out these sheets. Take a good look at them and make sure you're choosing the right job for you. Lopez would like to have them sooner than later, as we are already in a bit of trouble and we need protection. We'll have another meeting with Lopez attending a week from today at my place, men only, and figure out something to tell your families. Just remember, everything we speak about stays in this room. Thank you, my dear brothers, for coming tonight; I know there are big decisions to be made, and if you chicken out, that's fine too. I, for one, will proceed with a side job, 'cause I know the dangers that may come."

So, after Pete stops blabbin', we talk about who is interested in this job or that job; Tommy doesn't talk much, not sure he'll go for this kind of work. We all still have a week to decide, so no big rush. I guess we can lean on each other for help in deciding 'cause we can't talk to other family members, which will be hard, at least for me.

At ten pm, we decide to call it a night after a glass of brandy. On my way home, my mind is spinnin' with decisions to make and the thought of dealin' with Anna again. I think I'll call her and just tell her I'm too tired to pick up the kids tonight and will get them to school in the morning.

"Hello, Anna, I'm exhausted, and I'm going straight home; I'll pick up the kids first thing in the A.M and take them to school." I hang up before she gets a word in!

31

DANNY

It was a good meeting last night, but it may be too many choices for all of us to think about. I honestly believe that my idea is the best one. We work for Lopez, doing what he wants us to do; it may change from week to week, but who cares if we get the continuous protection, which is very costly for us to get by ourselves.

On the other hand, if we pick a specific job, it may turn out bad and frustrating in the sense of money, and who knows how much take we'll get; a lot of it will go to Lopez. I think I should call Pete and Ted to convince them of my idea; the others will follow if I can get Pete on my side.

"Hello, Pete, Danny here."

"Oh, hi, Danny, what's on your brainy mind these days? You're usually the quiet one at meetings and such; I guess you're more of a listener than a talker."

"I don't know about that, Pete; I can blab like

everyone else in the family, but I like to listen to others speak their opinions first, then I will talk. So, Pete, I did listen to all of Lopez's options last night, and as they were put before us, I am thinking that these side jobs may not really work for us; they sound too iffy and maybe not steady. We need a good relationship with Lopez, a steady one that will get us the protection we need. We work for him, and he gives us the top bodyguards we need twenty-four-seven. Now, as far as paying off our loans, we can try to get some bonuses or raises from our bosses. But at least our families will be safe from Boss Johnnie, who, by now, realizes that two of his workers are missing. That being said, we may be in big trouble."

"I get your point, Danny, and it is a good idea. My only worry is that Eddie keeps calling me and Frankie about loans. If I didn't have them, I think your idea is great because I know we need the protection really badly. I'm really mixed up now, don't know which option is better."

"Listen, Pete. Since I don't have kids to support, I can help you pay back some of your loans so that Eddie doesn't bug you for a while. Would that help you out?"

"Gosh, Danny, that's too generous; I probably could never pay you back unless I can get a raise at work."

"But, Pete, I'm not asking you to pay me back. This is a gift, and I can help out Frankie too. I think the rest of us are okay. Look, Pete, I've been single all my life, no kids to feed, clothe, put kids through school, and I have a small place with my mortgage paid off. So, I've been able to save money, and it's cash in a safety deposit box at the bank near my house. Why don't you figure out how much you need now to keep Eddie and the Boss quiet for a while; then we'll play it by ear; does that sound reasonable?"

"More than reasonable, Danny, you are a living gem!"

"Not exactly, Pete, I'm trying to do the best thing for our family, and that is protection. Now, we have to discuss this with Lopez to see if he'll agree to this deal, but if we work for him, I think he'll go for it."

"Who should talk to Lopez about this exchange plan, and will he decide what work we will do?"

"Of course, he'll decide, but look what we're getting in return. I think you or Ted should talk to him. You guys know more about this than any of us.

"Okay, Danny, I'll talk to Ted, and we'll reach out to Lopez before the next meeting. Again, I can't thank you enough for your generous offer to me and Frankie. Maybe if we pay off some of the loans, they'll shut up for a while. In the meantime, we'll be working for Lopez and getting protection.

"Okay, Pete, let me know what happens, and in the meantime, I'll call Frankie and let him know I can help him out with his loan. Don't tell the rest of the family yet, as I think they are okay for now, in terms of Boss Johnnie going after them."

"Okay, Danny, I'll let you know what happens

after you talk to Frankie; If I go along with it, he will, and so will the rest of the family. Bye now."

I hang up the phone and think to myself, what on earth am I doing? Giving money away as if it was candy. But I do have money, and they don't, and I'm afraid they'll get knocked off eventually with those gun shots and phone calls to pay off their loans.

I have to do this to save my family.

Now I'm going to call Frankie to see if he'll accept my offer and to convince him that working for Lopez in exchange for protection is the best option on the table.

"Hey, Frankie, it's Danny here. How are you?"

"Just fine old pal, what's up?"

"Well, remember when I talked about working for Lopez in exchange for protection at our meeting last night? Instead of getting side jobs that may be a bit iffy, you would work for Lopez and get the protection twenty-four-seven which is expensive. And, I will help you pay off some of your loans so that the Boss' calls and the gunshot warnings hopefully will stop. What do you think about that idea?"

"You mean you're gonna help me pay off my loans, and we work for Lopez and get protection for our families?"

"That's exactly right, Frankie. I have money saved, so I can give you cash to help pay off some of your loans. Then we'll see what happens with Boss Johnnie and Eddie, who keep shooting off the gun fire and making threatening calls. Now, I don't want you spouting your mouth about my help because I'm only helping you and Pete right now; then, I'll see how much more I can spare. But I don't want the rest of our family to know. I believe they are better off than you and Pete."

"I'm definitely in on this deal, Danny, and you're such a great and generous bro. Do you think Lopez will go for it?"

"I think he will because it will be easy for him to keep track of his employees, and in return for your work, you'll get the protection. Pete or Ted will call Lopez before our next meeting to present this idea. He will say nothing about my gifts to you; that's totally secretive to everybody. I will call Pete back to let him know you're on; then Pete will call Lopez, then me.

You'll also know as soon as possible, and then the rest of the family. So, for now, Frankie, sit tight, and we'll call you. Bye now."

I hang up and find that my hands are a bit clammy. Maybe I'm a little nervous about the gifts. But I just checked on my stash, and I have enough saved for Pete and Frankie, who are more needy than the others. I'm still saving, so maybe I can help the rest too, at some time.

"Hey, Pete, it's me, Danny; I just spoke to Frankie, and he's in on the deal. I told him everything and that he would get help from me."

"That's great news, Danny, and now we have to get Lopez to agree to it. I'll give Lopez a call around five pm when I think he's least busy, okay with you?"

"Yup, it's fine, then call me back; I'm keeping my fingers crossed on this one because it's the best idea. Bye for now, speak later.

I'm pacing the floor at my house, hoping things will work out; it's only three pm, so two more hours in which I can do more work for my boss, virtually. In case I forgot to tell you, I do the accounting for various clients that my boss gives me.

So, I'm candid at work. No black money is involved here. Maybe some in my personal life, but very little. So, I'm kind of scared about working for boss Jim Lopez. But the family is involved, so I guess I am too.

LATER THAT DAY

I get a call from Pete after six pm; he tells me that Lopez agrees to our idea because he needs workers and, in exchange, will give us protection. He says that we have to put in many hours because protection twenty-four seven is very costly, and he will assign us to various jobs according to need.

So, we can't pick what we want, it's his priority now, and he is our new Boss. Now, if Boss Johnnie tries any tricks on us, at least we'll have our families protected.

After Pete calls, Ted calls.

"Hi, Ted, how are you doing?"

"Just great, Danny; I just heard from Pete about our new deal; sounds good to me. I'm not really in debt with loans, so protection for my family is the most important thing. I make a pretty good living at the pawn shop, and I've been able to make our loan payments and still save a little. I really hate to do these jobs that Lopez is suggesting, plenty risky, but we're one big family, and you do what you have to."

"I'm glad you understand that it's the best way for all of us, and Ted, if you ever get in trouble financially, I'll help you out."

"You're such a great guy, Danny; your idea is really well thought out. These jobs are very risky, but I think we can all handle it, and hopefully, Boss Johnnie will stay quiet."

"I doubt that Ted: I think he knows now that two of his men are missing, therefore the gunshots and Eddie's annoying calls. He'll be on some of our tails sooner than later. That's why we need the protection."

"Yeah, I guess you're right, Danny; I just hope we can handle these jobs. By the way, have you spoken to Tommy or the others?"

"Not yet. First, I want to talk to Pete about that to see if they're in or out. Tommy seems to be a bit reserved about going in with us, I don't know about the others yet, but they will be called."

Now, I feel a little bit better knowing that Lopez is okay with the deal. I take a deep breath and think about my wonderful family and how much I love them. A minute after I take my deep breath, I get a call from Frankie; he says more gunshots around his house.

32

PETE

Viv and I are sipping our after-dinner drinks, usually some kind of brandy, when I get a hysterical call from Frankie.

"Hey, Pete, I got home tonight. I heard the shots around the house again. This time though, I saw a dark-colored car about fifty feet away just sittin' there in the street. I was afraid to go out, even with my gun, cause It looked like there was more than one guy in there...oh geez, I'm meat!"

"Take it easy, Frankie. I'll be over in a few minutes, just take a drink of bourbon and keep your gun handy."

"Okay, thanks, Pete, I'm really getting scared now, and I have the kids tonight."

"Stay calm, Frankie. I'm on my way over."

"Hey, Viv, Frankie just called, he heard more gunshots around his place, and he's got the kids tonight, so he's quite frantic, to say the least; I have to go over and calm him and or help protect him."

"Oh, Pete, he's a real whiney one; can't he just lock himself and the kids in and put on the radio instead of poking his head out the door?"

"I guess not, Viv, I'll go, but it won't be long, okay? You just keep sipping Brandy so you won't get nervous."

I give Viv a kiss on her forehead, take the car keys and dash out of the house. While driving, I have all kinds of thoughts running through my mind, but I put my foot on the gas, and I go as quickly as possible without being stopped by a cop.

I arrive at Frankie's place, and he's got all the outside lights on; he opens the door and smiles at me.

"Should we take our guns and slowly walk over to that parked car near the bushes so we won't be seen?"

"If you feel comfortable doing that, Frankie, sure we can."

We both strap up with our pistols hidden in our clothes. We have on dark jackets, so that's good. Frankie goes to check on the kids, and both are sound asleep. He leaves the radio on pretty loud, and the cars are in front.

Before we even open the front door, we hear more gunshots coming from that car, but the shooting is up in the air, like a warning. We step outside and wait a minute to know if there will be more. Silence.

I lead us down the few steps and along the deep

hedge on the sidewalk; we walk gingerly with our guns now in our hands, pointing them low so as not to be seen. We continue on our path, stopping every few seconds; another gunshot.

We wait until I give Frankie the sign to move; we're getting a bit closer to the car, but it's so dark, they can't see us, I hope. I take my night binoculars, so I look through them and see the tops of two heads in the car.

My heart starts to flutter. Frankie is still behind me, hands shaking. We pause for a moment and whisper to each other to try to make a plan.

Should we just go back or try to knock them off? Hard decision to make; what are the risks?

Indeed Boss Johnnie or Eddie will find out it's us. We could get ourselves killed or maimed. I have a thought right now. Maybe send Frankie home because it seems like they're after him more than me.

Then I'll sneak up a little and fire some shots in the air to let them know we mean business. Frankie whispers that he doesn't want me alone, but I assure him I'm okay. He starts walking back towards his place.

When I know he's safe, I start firing shots in the air, dead silence for seconds, and then more shots. I jump back, think for a moment, and again use my binoculars to get a better description of the car.

Now, it looks like only one head is sticking up, but the guy is wearing a mask. I get angry and frustrated because I can't identify the person. I have to make a quick decision; I think it's better to get one of Lopez's hitmen to go with me next time this happens.

I turn around, always looking behind me. The gun points down, out of sight, until I reach Frankie's place. He looks out the window, sees me coming, and opens the door quickly. Now I'm inside, and I can put my gun in my pants.

"What happened, bro?"

"I guess I chickened out, you might say, but I made a decision not to do this alone, but try to convince Lopez to get me one of his sharp shooters to come next time. I'll give him the scoop and let him know I need his help. I think he'll cooperate. I'm so sorry, Frankie, that they seem to be picking on you more than me. I may call Eddie to see if he knows about this. He'll probably deny it, but I can tell from his words and voice if he's lying."

"You sure you want to call him, Pete?"

"Yeah, I'm not afraid of Eddie. He's just a pawn in the game. I think it's too late to call now, but first thing in the morning, I will. Do you want me to stay a bit longer?"

"Well, do you think that car will be there all night?" Frankie asks.

"How do I know? I doubt it, and you know it could be just a bunch of kids doing this, not connected to Boss Johnnie."

"I doubt it, it's happenin' too often, and I know they're after us. Why don't you go home? Viv is probably nervous about you bein' out so late?"

"You're right, Frankie, but are you okay now? Double lock the door after I leave and let the radio stay on loud, so someone thinks you're up, like an insomniac."

"What's that?" asks Frankie.

"Someone who can't sleep. Now I have to sleep. I have work in the morning, and I'd like to see Viv before she passes out."

"Okay, buddy, have a good night, and let me know what Lopez says about coverin' us if this happens again."

"I will; goodnight, Frankie."

I'm thinking now about what maybe I should have done; that is, shoot the bastards in the car. But I'm a pussy, not a cop. So I will need help to carry this out. Frankie is no help. He's worse than me. I'm so happy that we're getting protection soon. We need it, at least some of us.

I arrive home, and Viv is still up and looks scared.

"What happened, honey? You're so late."

"I know, and we really didn't accomplish anything either."

"What do you mean by that?"

Well, there were more shots, so we carefully crept outside with our guns in hand, ready to take them on, and I couldn't do it. I sent Frankie home, and I was alone...scared and afraid I would get harmed."

"You poor baby, let me get you a brandy, and we can sit in the living room for a while."

"I'm such a pussy, I should have pointed the gun at the windshield and shot, but I didn't."

"I'm so glad you didn't, Pete. I could have lost you." Tears in Viv's eyes.

THE NEXT MORNING

I wake up with a raging headache from last night's ordeal, have my coffee, chat with Viv, and then get busy with everything that must get done before work.

On my list is to call Eddie and feel him out.

"Hey, Eddie, it's me, Pete; Lately, Frankie and I have heard gun shots around our houses. What's going on? Do you know anything about this?"

"No, I don't, Pete, but maybe I can find out for you."

"Listen, Eddie. I don't believe a word you just said; I can tell by the tone of your voice that you're putting me on; now let's have the truth, or you'll be in big trouble; I have my means."

"I swear I'm not doin' it, Pete, but maybe some of the Boss' other men are shootin'."

"Okay, Eddie, I know your car, and Frankie and I heard shots last night at Frankie's place, and it looked like it was coming from a parked car similar to yours."

"But Pete, I went to bed at nine pm last night and didn't go out at all; besides, there are a lot of sedans like mine, and it was dark out; how could you see anything? No street lights either."

"Sounds like a good alibi to me, Eddie, but I still don't believe it. And, if it wasn't you, then you must know who it is, right?"

"Listen, Pete. I'll find out from Boss Johnnie if he tells me who was out last night causin' trouble. I don't know if the Boss will say, but I can try. By the way, he did let me know that Alex and Garcia are missing from work at the boss' companies. He's pretty sure you are a part of this revenge deal; I haven't said nothin' to him, but I know he's gettin' steamed up about it. Do you know anythin' about these guys missing?"

"Listen, Eddie, absolutely nothing. I don't have the means like you do to harm anyone. I'm just an ordinary guy who got caught up with loans from the Boss. And Eddie, you're really annoying me with these phone calls about the loans. I will have the money to pay them off very soon, so keep your pants on will you? And, stop bothering Frankie too; he's a hard-working man whose wife left him, and he has to pay for everything, even her screaming all the time! Bug off, we'll pay the loans, and tell your freaking Boss that we don't know what happened to those guys who are missing. Whoever is doing the shooting, you better tell them to end it, or else. Remember what I said. Bye now, Eddie."

I'm shaking after that phone call; I have to pull myself together and get ready for work.

I go into the kitchen to set my coffee cup in the sink. Viv is not there. I call for her, no answer; I call twice more and start searching the house. Then I start screaming for her, looking outside. Her car is still there, then in the basement, and all over.

I'm panicking, breathing hard, can barely speak; where could she be? Maybe she just went out for an errand or two, but her car is still here. I'll wait and have another cup of coffee; if she's not back in fifteen minutes, I'll call the police, no, maybe Ted.

Oh, God! Please let her be safe. I'm a wreck. I think back on what happened to Sylvia. Thank God the kids are at school. I hope she comes home quickly, or I'll have to do something, praying for her safe return right now.

33

TED

I'm in a light sleep when the phone rings, and I jump up to answer it. I guess it is about four am. I can't see the clock that well, and I'm thinking God who's calling me now. It must be bad news. I wipe the crap out of my eyes and answer it.

"Hello, Pete, you're hysterical. What's happening? Calm down. I can't hear you."

Pete is sobbing and can barely get the words out; my heart starts fluttering.

"What is it? Please say something!"

"Viv is gone!" More sobbing. "She disappeared late last night." Sob. "I was talking with Eddie, angrily and then when I went back in the kitchen to join Viv, she was not anywhere in the house or outside, and her car was still parked at the house. I searched the basement too. Now, what do I do? I'm so angry, scared, and exhausted."

"I'll get dressed now and come over. Just sit

tight, and we'll figure it out together; take a glass of brandy. I'll be there as fast as I can."

Oh my God, I don't believe this one! I'm almost sure the Boss sent someone to kidnap Viv in retribution for the money owed to him. That damn person probably chloroformed her, which put her out and then dragged her into a car and sped off because Pete didn't mention any screaming or other noises.

I'm getting dressed in sweats and a top; Margaret is still sleeping, and I don't want to wake her at this hour, but I'll leave her a note, nothing to scare her. I get myself over there quickly. Pete greets me at the door, tears rolling down his cheeks. Poor thing.

I hug him tight and try to calm him down. We sit on the couch for a few minutes until his sobbing stops, and we can talk. His eyes are red, and he keeps sniffling.

"Are you able to talk now, Pete?"

"I guess," he says, still sniffling. "Poor Viv, I know she's petrified. I wish I could hug her right now and apologize for getting involved with this mess."

"So, do you think it is related to Boss Johnnie, retribution for no payment of loans?"

"Yes, Ted, I do, but why not take me?"

"Because, Pete, that's too easy; this way, they go round about and make you suffer."

"Where do you think they took her, Ted?"

"Maybe to the Boss' mansion, to one of his interrogation rooms, or maybe somewhere else. Did

Eddie give any hints about loans when you spoke to him or anything about the gunshots?"

"No, he played dumb as usual, but I gave him the riot act, and maybe that's the reason he and the Boss are taking revenge, who knows? I'm just so worried about what they might do to Viv. I think I told you about the parked car and gun shots near Frankie's house the other night. We tried to see who was in the car, but it was too far away, and they had masks; we had our guns with us but decided to go back to Frankie's."

"Is it possible for you to get a little shut-eye, Pete? Before we start our search? Or are you eager to run?"

"I couldn't sleep if I tried, Ted, so let's call the Boss and see what he has to say about this"

"Let's see, Pete, it's only five-thirty am. I don't think the mansion will be open for business this early. So, let's try to relax and listen to the radio news; I know you're ready to run, and I don't blame you, but even Eddie won't answer the phone this early."

Pete goes over to a statue of the Virgin Mary in their hall and kneels. He mutters a lot of words, crosses himself, and cries. I feel bad for the guy; we don't want to involve the police, making it even harder to get facts and alibies.

I go over to Pete and put my hand on his shoulders. Then I cross myself. We stay in silence for a few seconds, then Pete agrees to sit down for a few minutes before calling the Boss. My thinking is they're holding her at the mansion until they get paid off. Pete falls asleep reading a magazine; now it's about eight am so it's time to get the ball rolling.

"Pete, wake up. It's time to make a call to the Boss."

Pete rubs his red eyes, yawns, and says, "Do you want me to call or do you, Ted?"

"I think I'll call because you just had a bit of a row with Eddie."

"Okay then, be sure to get us down there today."

"I'll do my best, Pete."

I walk into the kitchen to look for the Boss' number, noticing a cloth in the sink. I pick it up, and it's still damp and has sort of a sweet smell, like a mild disinfectant. I take another whiff, and now I'm sure whoever did this used it on Viv to make her pass out. Damn!

I'm going to call the Boss now.

"Hello, who am I speaking with?"

"It's the Boss' guard at the front door. What do you want?"

"I want to speak to the Boss."

"Who is this calling?"

"It's Ted. Just tell him Ted, Pete's brother-in-law."

"Okay, just a moment."

I'm holding on forever. It seems with Pete right behind so he can listen in.

"The Boss wants to know why are you coming?"

"Just tell him it's urgent!"

"Okay, sir, be right back."

"Okay then, the boss says to come to his office."
We leave immediately.

We arrive at the mansion; and are escorted by his assistant. We walk down the long hallways with many doors until we finally each the Boss' office. I knock on the door and let Pete enter before me. The Boss is smoking a stinky cigar and rocking back and forth in his oversized desk chair.

"What can I do for you, fellas?"

"You know exactly why we're here!"

"Slow down, Pete, now talk to me in plain English."

"Where is my wife, Viv? She was kidnapped last night in our own house, and your guys shut her up with chloroform so there would be silence; very cleverly done, Boss, I applaud you. Now, where is she?"

"Calm down, my friend; I will tell you she is alive and well. But I had to do this because you ignored all my warnings; telephone calls, gunshots, etc. It's quite simple, Pete. You have owed me money for a long time; you're not appreciative of my generosity."

"What generosity? Your loans have the highest interest rates than anybody in our world."

"But, Mr. Pete, we give you quite a long time to pay them back, right?"

"Not necessarily, Boss. Now, let's get to your many points; what do you really want from our family?"

"I want my money immediately, and I want to know where my missing workers are located. I heard they were missing last week from the two companies, and I suspect it was your revenge on me for the killing of your brother and the disappearance of your sister-in-law, not to mention the killing of the guard."

"You get nothing back until you show me my wife and let me speak with her, so I believe she's alive; then I will pay off the loan within a day or two. Do you have the exact amount on paper?"

"I will get my assistant to give you a bill. Let's take one problem at a time. Before you leave here today, you will have a bill. Bring the money in two days, and I will let you speak with your wife to prove she's alive, then you hand over the money."

"But, can't she leave when I pay you in full?"

"Not so fast, Mr. Pete. We still have to figure out the other problem; where are my missing workers?"

"Boss, I have nothing to do with the disappearance of your workers. There are many crime families around this town, and I have no idea who did it. You already ruined our family, and we're still grieving. I have no more strength for this warfare; I'm done."

"Maybe not," says the Boss. "I'll see you in two days with the money. And, by the way, your brother Frankie will be next if he doesn't pay in two days; you can relay that message to him."

"I will let him know right away, Boss, and I'm sure he'll pay you back in full. But could you do me a favor? Stop the gunshots, please. It's very disturbing."

"I'll think about that, Mr. Pete; let's see what you come up with first."

"Okay, Boss, we'll see you in two days."

We're escorted out of the Boss' mansion by his assistant. Pete has a bill in his hand, which is shaking. We leave the premises. Pete's head is down, walking slowly, not happy at all.

I'm concerned about the missing workers because we know where they are; I think Pete told me that he could get the money, that was no problem, but Alex and Garcia are another issue we must face.

"I'm so worried about Viv, Ted. I just can't imagine where they put her. She is a fragile person who must be quivering, crying, and sleepless. The Boss is being an asshole as usual. I hope that Viv is not prepped as to what to say; who knows what they did to her mind; it can happen quickly."

"Don't try to pre-judge anything, Pete. It will work out for you."

"I have to call Danny and Frankie as soon as I get home. Thanks so much, Ted, for coming with me to see the Boss. I really appreciate it. I couldn't do it alone."

"You're pretty tough, Pete, but I am happy to help anytime."

"I'll speak soon, Ted. I'll be on my way."

"Bye, Pete, keep me posted. I'm worried about you."

34

FRANKIE

Oh my God, I just got a call from Pete that Viv was kidnapped! I can't believe it. It's so insane. I'm quiverin' in my boots; they may come for me or my kids. I knew those gunshots meant something; now what are we goin' to do?

Why me, I did nothin to nobody, well except for Alex and Garcia, but I didn't do the dirty work either, and I told Eddie I am goin' to pay off the loans as soon as I can, but that's not good enough for them; they had to kidnap Viv, so upsettin'.

Pete is beside himself; he's waitin' angrily for two more days when he can speak to Viv, so he knows she's alive, poor thing. She must be out of her mind, not knowin' what will happen to her.

I invited Pete over to my place to drink and settle down a little. He told me he's sendin' the kids over to Viv's mother's house so that he can have a break. He is tellin' the kids that mom has to visit an old high school friend in Boston, and she'll be away for a few days.

The family will chip in with visits to the kids while Viv is gone. My sister, Margaret, Ted's wife, will be happy to keep them company and bring her kids over too. For a while, at least, they won't suspect anythin'.

We gotta pay off those loans fast; Pete said somethin' about Danny helpin' us, but I don't know 'til I speak with Pete in a few minutes. How we'll handle Alex and Garcia is another story. I hope Pete and the others can figure it out. I hear the doorbell; it must be Pete.

"Hey, buddy, come in, sit down and relax. I'll get you some Bourbon."

Pete says nothin', which I expect, cause he's so upset. I try to cheer him up with a few jokes but no laughs. I hand him his drink, and he slugs it down.

I ask him if he wants more, and he nods; another and another, and then he just about passes out. I feel for my brother, and I hate to see him like this; he's usually our leader, laughs, jokes, and is responsible for good decisions. He takes care of the whole family in a lot of ways.

I let him sleep like a baby for about an hour while listening to the baseball game. He snores pretty loud. Soon enough, I hear a yawn, and he's awake. I'll let him talk when he's ready. Just wait.

"Was I asleep for a long time, Frankie?"

"Na, just about an hour; I think you drank too

much booze and just passed out. I know you're under a lot of stress now, so I let you sleep. I'm listenin' to the news, and I'm sick of it, so I'll turn off the radio. Are you ready to chat a little?"

"Sure, Frankie; I apologize for my behavior, bro, but I'm so tired, and I feel so lost without Viv. I'm also very worried about her treatment and how she'll be when I speak to her in a couple of days. It's just so painful, Frankie."

I see some tears rollin' off his cheeks; I get closer to him and put my arm around him for comfort, poor guy; some sniffles too, as he reaches for his tissues. I decide to get him some cold water from the frig.

"Here, Pete, some nice, cold water, you've been sleepin' with your mouth open, so it must be dry."

"Thanks, Frankie, that water sure is refreshing. So, now I'm feeling comforted by you, bro, and I can chat for as long as you want. I have some news from Danny, which I think will make you happy."

"Oh yeah?"

"Yes, Frankie. When I was with Danny the other day, I told him about the phone calls and the gunshots and the urgency of paying off our loans to the boss. I don't think you know this, but Danny has been stashing money for a long time. He's single and has less responsibilities than the rest of us. So, he's being generous in offering to pay our loans off (meaning just us two). Don't say a word to the rest of the family. It's a secret."

"Why just us two, Pete?"

"Well, we're the "lucky" ones that the Boss chose to harass, you know what I mean?"

"Sure thing, Pete, I'm thrilled that Danny will do this. It's absolutely amazin'. But wait, what about the missin' men?"

"That's a whole other problem, my bro. Ted and I went to see the Boss yesterday and demanded Viv's return, which of course, he laughed at, and it infuriated me."

"I can certainly understand that, Pete. Did he say anythin' else about Viv?"

"Yes. He said she is still alive but wouldn't tell me where she is and said I could go back to the mansion and speak with her on the phone if I bring the cash we both owe him. That's where Danny comes in."

"I'm gettin' the story straight now. That's the reason for the threatenin' phone calls and the gun shots."

"Correct, Frankie, now we have to call Danny and him. I know we need the cash as soon as possible; only two more days, and I'll get to speak to Viv and pay the asshole off. Then I'm out."

"Out of what, Pete?"

"Well, out of the loan payment at least; then I think Viv may come home."

"But, what about the missin' guys? Are they goin' to hold her until they find them, which we know is impossible?"

"We'll have to figure out an alibi; we may have

to get Lopez involved to show him how angry we are about holding Viv."

"What can Lopez do, Pete?"

"I can't really dwell on it now, Frankie, but Lopez could set up a plan to kidnap one or more of the Boss' assistants or knock them off. We'll need a really good alibi. After all, we agreed to work for Lopez in exchange for protection, right? Oh, and don't forget to not to say a word to the rest of the family about Danny's gift to us, okay?"

"When will we get the dough?"

"I'm calling Danny right now."

Pete seems in a better mood now; his face has some color, and he's chattin', which is all good. I know deep down he's terrified about Viv. I'm prayin' that it all works out in the end. But I'm scared too.

"Hello, Danny, this is Pete."

"Oh, hi, bro. What's up?"

"Well, you know all about the guns shots and the other bullshit?"

"Yeah, you told me about the threats and the need for cash to pay off the loans."

"You know they took Viv as a hostage?"

"No, I can't believe it. Damn them. Is she okay?"

"I'll know in two more days; I'm heading to see the boss, give him Frankie's and my money and hope to speak to Viv then, and maybe get her out; I hope she's alive."

"Of course, she is, Pete. Let's think positively. I'm so sorry, bro. I just have no words, just prayers."

"Can we get the money from you tomorrow, Danny?"

"Sure; do you a have a bill for both of you? So, I can go to the vault and get the exact amount."

"Yup, it's in my wallet right now; do you want the exact amount?"

"Well, if you don't mind, and Frankie too, I think I'll come over and get the bill from you. Is that okay?"

"It's fine with me, and I'm sure Frankie is good with it too."

"I'll be over in a few minutes. Bye now."

So, Pete and I chat about the kids, asking how his kids are doin' under the circumstances. He tells me he hasn't said nothin' true about Viv, just that she's away visitin' for a few days. I think that's a good idea; these kids are busy in school and don't overthink about their parents, except when they're hungry or want their allowance.

Danny is knockin' on the door. I'll open it.

"Great to see you, Frankie and Pete!"

"I'll fix you a bourbon, Danny. And, oh, by the way, I have some left-over pizza I can warm up to keep our stomachs from growlin'."

"Sounds good to me, Frankie. You too, Pete?"

"Yeah, I was just going to say let's go out for pizza, but now we can be comfortable."

I put the pizza in my toaster oven, hearing quiet chatter between Pete and Danny. I think they're figurin' out the money situation. I'm not too good at math, so they should handle it. But, I'm just so thrilled at what Danny is doin' for us.

When the pizza is warm, I bring it out on a tray with paper plates and napkins. We all sit around the coffee table and gobble down our food and drink. When we're finished, I take the plates and throw them in the garbage; that's how I usually entertain, not very high class.

I feel that Danny needs a thank-you hug from me; I go over to him and put my arms around his shoulders. He holds my hands, no words, but he knows what I mean. He's the best brother when it comes to a jam.

Thank God for his generosity, or we'd all be held hostage. I will pray for Viv's safe return every night at church. And, of course, Pete's recovery from all of this.

"Okay," says Danny. "I'm giving Pete the money for both of you. I looked at the bill, and he has the right amount. I hope this settles things down for some time and that Viv gets out of that hellhole quickly. Then we can all rest, at least temporarily."

35

TED

TWO DAYS LATER

I just heard from Pete, and he says he has the money to pay off his and Frankie's loans. He didn't tell me where he got it from, but I assume it is Danny because he has been socking away dough for years.

I don't care that Pete doesn't want me to know; as long as he has it, that's great; and that goes for Frankie too. They are the most in debt of the whole family.

The problem now is Viv; if they pay off, will she be released, or will the Boss decide to play tricks? Pete may need some extra support today because he's going down to see the Boss, hopefully, to talk with Viv on the phone.

I don't think it will be a video call 'cause the Boss

doesn't want to tell much. I feel for Pete and Viv. They're such a wonderful family, always ready to help us and host dinners!

I don't want Pete to see the Boss alone, so I'm going to join him if he wants. I think I'll call him back and see if he wants me to go.

"Hey, Pete, I forgot to ask, would you like me to come with you to see the Boss? I won't interfere at all, just company."

"Sure, Ted, you're very cool and level-headed as opposed to Frankie. Danny may want to come too."

"That's even better, Pete; he's calm, cool, and collected, and it will be fine to have him there.

"We need to be there in a couple of hours; want to grab some lunch first? Let's all meet at Aztec Mexican. They're pretty fast there. I'll call Danny and tell him to meet us there ASAP."

"Okay, Pete, see you there soon; we can get a few beers too, may relax all of us."

"I'll call Danny, Pete, and invite him if he's available. See ya in a few."

I call Danny, and he says he's delighted to join us but can't make lunch. He's busy with work; he says to call him when we're ready to visit the Boss.

I'm glad I can be with Pete, who needs some comforting now more than ever; he's tied up in knots, and he thinks the immediate future looks bleak. I try to be positive and give him some hope.

I meet Pete at Aztec in Brooklyn, a newish restaurant that's usually slammed for lunch; the margaritas are fantastic but will give you a quick buzz. We each order a chicken quesadilla and a beer; lots of chips and salsa on the table while we're waiting for our main dish.

"So, Ted, what do you think will happen at the Boss' place?"

"Gosh, Pete, I have no idea what's up the Boss' sleeve, but you told me that you're paying off your loan, right?"

"Yes, and the deal is I get to talk to my wife on the phone. And, I'm sure they've prepped her to say what they want."

"Yeah, Pete, that's usually what they do, but you know better than to believe the shit that will come out of her mouth, right?"

"I guess so, Ted. I'm also concerned about her physical safety; is she tied up, taped up, or what? And the Boss really won't talk. Then we got the other problem of the missing workers, Alex and Garcia; he knows about it now and is questioning us; that's a real problem unless we get some help from Lopez."

"Lopez? How would that solve anything, Pete?"

"Well, it may not Ted, but one thing I've been toying with is to try to get Lopez to knock off some of the Boss' assistants, lessening his strength and then making up an amazing alibi."

"Do you think the Boss will know who killed them?"

"No, because we're not doing it, Lopez is."

"Yeah, I know, but we have to pay Lopez. It's not free."

"But we'll be working for Lopez anyway in exchange for protection."

"So, I don't get it, Pete."

"We'll get the money; I have my sources."

I look at my watch and realize we have to go soon. I decide to treat Pete 'cause he's so damn nice and is having so many problems. I wish I could be more of a help, but I guess giving him moral support is good.

"Okay, buddy, it's time to get the check and leave. I'm treating you today. You deserve it."

"Thanks, Ted. I really appreciate your support; you got a good head on your shoulders; you're a great husband and father too. Shall we grab a taxi to the Boss' place?"

"Yea, let's splurge. While you're paying the bill, I'll get us a taxi."

"Fair enough, and I'll pay for that."

We discuss things we will say to the Boss on the taxi ride. But, we're not going to give in like wimps; we're going to try to stand our ground and demand that Viv be released as soon as the money is transferred. And, if it were me, I would demand to see her on video.

We arrive at the Boss' place and are greeted by one of his assistants, who lets us in after saying our names. It's a long walk to the Boss' office, which we've done many times. The assistant knocks on the door.

We can hear the Boss say, "who is it?" The assistant says to wait for a few seconds, and then we're allowed to enter. The Boss, as usual, is smoking a stinky cigar and spitting into a dish next to him.

The cigar smoke smells very stale. I wish he'd open a window. We both sit in front of him, and he asks us to remind him why we're here (dummy)! Pete tells him.

"Good afternoon, Boss Johnnie. As I recall, you said to come here today with the money my bother (not this one) and I owe, and then we would have a chance to speak to my wife Viv, who has been kidnapped by your men."

"Oh, yes, I remember now. Of course, you've come to pay your loan off, right?"

"Exactly, sir. I have the cash and am ready to give it to you provided I get a signed letter by you, promising to let me speak with her and hopefully see her in a video conference."

"Well," says the Boss, "first hand over the cash, and I will have my assistant count it, so hold on a minute. Is it large bills?"

"Yes, sir, it is."

The assistant goes into another room with the bill and evidently counts the money. He comes out about ten minutes later and says that it is correct. Thank God for that.

"Is everything okay?" Pete asks.

"It seems so," says the Boss.

"I'd like to know why you are hiding my wife?"

"Ah, that I can't tell you right now. We still have some other problems to solve, and you know what they are."

"But what does that have to do with my wife?"

"Well, it's a long history we have, Pete, much of it not very pleasant. We have some outstanding business, as I said, so let's try to solve our differences."

"Okay," says Pete, "let's discuss it right now.

"Can't do that now, tomorrow at five pm."

"Can I speak with my wife now?"

"I will arrange that for you. Let me speak to my assistant to set up the call. No video allowed today, maybe another day; we'll see."

Pete and I wait, it seems like hours, when finally, the assistant calls us to come to another room. They have a phone there that I guess connects to wherever Viv is being held. Pete looks very nervous and shaky, but he'll be okay once he sits down. The assistant dials a specific number that we can't see, and another voice picks up.

"Yes, who is this speaking?"

"This is Vivian's husband. I have permission from the Boss to speak with my wife now."

"Just a moment; it will take a minute or two."

Pete is all sweaty, probably wondering why it's taking so long.

"Okay, sir, here she is, you have ten minutes to talk, and I will be standing next to her."

"Hello, Pete, it's me, Viv. I'm so happy to hear your voice."

"Oh Viv, I have tears in my eyes just listening to you. How do you feel?"

"I'm okay, honey, hanging in; they're feeding me, and I can bathe, and they are treating me decently."

"Viv, is this all bullshit? Just answer yes or no."

"I can't, Pete. I think they can listen in."

"Don't worry, darling. I know why they took you, sort of as a bargaining chip."

"How are the kids doing, darling?"

"The kids are great, Viv, well taken care of by the whole family, everyone chips in, so they get a lot of attention. The problem is, I told them you'd only be gone a few days, and it doesn't look like that. What should I tell them very soon? Never mind, Viv, that's not your problem. I'll figure something out. I miss you so much, and I don't know what the immediate future is like. I'll try to negotiate a way out; I just need some time to think about it. I asked to see you on video, but the Boss says no, not at this time. By the way, the loan is paid off, so that's a good thing. Have faith in me, sweetheart. It won't be too long."

"Thanks for calling, Pete, so happy to hear your voice. Please give the kids a big hug from mommy, but don't say a word. They'll never recover."

"I know, my love. I'm throwing you kisses now, and I will find out when we can speak again. In the meantime, take good care of yourself; I love you very much. Bye."

When Pete hangs up the phone, he cries like a baby, just sobbing, like a fountain. I let him go on this way, so he lets his emotions go crazy. That's the best thing. He composes himself, and the assistant walks us back to the Boss' office. Can't wait to hear his bullshit again.

36

PETE

After sobbing for what seems like hours, I finally get over it and calm myself down to a sniffle. Thank God Ted was were to quiet me, or they might have thrown me out of the place.

When I heard Viv's voice, it was just too much. I'm still so frightened for her and angry at the Boss. I'm in the mansion outside the door where I talked to Viv. Ted went to the restroom, so I'm just waiting for him, and then we'll talk to the Boss again. I feel like he's got something up his sleeve, but then again, so may I.

"Hey, Pete, you feeling a little better now?"

"A little, Ted, but I still can't believe what's happening before my eyes. I hate to say it 'cause people say don't look back, but maybe be shouldn't have knocked off Alex and Garcia, 'cause look at what the result is now. The Boss knows that they're missing or dead, I guess, and we don't have an alibi yet. Let's try to avoid the subject when we go back to talk to him."

"First of all, Pete, let's listen to what the Boss has to say, and then we'll double-talk him and leave."

"Yeah, you're right, we have to listen, but let's not give any specific answers yet, okay, Ted?"

"Okay, let's tell this guard that we're ready to see the Boss."

Now we're back in the Boss' office, that stinking stale awful place where he chomps on his cigars. He could also lose about a hundred pounds. I want to make this fast until I get my head together and speak with Lopez.

"What do you guys want now?"

"I demand my wife's release. That's what I want!"

"Well," says the Boss, "that may be negotiable."

"How?'

"If you can find my men, Alex and Garcia."

Pete remarks, "I don't know anything about that. Why don't we set up another meeting next week to talk about the release of my wife and why you're keeping her. I'll have answers for you. I'm very tired now, and I need to go home; just remember to tell Eddie to call with a date next week."

"Don't threaten me," says the Boss, "or I'll have you all captured or knocked off."

"We're leaving now. I'll hear from Eddie."

The assistant walks us to the front door; now I'm smelling cigar smoke, damn!

Ted and I get a cab back to my place. I'm pretty

silent during the ride while Ted talks, but I'm not listening. I'm thinking about Viv, her beautiful face, her smile, her cooking, just everything about her. Then I think about the kids. What the hell am I going to tell them

I take two aspirin and a stiff bourbon when we get home. Maybe Ted has a good idea of what to tell the kids because I sure am stumped.

"I'll get the cab ride, Pete; you stay inside until it comes."

The house has been filthy since Viv was kidnapped. Luckily, the kids haven't seen it this way since they're staying with family. Dishes are piling up, not from my cooking, but from takeout and frozen food.

After Ted leaves, I think I'll straighten up a bit so even I can stand living here. It's very lonely, I must say, but I can't have the kids here; thank God for my family. They're taking good care of them and making sure they do their homework. I visit every day, sometimes evenings, and I take them to Coney Island for cotton candy on weekends.

It still feels like we're not a complete family without Viv. Now I must think of something to tell them because I don't know when Viv will be released. I guess I could say that she's had some minor plastic surgery done on her face, and she has to heal before she wants anyone to see her.

So, she will stay with her aunt in the Catskills until she feels comfortable enough in public. I'll have to discuss that angle with Ted. He may have a better idea.

I offer Ted a bourbon, and he gladly accepts. While I'm fixing it, the phone rings.

"Hello, oh, Frankie, how are you?"

'I'm doin' okay, but I wanted to know how the phone call went with Viv."

"It was short, and she couldn't really talk truthfully because someone was standing next to her. But at least I know she's alive. They're not letting her out, Frankie. I'm so angry and upset. You need to help us think of what to tell my kids and also how we're going to answer to the Boss about Alex and Garcia. I'm sure that's why they're holding Viv. We have to get Lopez involved again to knock off some of the Boss' key men, and that will weaken him, I hope. Then we need a good alibi."

"Yeah, good idea, Pete, I'm with ya on that. Now about tellin' your kids where Viv is at the moment. Whew, that's hard, 'cause we don't know when she'll be out. Hey, I got it. Tell the kids that mom is on a transatlantic cruise with her female cousin, 'cause she's always wanted to do that, and it takes a long time to cross the ocean, ya know? And then she could visit England and maybe France, and you could say that you didn't really want to go, because of them. What do you think about that idea?"

"Not bad, Frankie. I'll consider it. Can I call you back? Ted is here, and we're about to drink some bourbon. I'll call you later or in the morning. Thanks, Frankie, Bye."

I think about Frankie's ideas about telling the kids where Viv is. They're ten and twelve now; you think they're going to believe this bullshit? I don't know. I may just tell them that she is very stressed out and wants to go to a place where they take good care of you, and when you leave, you feel like yourself again.

I will say that sometimes it takes a few weeks or a month of care until they release you; no visitors are allowed, but I can talk to her, and you can write letters. I'm thinking about that idea because they have noticed that she's yelling at them a lot lately, so the stress part is realistic. And we all want her to get better.

Ted and I sit in the living room and sip our bourbons.

"What did Frankie want?" asks Ted.

"Well, basically, he wants to know how Viv is doing and to speak with her. Then I asked him for ideas about what to tell the kids. That's it."

"Did he have any good ideas, Pete?"

"I don't know. I'm so sick of gabbing about it, maybe he does, but I'll have to think them over. In the meantime, my focus is getting Viv out of that damn place. I think our only option is to have Lopez help us out. We need to set up a meeting with him soon to see what the price is for killing some key men to weaken Boss' power. We may have to ask

Danny to help us pay for the job; some of us should start working for our new Boss Lopez to let him know we're on for whatever he wants us to do. Then at least we'll get protection which we need right away; Boss Johnnie is the move!"

"You know, Pete, we may be able to give the Boss an alibi anyway, without knocking anyone off. If he asks, we just let him know where we were when Alex and Garcia went missing. What do you think?"

"Well, we can certainly try to convince him we had nothing to do with it, and I don't think he knows about Lopez; he's just trying to put the blame directly on us. But he can check our guns, our houses, and he'll find nothing."

"Okay, Ted, not a bad idea; let him hunt for evidence that we did the job, and he won't find anything."

"Yeah, Pete, let's try the cheap way first. We may be able to convince him enough to get Viv out. You know, I think I'll call the Boss, make another appointment, and you come too so you can speak with Viv. I'll be tough but not angry, more like negotiating a deal. What do you say, buddy?"

"I'm willing to go along with that, Ted. Why don't we try calling Lopez now and let him in on some of our thoughts? He doesn't know about Viv either. He'll be pretty shocked. It's about six pm now, so he should be available."

I think the alibi with our co-workers may be a good idea, but I still don't know if it's enough to get

Viv out. The longer she's there, the more worried I get. They better keep their foul hands off her. I'm sweating again and nervous about the kids.

"I'm calling Lopez now."

"Hello, is this Jim? Great, this is Pete; listen, we may need your help. And, I'm sorry we haven't started working for you, but I have some sad news."

"What's that?" says Lopez in a surprised voice.

"My wife was kidnapped by Boss Bellini a few days ago."

"Oh no, that's terrible. What can I do to help?"

"Well, I'm not sure yet; They took her, I'm sure, because of what we did to Alex and Garcia. As soon as he got word that two of his workers went missing, he blamed us for the knockoff; that's his revenge. I'm trying to think of ways to get her released ASAP, without too much bloodshed, at least at first. We're going to try with some alibis of our whereabouts when they went missing. Do you have the exact dates and time of the shootings, Jim?"

"Let me look in my book for a minute; let's see, um, the exact date is Thursday, September thirteenth at nine-twenty-three. You know we mostly work at night. So sorry about your wife. Call if you need me."

37

DANNY

I'm upset about Vivian. She doesn't deserve this. She is an innocent pawn in a family mess. The Boss should have taken one of us, but he has a plan, I guess. We know nothing about it, though. I know that Pete has spoken to Lopez.

I told Pete that I would fund a knockoff if that's what he wants. But I also agree with the idea of negotiation, as does Ted. We have a good alibi, and we should use it first before becoming violent. It looks like there are only four of us left.

The other family members, like Tommy, are out. I think we should try to get some information from Eddie first, although he'll probably play dumb. I've had two cups of coffee, and I'm on my third; this is pretty usual for me.

I met a woman the other night. She seems pretty smart, good looking. She is sitting at the bar I frequent, appears pretty lonely, has no smile on her face, and her lips sort of turned down, although I really shouldn't say that.

She could have a million guys after her. I quietly sneak over to her and introduce myself. We start up a conversation, and it's pretty pleasant. So, as the night wears on, I buy her more drinks, and before you know, it's midnight.

We exchanged telephone numbers, and oh, by the way, her name is Lois, Lois Borzofsky, maybe a Russian. I put her in a cab and thought to myself; she's a catch—more another time.

Pete's calling me.

"Hi there, buddy, what's up?"

"Well, I just want you to know, and I'll tell Frankie and Ted what I told my kids last night."

"Yeah, what is that, Pete?"

"Well, there were several options. I sort of mixed them together. I think the best one is the idea that Viv is very stressed out at the moment and can't take proper care of the kids. So, she wants to go to her aunt in Colorado and stay for a few weeks, look at the mountains, get some fresh air, take some hikes, and so forth. I think I told them the best lie I could, that they would believe. I don't want them to freak out and say she's in a mental hospital, so this is calmer and more understandable for them."

"But, Pete, what about speaking with her and all that stuff?"

"I think the only way they can communicate at the moment is by letter. But the Boss may ease up a bit, and hopefully, he'll allow them to speak with her. Next time I speak with her, I will alert her to this plan. Look, Viv's going to be upset about everything, so this works as well as any other idea."

"Are the kids very upset now?

"They think she's away for a week or so, looking for new furniture. They're okay, getting a lot of family attention, probably getting away with murder (oops, I shouldn't say that)."

"Hey, Pete, do you think one of us should call Eddie, or is it a waste of time?"

"Danny, talking to Eddie is like talking to a wall. He only knows one sentence, and that is where's the money; so, I think we're wasting our time doing that."

"Okay, then let's leave him out unless we decide on plan B, knocking off those closest to the Boss."

"I think that's best, Danny. However, we should have a meeting of the four of us to discuss our strategy because I'm going down there again tomorrow, hoping to actually see Vivian."

"If you want company, just let me know, kiddo. What time do you want to meet tomorrow? "How about you all come to my place; I'll order some food and pick it up, and I always have booze, you know that. How about six pm; we should all be out of work by then."

"Sounds great, Danny."

"I'll even call Frankie and Ted for you and let them know what going on; I'm pretty sure they can make it; after all, this is heavy stuff, and our goal at this moment is to get Viv out of that rathole."

"Yes, that's it, Danny; so, I'll see you tomorrow at six pm at your place. Good enough."

"Hey, Pete, get some rest. You really need it. I'll take care of the others."

"After I see my kids, I'm going to crash, if I can. Bye now."

Pete is looking paler each day. He probably is losing a pound a day. He's drinking but not eating, according to him. I wish I could wave a magic wand, and this whole mess would be over once and for all. It seems to be dragging on.

If we could kill the Boss, I think the Bellini family will die out; but, that's almost an impossibility; we'd never get close enough because he has guards with guns twenty-four seven. I'm not sure that Lopez could even get him, but maybe.

"Hey, Frankie, it's Danny. You at work? Your voice sounds funny."

"Yeah, but I can talk for a minute. What's up?"

"Pete wants to call a meeting for tomorrow at six pm at my place; we'll have booze and food. Sound inviting? We'll talk about our alibi concerning Vivian and releasing her."

"Wait, let me check my calendar to see if I have the kids. No, I'm free, so I'll be there."

"Great, Frankie, it's really important for Pete. He's not looking well these days, and we really need to support him."

"Oh, no problem, Danny. I know exactly what you mean, and I agree, so I'll see you tomorrow. Goodbye."

"Goodbye, Frankie."

"Hey, Ted, it's Danny, calling; we have a meeting at six pm to plan our alibi with the Boss regarding Viv's release; can you come? Are you at the pawn shop now?"

"Yes, I am, and we're pretty busy; I even have Margaret here to help me. I believe I'm free tomorrow, so I'll see you soon. Gotta go back to work."

"Okay, Ted, see you tomorrow at my place. Bye."

Well, I think that does it, so I'll finish my work at home and then maybe I'll call Lois to see if we can meet for a drink. I've been thinking about her since we met last night; it sounds stupid, but you never know what will happen. I haven't felt this way about other women I've met at bars or other places.

The phone is ringing and ringing; damn, all I get is a voicemail. So I'll leave a very low-key message not to come on too strong.

"Hi, Lois, this is Danny. I met you last night at Rico's Bar. I think it might be nice to take you out to dinner sometime soon. Please return my call. Goodbye."

Whew, I did it. I'm acting like a God damn teenager. I need to settle down. I hope she calls back tonight. In the meantime, I'll have a brandy to ease my nerves; too much going on with Viv and all.

I'm also wondering how this extra work for Lopez

will turn out. He's probably only giving us night protection because we all work days, and we probably don't need protection twenty-four seven.

I know Tommy is out, and thinking about it now, I don't really need the work, but I'll make that decision later. I'm feeling for Pete and Viv, their kids too.

This has got to stop. I'm going to call the Boss and insist that Pete be allowed to see Viv, not just talk to her on the phone. He has his money from the loans by God.

"Hello, this is Danny, Pete's brother calling. I need to speak with the Boss; it's urgent."

"Let me see if the Boss is still in his office."

He has me holding for ten minutes.

"Just a minute, I'll connect you."

"Hello, who is this at this hour of the night?"

"I'm sorry, Boss, but I'm calling for Pete, and it's important."

"How important could it be?"

"Well, Pete is supposed to come to speak with his wife tomorrow at your office. I am asking and begging you to let him see her as well, please."

"Do I have your loan money?"

"Yes, you do, all of it."

"Well then, I guess I could grant a ten-minute visit with her, but that's it. What time is he coming tomorrow?"

"I think about three pm, and I will escort him but not see his wife. Thank you, Boss, for doing this. I'm sure Pete will be greatly relieved."

"Only ten minutes, that's it for tomorrow. Now, I must rest."

And, he hangs up.

Boy, Pete is going to be so overjoyed at this news. Sometimes the Boss can even be reasonable, not much, but this time yes. I can't wait to call Pete. He'll be up.

"Hello, Pete, guess what?"

"I can't imagine, Danny; you won the lottery."

"I wish. No, Pete, good news. I called the Boss just now, and surprisingly he was civil, though tired. "I asked him if you could see Viv tomorrow, and he actually said YES, but only for ten minutes."

"WOW"! That's amazing Danny, what time?"

"Three pm at his office, isn't that great?"

"Yes, it is, and I'm very excited and, of course, curious to see how she looks."

"I'm going to be your escort, but not to see Viv. That's only you. I'll pick you up in a cab at two-thirty pm."

"I'm speechless, Danny. What a terrific brother. I owe you."

38

PETE

On the cab ride home, I feel so elated that I'm going to see my beautiful wife. I can picture her in my mind's eye; her perfectly formed face, silky hair, graceful legs, and everything else.

I wonder if they'll leave us alone for ten minutes so I can hug, kiss, and feel her body next to mine. Wouldn't that be great? I'm not asking for much, you know. I am so appreciative of Danny's help in getting me down there and paying off my loan, not to mention getting Eddie off my back.

So, when I arrive home, I'm going to call my kids, just to see how they are doing. I miss them so much, but honestly, they're doing fine without me. The one they miss the most is their mother, don't blame them at all.

But they seem okay with the story I made up about her. And, if the Boss will agree, maybe they can even get to talk to her; depends on his moodiness; he can be a real shit head, we all know that.

The house is ghostly-like. My voice echoes off the walls. I make myself some hot tea, put a shot of brandy in it to make sure I sleep well tonight. Before I call the kids, Danny calls me.

"Hi, Danny, you still up?"

"Of course, bro, I'm listening to the eleven o'clock news, but I want to check on you to be sure you're okay with tomorrow."

"I'm so excited to see you, Viv. Are you kidding?"

"I'm sure you are, Pete. Maybe next visit we'll be to pick her up and take her home, you think?"

"I doubt it, but we'll try to negotiate for it."

"What if he brings up the missing men?"

Then, we'll have an alibi, Danny."

"What alibi, Pete?"

"Well, first we say that we know nothing about it, nothing!"

"And?"

"He'll want us to explain who did it."

"Yeah, Danny, and then we say we have no idea, play dumb."

"Yeah, but he's going to want detailed information."

"I know, and then we ask specifically what he wants? If he says something like I know the day they went missing, then we have our alibi straight out. We were all at work, and we can prove it. We shouldn't say anything else. I hope he accepts our alibi. He'll have to find someone else to blame."

"Pete, do you think that garbage will be enough to get Viv out and leave us alone?"

"I'm not sure. He really has no evidence. He's just shooting from the hip, as they say. I mean, he can try to kill us, but that won't bring back the missing, although it may satisfy his anger. The fact is, he's unpredictable; that's why we need the protection, at least at night when we're home. Which means that we have to start working for Lopez on our off hours, at least I do. But I can't do anything until Viv is back and can take care of the kids. And, you know, Danny, you may have enough dough so that you don't need to work for Lopez. Me, Frankie, and Ted definitely have to work, mostly for the protection, cause I think we're the main targets of the Boss. You are more of an outlier, a negotiator, so I don't think he'll bother you. And, obviously, he struck a chord with you, as you paid off the loans for us, and he knows it, and he allows me a visit with my wife."

"I think what you're saying is probably true, Pete, but let's see what happens tomorrow, and how the Boss conducts himself, what mood he's in and on and on. We should both pray tonight. Let's also keep our fingers crossed, and I'll pick you up by cab tomorrow at work, two-thirty pm; have a good evening, bro, lot's going on."

"Okay, Danny, see you tomorrow. Bye."

I'm calling my kids.

"Are these my little cutie pies?"

"Yes, Dad, it's both of us on the phone."

"Do you miss us?"

"Like hell, I miss both of you so much, but I'll be there to see you tomorrow night after work."

"Will you bring us some presents?"

"What do you want that is reasonable?"

"Some pictures of mom, is that reasonable?"

"You're making me cry, kids, stop it! Okay, you got a deal! How is Aunt Margaret treating you?"

"Aunt Margaret is funny, tells a lot of jokes, tucks us in at bedtime, and we like being with our cousins, and she lets us have ice cream for dessert every night. We miss mom a lot, but we're happy she will get better staying in Colorado."

"You're absolutely correct, guys, and she misses you too, believe me. Anything else you want to tell me? How about school?"

They both say, "It's pretty good. We're up to date with our homework."

"Great, I'm proud of both of you, keep up the good work and always be polite, right?"

"Yes, we are, dad; we love you."

"Love you both too, see you tomorrow eve. Bye"

I get off the phone, and tears start coming down my cheeks. This whole ordeal is so horrible for the kids, me, and mainly for Viv. If I could, I would start my life all over, be a clean guy, not involved with crime in any way; it would be so much better, uncluttered, and happy.

But, instead, I'm in deep doo and can't seem to get away from my own shadow. I was born into this life cause my dad wasn't exactly "clean."

So, it is passed down to us, and we can't seem to get out, no matter what we do or don't do. It's like a vicious cycle, round and round in the underworld. I have a beautiful family, all torn apart now; that should never happen to anyone, even a crook like me.

Maybe I should talk to the priest, not confess, but just for counseling purposes. Maybe that will help me understand my situation better. I wonder if he's still there or keeps regular hours. Nay. I'll skip that and put on some soft music, get me some brandy, and think about tomorrow.

The phone rings.

"Hey there, Frankie."

"Hi, Pete, just calling to find out if I'm goin' with you tomorrow to see the Boss?"

"I'm afraid not, bro, it's too risky because the Boss hates you, as he does me, so I'm taking Danny with me, 'cause he's not on the Boss' shit list, got it, bro?"

"Yeah, I got it, Pete; well, let me wish you all the luck, fingers crossed, things work out with the Boss and Viv. Will you keep me posted?"

"Of course, pal, you'll know one way or the other. Now I have to rest up for tomorrow. Thanks for calling."

So, I continue to think about tomorrow as I sip my brandy. My mind swirls around in different directions. I can't help it. It won't settle down. I take another sip and another, and now I'm starting to feel a bit sleepy, so I turn off the music and walk upstairs to my bedroom.

I'll get into my pajamas and maybe read a magazine called "True Crime," no, that's ridiculous, what am I thinking! I should just close my eyes and count sheep. While I'm counting sheep, the phone rings.

"Hello?"

"Pete, it's me, Ted. Did I wake you? You sound groggy."

"Well, Ted, actually I am counting sheep, trying to fall asleep, not much luck though."

"Sorry, bro, I just wanted to wish you luck tomorrow. The kids are doing great here, all of them. They love being together, and they don't talk much about you and Viv."

"That's not great Ted, that means they don't miss me?"

"Nay, I'm just kidding, Pete. They miss you and Viv a lot. I suspect you handled the Viv situation okay with the kids?"

"Yeah, I lied pretty well, but they're only kids, so they don't have to know the ugly truth, right?"

"Absolutely, Pete, you did the right thing. All's well here, so don't worry. I just want to wish you luck with shit Boss tomorrow, and let me know what is going on."

"I sure will, Ted, and thanks for everything that you and the whole family is doing to help me and Viv."

"It's our duty and our pleasure to help. We're

family, and we're close. We have a strong bond that can never be broken, no matter what. Speak soon, pal."

I can't count any more sheep, so I think I'll go to the church, light a candle for Viv, and if the priest is there, fine, and if he isn't, I'll sit there and pray. I can walk to the church in about ten minutes.

When I get there, it's eerily quiet. I can almost hear my breathing. It's dark, except for all the lit candles. I stroll to the front pews to gaze at Jesus on the cross and the Virgin Mary.

I kneel and start to pray when someone gently taps me on the shoulder from behind. I look around, and to my surprise, I see the priest. I'm thinking to myself, what on earth is he doing up this late.

This is really weird. Maybe he knows about my problems and my visit tomorrow. He speaks softly to me and leads me to his chamber. I follow, not knowing what will transpire.

He tells me to pray with him, and then he puts his hands on mine and says some more prayers. Then he walks out, and I'm alone.

On my walk home, I feel refreshed, not tired, but it's one am by now. I have to go home and count sheep, or I'll be in no shape to face the Boss.

39

DANNY

I woke up pretty early this morning. I couldn't sleep well last night worrying about Pete. I got home late because I had a date with Doris. I'm starting to feel more comfortable with her. She's really easy to be with; relaxed, funny, intelligent, pretty smile, one dimple on her left cheek.

We went to a French Restaurant called Henri, very chic, and we ate well; onion soup with lots of gooey cheese, snails, steak fries and for dessert we had chocolate mousse. And then back at my place, we had brandy and mints.

I shouldn't tell you, but I smooched a little, nothing drastic, we didn't hit the sack. I think she likes me too, or else she wouldn't accept my invitation. We'll see what happens next time.

Anyway, back to Pete, yeah, I'm stressed because our alibi may not pan out.

We were indeed at work, and our bosses will

vouch for us, but that's all we have to go on. If the boss knows what date the men went missing, we were at work because we know from Lopez, and that was a weekday. But we don't even mention Lopez in our conversation.

I'm making myself some strong coffee, and then I'll call Pete to see how he's doing. I hope he got some sleep.

"Good morning, Pete. You sound a bit groggy."

"Yeah, bro, I went to sleep really late last night, trying to count sheep. I have no idea how long it took; I'm pretty tired now, but more nervous, as it's soon that we see the Boss. You'll never guess what I did last night."

"You went to church, right?"

"Yup, Danny, but I went after midnight to pray, thinking I would be all alone. And, guess who was there that late?"

"The priest, bingo?"

"How did you guess? You got it, bro. I couldn't believe it; he sneaked up on me. Then he said we should pray together, and we did, and then I stayed a bit longer and left. That's why I went to sleep so late."

"Well, Pete, I think the two of us have enough nervous energy to make it through the day, don't you?"

"I have to, Danny; I'm seeing my wife today. I don't want to look like a schlump; I want to look rested, so I think I'm going to call in sick to work;

they'll understand. I think I'll lounge around the house, read the newspaper and then go for a nice long walk."

"Sounds like a plan Pete, I'll be here doing my paperwork if you need me. Otherwise, I'll pick you up in a cab around two-thirty pm, okay? Don't do too much exercise. Save your power for the Boss."

"Okay, Danny, I'll see you later, fingers crossed."

I have a lot of paperwork to do for my financial boss, but at the moment, I'm thinking of Doris; why not? She's so pretty and nice to me. It's only natural she should occupy my mind. She works in a library, so I can't talk to her now.

But I know she takes a lunch break from one to two pm, so I'll wait and call her then. It's almost noon now, and I haven't done any work.

My boss, he's a senior man at a company that takes bets from hundreds of people who bet at the race track. I work for him, keep up with all the bets and figure out the money. Even though they don't race every day, I still have to be up to speed with it.

I get a percentage of everything that comes in, so that's why I'm called the money man in my family. By the way, Doris doesn't know anything about our family dealings.

The phone rings.

"Hi, Danny, Pete here. I just want to touch base and let you know I've been running around to help one of my boys, who got hit in the wrist playing soccer. The x-rays show a clean break. So, he's in a cast and home with Margaret. I'll visit him again, hopefully after our meeting, which is soon, and I'm getting very nervous."

"Don't worry, Pete, we've got an alibi, just in case, and you're going to see your beautiful wife. Put a smile on your face. bro."

"I'll try. See you at two-thirty pm sharp, Danny."

Poor Pete, he's so lost without Viv and the kids. If the boss disagrees on a release for Viv soon, I can only imagine a scenario. It may come down to a showdown, a real ugly mess if you know what I mean.

And that may be the end of some members of our family. Or, on the other hand, we could get Lopez and his hit men to kill the assistants and then the boss. Either way, it's ugly, and there may still be retribution from the Boss and his gang

Well, it's almost two pm. I did speak with Doris, and she is happy I called. We talked about going to Coney Island on Sunday, weather permitting. I love hearing her voice. It's so soft and clear.

Oh well, I must get respectable to see the Boss, so I'll clean up and put on a jacket and tie. I hate ties and seldom wear them because I work from home, only see my boss weekly,

I'm ready to leave and pick up Pete. He knows to look decent for the Boss' visit.

"Hey, Pete, jump in the cab, there is so much traffic, but we'll still make it there on time."

"I did my praying and sweating, and now I'm ready."

"By the way, I spoke to Doris again (wink wink),

and we're heading for Coney Island Sunday, not bad for an old bachelor, eh?"

"Ah, come on, Danny, you're not old, and you're handsome like the rest of the Valenti Family.

We joke around during the cab ride, but I can see Pete go silent pretty quickly as we near the Boss' mansion. Finally, I pay the driver, and we both head for the front door.

The assistant opens the door and by now recognizes our faces. He tells us to wait in the study.

Pete's hands are trembling; he takes out a small handkerchief and blows his nose, wiping the sweat off his brow. A few minutes pass, seeming like hours, and he motions us to follow him. Again, down the long halls to finally reach the Boss' office.

Once more, we can smell the cigar smoke before we even get close to it. Pete starts coughing a bit and takes a deep breath.

"Hello again," says the Boss, puffing on his cigar, looking even heavier than the last time we saw him. "Please sit down. So, we have negotiated a visit with your wife today. This visit is a favor for paying off your loans. It doesn't mean that your wife is released. You may have a ten-minute visit alone with your wife. We will have a guard standing outside the door. He will tell you when the visit is over. Any questions?"

"Yes," says Pete, "What is necessary for her release?"

"Well," says the Boss, "we still have two of our workers missing. And, I have more information on the date they never showed up at work."

"And, what was that date?" asks Pete.

"September fourteenth at eight am, according to their superiors, and after that, they never showed up again. How do explain that?"

"I know nothing about your missing workers, nothing. My brothers and I were at work that day, and we don't end our work until five-thirty pm any day, and we can prove it because our superiors will vouch for us. So, go find someone else to blame, not me, not my brothers. We're not killers, period. We're hard-working men who love our families and will not put them in any kind of harm. We are providers, and we love our kids. You've got the wrong people. Now please let me see my wife."

The Boss says nothing, just tells us to follow the assistant to where his wife is kept. Pete is red in the face, and I can predict anger and frustration in his voice.

"Calm down, bro. You don't want Viv to see you angry, okay?"

"Yeah, you're right, Danny."

The assistant unlocks a door, Pete enters, and there, standing in a jumper, is his wife, Viv.

PETE

We look at each other in silence, then rush to embrace, standing there for many seconds. "Oh, my dear Viv, at last, I can feel you, kiss you, gaze at you. Other than your hair turning a little gray, you don't look too bad. I mean, you look thinner; have they been feeding you well?"

"Yes, pretty well, not that it's good tasting food. Oh, Pete, it's so good to see you; how are the kids?"

"Doing well, under the circumstances. I had to tell them something about your absence. So, I told them that you went to see an aunt in Colorado for a few weeks to rest."

"Did they believe you, Pete?"

"I think they did, hon. They're staying with Margaret and Ted, and they are doing well. Other family members come to visit often. And, of course, I visit every day. Oh, Viv, let me hold you again. I miss you so much; I shed tears every night and find it hard to sleep without you."

"My bedtime is ten pm," says Viv. "There are others here too. We don't talk about how we got here; the guards are all over the place. When will I be released?"

"Soon, darling. I have evidence that neither I nor any of the family killed anybody, but the Boss will have to check my alibi carefully. It won't be long now, sweetheart; please pray every day and be strong. They haven't laid hands on you, have they?"

"No, but their language isn't very nice. They use curse words frequently. I have some books to read, and they have some games that me and others play sometimes. But I want to come home, Pete. Please try your best."

40

THE BOSS

Ah, that cigar tastes good. Much of the time, it just sits burning slowly in my ash tray. Most of my buddies hate the smell, but I'm the Boss, so they have to put up with it. You know something? I'm getting tired of this job. After all, I'm seventy-two years young, but I got plenty of aches and pains, not to mention stress.

I'm getting to the point where I can't keep track of things; I tend to forget stuff now, so I'm thinking of making my younger brother Victor my immediate and highest associate. He will keep track of the money owed to me.

He will also do all the dirty work like keeping track of all the records, who is out to kill me, who is still here as a hostage and why, and working with my hitmen to keep them in line, among other duties.

It's a big job, but I'll still be here to help. I just don't want to have such responsibility. I'd like to die a normal death, not be killed by a bullet from someone wanting revenge, and there are a lot of them, believe me

Victor is in the black money business; he's a carrier and makes a lot of dough, right off the top. He could easily be the next Bellini Boss and still keep his job, or quit, and he'll still make plenty of money off of my businesses.

So I have to get my associates to train him to be just like me. Not so hard, he's got guts; it's in our genes. I think I'll call him right now and get him over here if he's not out of town 'cause sometimes he's traveling for the company.

"Hello, Victor, hey, this is Johnnie. How are you doing, pal? Haven't chatted in a while. Listen, I gotta speak with you. It's important; are you in town?"

"Yeah, bro, you caught me at a good time. I have a few days' break until I'm on the road again."

"Boy, this traveling is getting to me, you know?"

"Yeah, I know Victor, and that is exactly why I'm calling you. I've had it with my job. Look, I'm ten years older than you, and I'm getting too tired to be in this business much longer; plus, I still have many enemies, and I can't handle it anymore."

"I gotcha, bro, well how about I come over, and we can have dinner at your place. You got plenty of help, so let them cook for us. Can I bring you anything?"

"Nah, I'm good, just bring yourself. Come over around six tonight. See you then."

Well, I may be in some luck, just coincidentally, Victor is getting sick of traveling as a runner, so this whole scheme may work out. He'll have a desk job with many associates to help him, not to mention all my hit men.

I think he's pretty good at ordering people to do things, some pretty nasty. Look, this job won't be that different. I mean, he works for a crook now anyway.

At six-fifteen pm, I tell one of my assistants to bring my brother into my study.

I haven't seen him in a while, but we talk regularly. My mother thought she couldn't have kids after me, so Victor is a total surprise. That's why he's ten years younger.

And, believe it or not, we were all clean then, and I helped take care of him as a baby. It's easy, though, to get hooked into this kind of business. As long as you keep a low profile, you can do very well. I do not have to worry about money, just my life.

"Hey, bro, it's great to see you, step back a little, so I can get a good look at you. Wow, my little brother, you look different to me, and you have much less gray hair; mine is all white. Sit down, take off your jacket and let's have some bourbon before dinner. I'll get Troy, one of my assistants, to get us some drinks."

"Wow, you look great too, Johnnie, a bit older, but hey, we're all aging. How's Veronica?"

"She's hanging in, getting old like me. She

crochets a lot, makes beautiful pillow covers, and seems to keep busy. At this point, she's in sync with me about getting out of this business, so we'll grow even older together."

"Should we eat first and then talk? I think we should go to the dining room; dinner is probably ready."

"Let's do it."

On the way there, I'm thinking how lucky I am to have a younger brother who is good-looking, smart, savvy, and willing to work hard. I hope he doesn't freak out when I tell him what the job is about. But he'll have plenty of underlings to do the dirty work.

"How's dinner, Victor?"

"I'm eating like a horse; the pasta and fish are terrific. I wish Margie could cook as good. I think she picks up ready-to-eat food when I'm away, don't blame her. We eat very simple when I'm home."

"We always have delicious food. Our cook used to be in an Italian restaurant, so it's like eating out every night. We almost never eat out, except at certain restaurants where we know the owner. What's for dessert, Troy?"

"An Italian cheese cake, sir."

"Perfect, thank you, Troy."

So, we stuff ourselves with dessert, and then we move back to my study for a nice cigar. My father is to blame for that habit, and we both have it. Troy also brings us some Strega Liqueur to polish off the excellent meal.

There is a moment of silence between us, and I wonder what is going through Victor's head. He has a determined look on his face, and I decide to let him be for a minute. Then he sort of pops out of it and smiles.

"So, my dear Johnnie the Boss, what is on your mind for me?"

"Well, let's start with the good stuff. You'll make loads of money; you don't have to travel; you'll sit in your chair, boss everybody around, smoking your cigar. Pretty nice, eh? Your underlings will take care of all the details; you'll have body guards all the time, and you'll live in this mansion.

So, here's the current situation. I have at least a dozen or so people who have it in for me for knocking off some of their underlings and various other things."

"Do you have a list of those people who are out to get you, Johnnie?"

"My associates have lists which we go over frequently."

"What else?"

"We are holding hostage five women whose husbands killed some of my men for revenge on me. In addition, I have many out there who owe me money, and I want my money; it's been too long."

"Why did you loan them money?"

"Well, these are families loosely tied to us and or work for us, so we like to be kind once in a while, you know. But not too kind, then it gets testy. One of my associates, Eddie, is to take care of that and is to keep me informed. He's not all that honest, so for all, I know he may be skimming off some dough for himself, who knows. We may get rid of him and put Jimmy in his place. I can't stand my associates stealing money from me. As I said before, we are holding five women whose husbands may have killed some of our employees for us, killing some of their family members and guards who deserved it; and most of them have no good alibis. So, we thought capturing their wives would force them to fess up, but so far, it hasn't panned out that way. You're not used to this lifestyle, Victor; there's a lot of bloodshed and death, but if someone crosses me or one of my associates, I get my hit men in action."

Victor has a frown on his face listening to this. I can tell he's taking it all in and wondering if he can become as dirty as I am. He's not so clean now, you have to understand, but he's not dealing with as many people as I am in my empire.

He's thinking while crossing his legs from one side to another. I let him alone in his world to ask questions if he needs to or just enjoy his silence before he speaks.

"How long are you going to hold these women, Johnnie? Do some of their husbands have alibis?"

"Most of them are ready to leave soon. I got the alibis, and they are okay. There are one or two whose husbands are not fully checked out yet; I'm patiently waiting for them to satisfy me."

"Are you treating them well, Johnnie?"

"Oh yeah, they get plenty of food, sleep games, radio, but it isn't Shangri-La, I can tell you that. They have guards watching them, so no funny business. They do get visiting time.

"I got two, named Pete and Frankie, who, recently, from all accounts, killed two of my men. I know this because they were reported missing the next day by one of my highest managers. I'm holding Pete's wife until he checks out. Pete and Frankie said there were threats to their sister-in-law, and my hit men killed her guard, made the wife run to protection, and killed their brother, Robbie but for good reasons. Robbie stole money from my company, and boom, my hit men took care of him. But to answer your question, Pete's wife is one of the women still here. His alibi is being checked out as we speak. It's very complicated, and you know we can't work with the police or the F.B.I., or we'll be in the clinker ourselves."

Victor's eyes roll back and forth as I speak, but it will take time to slip into my position. We all know that. He gets up, puffs on his cigar, and walks back and forth, pacing the floor. Then he sits down, still puffing. He's still silent; I hear him take a deep breath.

"Well, Johnnie, this is a big deal. First, I have to know how much money there is in it for me personally. I'm very comfortable with my job now. I earn a good living. I keep my cash in a bank vault. Nobody knows it's dirty money. My wife is happy and doesn't mind if I'm away on a "business" trip. She knows what I do, and she's comfortable with it. So, when you have the figures, please let me know, and I'll think carefully about your offer. Stay safe, bro."

41

PETE

I was very drained after my last visit with Viv. Even though she looks okay, I am still nervous about her release because our alibi doesn't cover where we were after work the day Alex and Garcia went missing.

The boss knows about work, but what about that evening? I usually go directly home, but can I prove that? Probably not; it's our words against the Boss' word. I don't think they are sophisticated enough to have cameras in our houses, but they could have guys watching us, following us around by foot and in cars.

How am I ever going to get Viv out of that stinking place? This is going on much too long; something's gotta give. We may have to get Lopez's opinion on this. My phone's ringing.

"Hello, who is this? Oh, Eddie, what do you want from me? I'm really in a bad mood, man."

"Well, I just thought I'd tell you some gossip you might want to know about."

"Oh yeah, what?"

"Well, I was at the Mansion yesterday after my errands for the Boss, and I overheard one of the assistants say that the Boss is thinkin' of retiring and gettin' his brother to take over, at least most of the business."

"Is that so, Eddie? Well, I'm really surprised, tell me more."

"Well, I don't know too much, but from what I've heard about him, he's much kinder than the Boss, you know, he's a nicer guy."

"What does that mean, Eddie?"

"It could mean that your wife might be let out sooner than you think; he doesn't know much about the business, 'cause he's in a totally different one. But he's smart and can learn quickly."

"Do you know for sure that he's taking over? "

"No, it's not definite yet, but I'll probably know in the next few days. Want me to spy a little more for you?"

"Whose side are you on, man?"

"Well, I like ya, Pete, and I feel sorry that your wife is a hostage. Sometimes I cheat a little on the Boss if I like somebody, and you're basically a good guy. I know nothin' abut the killin' of those two men, and I'm not gonna ask you nothin' either; that's between you and the Boss.

"Okay, Eddie, if you want to help us, I have no

problem with it. Just don't get us in more trouble than we're in already."

"Yeah, okay, well I'll try to find out more about his brother Victor if I can, no guarantees ya know."

"I understand, Eddie, and I thank you for turning the corner. I really appreciate anything you can do for us; the more stuff you can feed to me, the better."

"I'll do my best, Pete, and I'll get back to you as soon as I find out more. When is your next visit with your wife?"

"At three pm today."

"I should be there unless I'm running errands for the Boss."

"I have an important question for you, Eddie."

"What's that?"

"Do you know if the Boss uses anything to spy on us, or does he have men to watch us by foot and car?"

"I don't think he has microphones, but I know for sure he has men tailing certain people. But I shouldn't be tellin' you this, Pete, so you swear it's between you and me?"

"I swear to my God and Jesus that I won't say a word."

"Maybe I can persuade the Boss to let up on your wife. But you still need your alibis."

"Well, Eddie, you say you follow people around, sometimes collecting loan money, right?"

"Yes, I do when the Boss asks. He didn't say to

follow you and Frankie. But I can do it, and this gives the boss the alibi you're lookin' for. I don't think he'll know nothin'; he's been a little cranky with me lately."

"Why?"

"I can't really say; he might think I'm a little dishonest or somethin'."

"You mean he might fire you or, even worse, kill you?"

"You never know, but the money is good, and I ain't trained to do nothin' else. I've been workin' for the Boss since I'm a kid."

"I'm sort of confused at this news and the fact that you've taken our side, in a way. I don't want you to get knocked off by the Boss, Eddie, so please, whatever you do to help is great, but be careful, okay?"

"I can tell the Boss that me and another guy have been followin' you for a while to see what you do after work since those guys went missin'. I can tell him about the gunshot warnin's too.

Then he might believe your alibi that you were home that night. What do ya think?"

"Listen, Eddie, whatever you can pull off without getting hurt is great for me, especially in getting my wife out of there. And, if his brother takes over, it might be a whole new ball game."

"I've been doin' this a long time, Pete, So, I know the Boss well. He will believe you. If you tell him your whole alibi, then he'll check with me, and it will be cleared up. So, I may not see you later, but I'll be in touch, Pete."

"Just be extra careful, please."

"I will, Pete. Gotta go, I have work to do."

Man, when I finally hang up, I'm stunned and a bit worried. Why would a guy who's been working for the Boss for so long suddenly become a turncoat? I can't wrap my head around it. Maybe if the Boss' brother takes over, things will be different, who knows.

But I don't even know if it's true; this is all hearsay from Eddie. Though I must admit, Eddie can be pretty cunning when he gets in his certain mood. I feel like shouting out this news to the world.

But I will keep my promise to Eddie, that's for sure. I know he'll also help Frankie too, don't know about any other family members. So, I guess I better get ready. I sure don't want to be late for my visit.

I wonder if the Boss will tell me anything about his brother, probably not. I'll wait to tell him the whole alibi when Eddie gives me the signal. I hope that will be soon because I miss my beautiful wife and want her out as soon as possible.

I only have fifteen minutes to get ready, so I'll go upstairs and put on a clean shirt and some nice cologne for Viv.

"So, how are you feeling, Pete?"

"Great, Danny, how about you?"

"Well, I saw Doris again last eve, kind of a late date. We had a nightcap together, a little smooching, but she wouldn't stay the night, shit."

"Give her time, Danny. You're not in your twenties anymore, you know."

"I know, but it's a bit frustrating. It will happen one of these days. You look especially happy, Pete. Did something change? Is it Viv? Come on. Something's different in your manner."

"Absolutely nothing, Danny, just excited to see Viv."

We arrive at the mansion, and it's the same old thing. Eventually, we follow the assistant to the Boss' office. The cigar smell hits us in the face.

"Come in, Pete and Danny, sit down. Before you visit your wife, I need to know if you have more information for me about the missing men. I need the whole alibi from morning until you went to sleep that night."

"I already told you, Boss, that I was at work, and you can reach out to my manager to prove it."

"And, then what happened, Pete?"

"I believe I already told you; I went home to have dinner with my wife and kids."

"And how can you prove that, Pete? It's your word against mine, right?"

"I will prove it soon enough; don't you worry, Boss, I had nothing to do with those killings. Now I want to see my wife; you've been holding her long enough; this is cruel."

"You have fifteen minutes," says the guard.

"Hello, my darling, how are you? I miss you so much, and so do the kids. I put on a clean shirt for you and the special cologne that you love. You look a bit thinner, and your face is pale. Are you okay?"

"I'm existing, that's all. I need to leave this ghastly place; it's getting to me now, and I miss you and the kids so much. Can't you pull some strings, Pete?"

"I can't really talk now because the guard is right outside the door. I'll try to whisper. There is a good chance that you will be let go soon. Someone is helping me with this. I can't mention names, but there has been a big turn of events."

"What it is, Pete?"

I whisper, "Someone close to the Boss may be taking over the business. That's one positive thing, I think. Then, one of the Boss' associates/hit man tells me that he can help us. It's all very complicated, but basically, you should be out as soon as this person talks to the Boss, hopefully in the next few days. That's all I know right now, but it's all positive news, Viv. Please hang in there, sweetie, I know it's painful, and it's just as painful to me. You have to believe in me, Viv. I promise you are a short-timer now. Give me a hug. I've been wanting to hold you so badly, feel your skin against mine, kiss your hair, your ears, your mouth, just everything. I love you so much. The kids are fine, but they do ask questions about when you are coming home. They're pretty patient, though, and they think you're getting good rest in Colorado."

"Time's up," says the guard rather abruptly.

"I've got to go now, Viv." She starts crying. I give

her my tissues; tell her I love her, and the guard whisks me off.

"That was pretty tearful, Danny."

"I can imagine, Pete."

"No, you really can't."

42

THE BOSS

THREE DAYS LATER

I was feeling kind of nervous for the last three days cause I hadn't heard from Victor. I know he's a busy man and travels a lot for his job. He's not very communicative. He sure doesn't take after me. I hope he's thinking hard about taking over the helm here; my arthritis is kicking up, and my knees are killing me.

I don't need this pressure anymore, and my wife thinks I should slow down. So I have to find out how many people still owe me and how many are out for revenge on me, and if my assistants are on top of it, they better know because that's their job.

I need to check on some of my men, especially Eddie, who's not too reliable, can be a little tricky sometimes, and needs some talking to.

Someone is knocking at my door.

"Come in."

"Oh, James, good thing you stepped in. I was just going to call you to get some of the numbers for me. You're the math genius, and you are keeping the books, right?"

"Yes, I am, and I have some numbers here for you. Generally speaking, you have nothing to worry about Boss, as far as our cash fund, it's in the many millions after you've paid off all your staff. You're still owed money from a few people, which amounts to several hundred thousand."

"Do you have the names of these people, James?"

"I do, but not on me at the moment, but I can get them for you."

"If it's the few families that I think it may be, we need to get the money now, or we need to threaten and pressure them. I'm not tolerating any more favors or extending their loans, so don't forget to get me the names."

"I will get them as soon as I get the files on them or others, for that matter."

"James, is most of the money coming in black money, you know, laundering, drugs, etc.?"

"I believe so, Boss, but I really need to check. I'll be back soon."

"Oh, and by the way, James, tell Eddie I need to speak with him about Pete Valenti, and maybe Frankie Valenti too. I'm still waiting for alibis in the killing of two of my men. I'm still holding Pete's wife as hostage."

"I know, Boss, and there are a few others in there too."

I know, and they will be out soon if I'm satisfied with all the alibis."

Phone rings:

"Hello, Johnnie?"

"Yeah, how ya doing? I am sitting here on pins and needles waiting for your answer. Do you want to come over for some Bourbon and some bites? It's about that time of day, right?"

"Yeah, I think I can sneak out for a bit, but I've been on the road, so want to spend some time with the wife, you know."

"Sure Vic, I know. I got the same problem with mine too."

"So, I'll leave in a few and be there in an hour or so, good?"

"Perfect, I'll have the drinks ready in my office. Just tell the guard you're my brother."

As I'm waiting for Vic, I can't figure out whether he's interested; he sounds pretty tired, but hey, he's been on the road so much. On the other hand, he must be raking in the dough, so maybe that means he's not interested in my deal.

I mean, if he's making more money than me, then why would he take over my job? But I do clear quite a bit of dough after expenses; he could also stay in his own home if he wants to; I think the mortgage is paid off, so it's all gravy for him.

The phone rings.

"Hello?"

"Hi, it's Pete. I was just wondering if I could come by soon and see my wife."

"I think we may be able to arrange that. Do you have more news for me?"

"Well, I may have some more information for you soon."

"So, you want to come to my office to tell me nothing!"

"No, Boss, not exactly when I get more information. I think you'll be satisfied with my alibi."

"Let me think about it, I'm kind of busy now, but I'll get back to you soon; I'm curious as to what news you have for me."

"Okay, Boss, I'll wait for your call, but I'd really like to see my wife."

There's a knock on the door.

"Come in, oh hi, Vic, come sit down; want a cigar? I was just about to light up. Excuse me for a second."

"Hey, James, do you have all the stuff ready yet?"

"Not all yet, Boss, but I'm working on it."

"James, tell the bartender we need two bourbons on the rocks right now in my office."

"Yes, sir, coming up."

"So, how's the wife?"

"Just fine, Johnnie. We've been talking about taking a vacation, maybe to the Bahamas."

"When would that be?"

"Maybe two weeks from now, maybe a little

later. We both need it, 'cause I've been on the road a lot, not complaining. The money is good."

"Well, have you thought about my offer?"

"Yes, I've thought about it a lot."

"And?"

"I'm not sure I'm the right person for this position, Johnnie. My job, though it does take me away from home, is really a good one for me. You can't beat the money, and we can live very comfortably, take vacations, lead a sort of normal life, and nobody bothers me, at least so far. My mortgage is paid off, and we only have one kid, Michael, who is almost out of college. You know I'd love to help you out, Johnnie, but I guess the timing is bad for me. I feel awful, but maybe I can find you a good replacement; I'll ask around. Your job is immense and involves lots of risks. I don't think my brain could handle it, bro. It's just so complicated; it's not even the money. Believe me. I make plenty. Now, don't get mad at me. I'm not doing this to hurt you in any way. It's just not the right fit. One thing I could do is some consulting if you want to run something by me. I'll do that just cause you're my brother, and we should stay closer than we've been. So, are you mad at me?"

"No, no, not at all. I just want somebody I know to help run the business. But I'm okay and still have a few more years left in me, Vic."

"Well, Johnnie, if you ever need to bounce something off of me, don't hesitate to ask. I'm happy to help you, no charge."

"I'll figure something out, Vic, not to worry. You're

perfectly right in your decision. It's your life, and you must decide what's best for you and your family."

"So, let's drink to our families, meaning all of us, and hope that we all stay healthy and alive for the next few years."

"I'll drink to that, Johnnie, with pleasure. Hey, one of these days, we should go out to dinner, just the four of us."

"Sounds like a plan bro, it will be my pleasure to treat."

"Listen, Vic, you have a great vacation, and we'll be in touch when you return. I've got lots of work to do, and I may promote one of my assistants to help me keep track of things and, of course, raise his salary quite a bit."

"Now you're talking, Boss; great idea, you're too loaded with things on your mind; who owes you, who's out to get you and other things. Do you have someone in mind?"

"Actually, yes. You know my assistant James?"

"No, I don't think I know him."

"Well, he's been keeping my books and helping with other things too. He may be a good choice; he's trustworthy, reliable, and pretty smart. The other guys are good at hunting people down, knocking them off, etc. Then I have the body guards, who are really good, wouldn't trade them in for nothing."

"Well, Johnnie, it sounds like you're in pretty good shape. Is the dough coming in steady?"

"Oh yeah, no bones to pick about that. My family is very comfortable, like yours, Vic. We're not wanting; It's just my age and my arthritis that tells me it's about time to kick the bucket."

"I gotcha, Johnnie; just hang in there for a few more years, and someone will pop up to take over."

"Let's slug down another bourbon, and then, I'll take a rest. I have to call Pete back 'cause I'm curious to find out what he has to add to his story. You already know I'm holding his wife for a good reason."

"Yeah, Johnnie, you told me that. You think she'll get out soon?"

"Depends on Pete's new alibi. We'll see."

"Okay, bro, I've slugged down my bourbon and time to go home. Let's keep in touch and try to have dinners more often, okay?"

"Definitely, Vic. Say hi to the family and keep in touch."

I'm a little tipsy and worn out with my brother's response. I thought he might take it, though there was a little spot there that made me think he would say no. I'm bummed, to be honest. I have to put my thinking cap on to get a replacement for me.

But in the meantime, I think James will do a good job as my head assistant. I'll start teaching him the ropes very soon. And I'll start replacing some of my henchmen who aren't doing such a great job.

I just hope I live long enough to hand over the baton, as they say. Oh, I need to talk to Eddie; he's been a little sneaky these days. I don't know what's up his sleeve. But I need to find out. He's my oldest employee, and maybe it's time for his retirement.

43

PETE

I'm still waiting for the Boss' call. It's been three days of hell. I miss Viv so much, and the kids are starting to act out a little; one of them missed school the other day, just making like he was sick.

But Margaret is a softy, so she let him stay home. I guess I'm a softy too now, cause they don't have their mother around. We're spoiling them like crazy, and you know what? I don't even care anymore; I just want Viv out of there.

And, I want Eddie to talk to the Boss and let him know that he's been following me and can swear that I was home after work the day of the killings. I want to get on with my life; I pray every night that Viv will come home very soon. I feel like there's an echo in this house, maybe a ghost too.

The phone rings,

"Hello, oh hi, Danny, how are you doing, haven't spoken in a while, bro."

"I know, it's been almost a week, but more importantly, how are you, Pete?"

"Not so good; Viv is still kidnapped, the kids are acting out because she's gone, and frankly, my head is a wreck. I've been waiting for days for the Boss to call me so I can have another visit. And, oh shit, I'm not supposed to say anything, but I'll tell you, lips sealed. I think we can satisfy the Boss with our alibi. Eddie has turned our way. I guess he's fed up with the Boss and is going to help me and Frankie with an alibi."

"How can he do that?"

"He can lie like everybody else; I can't tell you anymore, but he's a turncoat, and I'm delighted,"

"Wow, that's amazing, Pete. I won't say a word to anybody. Do you need more money from me to make things go smoothly?"

"I don't think so, Danny; this is more of a scheme that really doesn't need dough. But if it does, I'll let you know. You've done plenty to help me and Frankie; I can't thank you enough. One thing you could do is pray for us, including Eddie. That's all I can say at the moment. Tell me some good news, Danny."

"Well, you wouldn't believe it, but Doris spent the night; all I can say is that it was divine. We had dinner first at a Chinese restaurant. Then I invited her to come back to my place. She asked if I could go to her place? So, of course, I said yes, with a big grin, and we did. It's all history from there, Pete."

"So, are you guys a pair now?"

"Well, that's the next step. I'm sure we'll be seeing each other a lot more. I'm taking it slowly and gently. I don't want to lose her."

"I'm happy for you, Danny, and yes, that is very good news; thanks for sharing."

"Do you want an escort the next time you see Viv? Maybe we could have a drink first, settle your nerves a bit beforehand. What do you think, pal?"

"I think it's great; I'd love to have you with me. I need a crutch; I'm getting so weak."

"Okay, bro, I'm going to call Doris now, but do let me know when the time comes, I'll be ready for you, bye."

Danny is such a wonderful brother; not that I don't love all my sibs, but he's so reasonable and helpful during these dire times. My other siblings reach out, but not like Danny. I really should call Eddie just to see if he's still with us.

"Hello, Eddie, it's me, Pete."

"Oh, yeah, good, Pete."

"Eddie, did I wake you up?"

"Are you kiddin', no, hell, I've been up and doin' my job for hours, just stopped home to grab a sandwich. What's up, Pete."

"Well, I wanted to make sure that we're still on the same page. You know what I'm talking about."

"Hell yeah, I know, and I'm still with ya. I've been so busy that I haven't seen the Boss in a few days, but actually, the Boss called me yesterday and said he needs to see me. He didn't sound so good; maybe he didn't get a replacement. I think I heard that his brother didn't want his job; I can't say that I blame him. It's a killer of a job, even with all the help he has. I'm gettin' old and tired but am willin' to keep workin' for a while longer if he needs me."

"You've been a real asset to him, Eddie, over the years. You've helped him immensely; I hope you realize that. So, after you meet with the Boss in the next few days, you'll let me know when I should meet with him about the alibi.

"Definitely, Pete, it should be very soon, then maybe all your troubles will be gone. God help us."

"Okay then, Eddie, you take care, bye."

I just hope Eddie remembers his promise. He seems a little off today, but that may just be my craziness. I have a break at work in a minute or two; I think I'll go to the "mess hall "and get a bite, then I'll finish up my work and go home.

The coffee is the best thing here, and the food is like the army. I have to drink coffee to stay awake these days, 'cause I don't get good sleep. I'm up every couple of hours with my head spinning, thinking of Viv.

I'm not back in the office for more than three minutes when I get a phone from the Boss.

"Hello, is this Pete?"

"Speaking."

"This is Johnnie, the Boss. I am calling to set up a meeting with you. You may not want to miss this one."

"Will I be able to see my wife?"

"Of course, but first, we must talk. Are you leaving work soon?"

"In fact, I am."

"I want you here right after work, understand?"

"Has anything happened to my wife?"

"No, but it may be a good sign for her."

"Oh, well, of course, I'll be there; is five-thirty pm a good time?"

"That will work. See you then."

Wow, my heart is thumping; the Boss just says it's a good sign for Viv; I think that's what I heard. Whew, I wonder what he wants from me. If it's to kill someone, the answer is no. But it probably isn't.

I have no idea, a surprise, but I will be there on time. I'll call Danny and tell him I'm going alone. I arrive at the mansion, and the assistant is waiting at the door. He escorts me to the Boss' office.

"Well, here we meet again. Can I get you a drink?"

"No thanks, I'd really like to see my wife, Boss."

"Just a minute, I need a favor from you, and then you'll see your wife."

"What is the favor?"

"Well, this is not a usual thing. But, the cops and maybe the F.B.I. are after me for a botched job; don't ask any other questions, okay?"

"Okay, Boss, I won't."

"I need you to testify for me in court."

"Exactly what do you need me to testify for?"

"You need to come to court and be on my side. You know what that means. You'll have to lie a little bit. You are my friend, known each other for years, and I'm clean as hell, you understand? If you agree to do this, I will let your wife go free."

"What court is this, Boss?"

"I'm not sure, my lawyer knows, but you are safe; not one person knows you, not the judge, not the lawyer, not the jury, so nothing to worry about, but you'll likely save my butt. How does that sound to you?"

"I'm not sure; how do I know you'll let my wife go free?"

"Because we'll sign a paper, you and I and I'll put my blood on it. The trial starts next week; it could go on for a week or so, but even if I get the hatchet, you'll be free to go, and I'll alert James, my head assistant, to release your wife immediately. I think with you as a witness, I should win. And if I don't, you still win. But we still need the alibi, or else things will turn bad for you regardless of this favor. I've talked to my lawyer; he knows you'll be there, right?"

"Are you sure I'll be safe, Boss, and my wife?"

"I just told you this is a favor in exchange for the release of your wife. This is fair, right?"

"Well, to be honest, I'm a bit surprised."

"Yes, but early on, I told you that you owe me a favor, you remember that?"

"Yes, I do, Boss."

"Well then, here is the favor, plain and simple."

"Yes, but how is this not risky?"

"We're going to introduce you with another name, address, and work title. You'll have fake IDs. There's little chance they'll take the time to figure all this out."

"Don't they check backgrounds of witnesses?"

"My lawyer knows the judge and the prosecutor. That's how it's all rigged. I took care of them."

"Well, are you doing me this favor that's owed? Your wife and family will be thrilled as well as you."

"And, if I don't do you this favor, Boss?"

"Then we will keep her as a hostage, plain and simple. I don't think you want that, Pete."

44

FRANKIE

I've been so worried the last couple of weeks, mainly about Pete and when Viv will be released; Geez, this is goin' on way too long. And, what about the killin's of Alex and Garcia. The Boss is still after us for that. He wants an alibi. I can't blame him.

Otherwise, it's, "he said, she said," you know. I've been workin' real hard too, and Anna's buggin' me for more money; what else is new. I haven't heard from Pete in a few days, but I know he's got a lot on his mind; poor kids really need their mother, though Margaret has been doin' a great job, and Pete's been over there a lot to visit with them.

I've been hearin' rumors about the Boss retirin'; I'll believe it when I see it. He knows there are people after him, so he probably wants to die peacefully, not to be knocked off by some competin' family, that's for damn sure.

We're supposed to be startin' part-time work for

Lopez, but this Viv thing has us all delayed. I'm not complainin', but the extra body guard time would be nice and is needed. Those gun shots have stopped, so somethin' is in the works.

Oh, by the way, Anna and I are officially divorced. I think it's sad for the kids but sort of a relief for us. Anna is already datin' someone. As for me, I like bein' single; no one to account to, and it gives me more time with my kids.

Don't take me wrong. It's not that I don't date once in a while, but I'm not goin' steady yet. I really should call Pete; he should be home by now.

You know what I think? I think the whole family needs a break; it's been stressful for all of us. Maybe we should plan a day at Coney Island when the kids are out of school, like on the weekend.

I'll call Pete now.

"Hello, Pete? It's your bro, Frankie. How the hell are you?"

"Crazy, Frankie. I apologize for not keeping in touch. But I think you know, I practically live at the Boss' place, between visiting Viv, trying to get her out, and drumming up an alibi for you and me to get these killings behind us. Oh, and I forgot, I work five days a week, and I have children to help take care of too. It's a big load right now, and I'm very worn out."

"I can believe it, Pete, and I've been thinkin' about you every day. So, now instead of thinkin', I'm callin' to speak with you and get some information, if you'll share."

"Of course, I'll share what I can. I'm going to shorten the story, okay? To make it quick, the Boss wants a favor from me to get Viv out. I reluctantly agreed to this favor, which I'll explain another time, and this favor will get Viv out of that place, I hope. The Boss put blood on a written agreement between me and him to assure me this is a valid agreement. But do I trust him one hundred percent? I don't think so. But I had no choice. He backed me up against a wall, so to speak. So, the favor will take place next week. I can't tell you anymore because frankly, I'm afraid to."

"Boy, this sounds like a big favor, Pete; are you sure you're okay with it?"

"If I want my wife back, I have no choice. That's it in a nutshell, Frankie. I got another thing to tell you. I spoke to Eddie, he called me. He has turned our way. I'm almost positive."

"What does that mean, Pete?"

"Well, it means that he's going to help us with an alibi. Don't say a word to anyone, understand?"

"I don't get it; I thought he was a wimp for the Boss doin' whatever the Boss wants him to do."

"No more, Frankie. Listen, he told me on the phone just the other day that now he wants to help us with an alibi. He's going to meet with the Boss very soon and tell him that he's been following us all along; remember the gunshots? Well, that was Eddie in a car, following us."

"But does the Boss know Eddie is following us?"

"No, I don't think the Boss knows who Eddie is following at the moment, and he's kind of pissed at Eddie for being lazy, not in touch enough."

"So, you mean we have an alibi for those killin's?"

"Well, if Eddie was snooping around at night, the Boss would know we weren't out partying or out of town, right? I think he will know soon enough that we were together at home, not out killing people; so, he can vouch for us being home, that's it. I just worry that Eddie doesn't get into trouble with the Boss because of this. He's a good guy who has been loyal to the Boss for many years."

"Well, I must say, bro, you are doin' a great job with this mess. I thank you from the bottom of my heart."

"Hey, listen, Frankie, I appreciate your words, but it's not done. Eddie and the Boss haven't even met yet, so don't get all excited until we know it's a go. My opinion is that the Boss may believe it, but then Eddie may get into trouble. That's what worries me. You get it?"

"Yea, I get it. But there's still a lot of hope, right?"

"Yes, Frankie, I keep my fingers crossed every day,"

"By the way, Pete, how is Viv doin' there?"

"Well, they're not beating her, starving her, or poisoning her, but she looks drawn and lonely and is desperate to get out. I can tell you that the kids miss her terribly, and I do too. They don't really understand the seriousness of what's going on. They think she's in Colorado, visiting with a relative. They still question me every now and then, but my lies are still the same. They should never know what happened to her; they just couldn't handle it."

"What do ya say we all take a break over the weekend? You're not gonna know about the favor for another week, right?"

"That's what the Boss told me. But I can see Viv tomorrow."

"So, why don't I call the rest of the family and arrange for an outin' on Saturday, two days from now, weather dependent, of course. Does Coney Island sound like a good place?"

"It sure does, Frankie. You make the arrangements and let me know what to bring, like cooler, beer. You know the necessities."

"Okay, Pete, you take care now, and I'll be in touch."

Boy, that poor man is goin' through shit. I thought I had it bad with my divorce, but he is in the middle of so much crap, which also involves me, even though I don't know the whole of it yet. But Pete is smart and knows how to get along with different kinds of people.

He's smarter than the Boss and can out sting him. I just hope all these problems work out for both of us. I think a day off with the family will be good for Pete, even though Viv won't be there, but his kids will be.

We can rent two beach cabanas, I think that will

be enough, and we can bring food, drink towels and we'll all share. Geez, we haven't done this kind of thing in a dog's age. I think we all need it. I'll make all the calls, and we'll plant it for Saturday. I'll also check to see If I have the kids, now that we're on a sort of regular schedule.

The phone's ringing.

"Hello, oh it's you, Anna, what's up? I'm very busy now."

"Well, I thought we could trade weekends. I take them this weekend, and you take them next, just switch, yes?"

"I can't, Anna, we're havin' a family gathering at Coney Island this weekend, and it's my turn to have the kids, so no, I'm not switchin'."

"That's what I thought you would say, Frankie. Boy, you have no flexibility at all. It's just one time."

"No, it's not, Anna, and I'm sorry, but this weekend is out, done; don't bother me now."

Geez, I can never get a break. The one time I make a big plan, she wants a favor. So, I take it back. She's a pain in the ass. I'm tellin' it like it is. Bein' divorced can have its problems too. It ain't all peaches and cream.

Phone rings:

"Hi, how are ya, Danny? By the way, I'm thankin' you again for the money and invitin' you to a family gathering this Saturday. I'm gonna call everyone, but you beat me to it."

"Hey, Frankie, have you heard from Pete?"

"Yeah, I was just talkin' to him a few minutes ago. Why?"

"Well, I was just curious about what happened with the Boss. I was supposed to go with him the other day, but he told me not to come at the last minute. He said the Boss wants to see him alone."

"I don't know much either, bro, except he said somethin' about a favor for the Boss, but he couldn't tell me what it is. I know somethin's gonna happen next week that may be good for Viv; at least that's what I hear. Let's put it this way. I think he's tryin' to outsmart the Boss. But he also said that there's something else goin' on too, but I'm not clear on that."

"Seems like the wheels are turning. He told me a few things too, but nothing too specific, or he said the Boss would be really angry at him. It seems to be a deal between the Boss and Pete. By the way, the picnic sounds great. We do all need a family gathering. Oh, by the way, Frankie, I've made a new girlfriend recently. But I'm not really announcing anything yet like we're going steady. Her name is Doris, and she's very pretty. Can I invite her to the picnic?"

"Oh, absolutely, Danny. I'd love to meet her. How old is she, if I may ask?"

"She's about my age, but I'm not allowed to tell. You'll see her Saturday if she can join us. You know, I've been very lonely for some time, even though I've had dates. So, this for me is very special. I hope it lasts. She's so amazing."

"I'm really happy for you, Danny; I know you're alone a lot, and that's not really good for anyone. I'm kind of in that position too now, you know."

"Yes, but you have your kids to love. I had no one. I mean to love. I'm a lucky guy to be included in all the family stuff, I mean it. And, now I have Doris, thank God. I think she's really smitten with me; it took a little time, but now it's wonderful."

"So, let's talk about the picnic. Bring a cooler and some beer and whatever you and Doris like to munch on, and we'll share our food with the others. Now, I gotta call the rest of the family and invite them."

"Okay, Frankie, what time?"

"Let's meet at the fishing pier about noon. See ya there, Danny. Hey, I'm really lookin' forward to meeting Doris."

I'm smiling from ear to ear; so happy for Danny. He really needs a companion, and it seems he did get a beauty, accordin' to him. This gathering is what we need for the whole family right now. I pray every day for Viv, at home, and at church; I wish she could be there with us, but the Boss has other ideas.

45

PETE

ONE WEEK LATER

Boy, it was touch and go with this court case; I was sweating the whole time, lying through my teeth. They didn't force me to take a lie detector case because the Boss took care of everything. I did have to swear on the Bible, but I practically whispered it.

The Boss looked like a ghost, pale and twiddling his hands, knees bouncing up and down. I thought he might fall off the chair.

The prosecutor did his best to double talk and, of course, my lawyer, well, let's just say they were all paid off. So, in reality, it was a win for the Boss. But it drained him, as he was still not entirely sure the Judge was with him.

It took about one hour of testimony, and then

the jury went out for about two hours; they also were hand-picked, slanted, and in fear of the Boss. So, the whole thing was a circus, and the Boss went out with a big cigar in his mouth. He came over to me, shook my hand, and said to meet him back at his office.

I left, chuckling to myself and thinking that I lie a lot; I hate that about myself. But when you get involved with these mobster families, that's a normal thing to do. I'm a crook, just like some of my family and the Boss, and, once you're in, it's hard to get out.

I hope our meeting in the Boss' office will allow me to take Viv home. At least that would settle and hopefully bring closure to this particular chaos. Viv has been there for weeks, poor thing. I haven't said a word to the kids, but they will be happy and surprised if she's out.

As I enter the Boss' office, I notice that he seems to be breathing harder and faster.

"Hi, Boss, congratulations on winning your trial; that worry is over now, right?"

"Yes, Pete, and I thank you for doing me this favor, for acting perfectly, the way us crooks do."

"My pleasure, Boss, I'm very happy for you; are you okay? You seem to be breathing a little faster than usual."

"Well, my doctor came to see me the other day and said that my heart is getting weaker, probably my age, but he did put me on some meds."

"I'm sorry to hear that, Boss, and I hope the meds work for you."

The Boss keeps puffing on his cigars without saying a word, just sort of staring into space.

I let him rest his weary mind, and there is a long silence. Meanwhile, I'm thinking about how to bring up the Viv release. He seems calm and satisfied with the court, so he's generally in a reasonably good mood for him.

"So, I guess you want your wife released. It was a promise from me if you completed the favor, which you did. Therefore, I am allowing your wife to be released today, as long as there's no talking about this favor, agreed?"

"Definitely agreed, Boss, and I appreciate that you kept your promise. Can you tell the guard to get her stuff ready so that she can leave with me?"

"Yes, I will phone the guard's office to get her ready. It will take about ten minutes. In the meantime, you're still out of favor with me on the killings of my men. You need a really good alibi to be released from possible harm to you and your family, and don't forget it."

"I realize this, Boss, and I hope to have an alibi for you soon enough. I still have to prove to you that I was home the night of the killings."

"Yes, you do, and I want that alibi soon so I can move on."

"Can I leave to pick up my wife?"

"My assistant who is outside my door will lead you to the guard."

"Thank you, Boss, and I'll be in touch very soon."

"I mean what I say; you'll be in big trouble if I can't find my men. Goodbye."

The assistant leads me down the hall to where they kidnap wanted persons. The guard didn't crack a smile; he merely unlocked the door, and there, in that dank room, is my wife sitting on a folding chair with a laundry bag full of stuff.

She has an excited but nervous expression on her face, and I notice that she has a few bruises on her legs. I run to her, and we embrace, holding tight. The guard stands outside the door motionless. Then he escorts us to the main entrance, where we wait to hail a taxi.

As we are driving home, I notice that Viv isn't talking much; maybe it's because I am talking too much. I'm thinking how excited the kids will be when I tell them mom came home sooner than expected; Viv is shaking slightly. Maybe she's just very excited to see the family.

"Viv, what's wrong honey, are you okay? Did something happen in the last few days since I've seen you? Did they hurt you?"

Viv is visibly shaken; I can see it clearly. What the hell did they do to her? I put my arm around her in the taxi and squeeze her. She stares out the window. I even see a tear or two roll down her cheek.

Maybe this whole ordeal is overwhelming her.

I kiss her on her wet cheek, a faint smile appears. I don't want to force her to do anything at this moment. When we get home, she will feel more comfortable, I hope. I'll give her a warm bath with some of her favorite oils and then a glass of white wine. I hope she doesn't remark about the cleanliness of the house.

"We're here, honey, at last, a comfortable bed, a nice bath, and some wine, and you'll feel much better, okay?"

She nods, but still no words. I pay the cab driver, help Viv out, and we both climb the few steps up to our house. I put the laundry bag on the floor, taking her hand to sit in the living room. I don't say anything about the bruises on her legs, but now I see them more clearly, poor darling. It's a bit hot, so I turn on the fan to cool off the room.

"Shall I get you a glass of chilled white wine, Viv?"

She nods, and then she says: "That would be nice."

I go to the fridge, and though there is not that much food in it, there is a fresh bottle of white wine. While I'm opening it, I'm trying to figure out the problem. Why the bruises? It worries me. Did they hit her, rape her, or God knows what?

I bring the wine to her in one of our fancy glasses, she accepts it and thanks me. I make myself a bourbon. We clink glasses, and she takes a small sip. This is not the time to bring up anything from the kidnapping.

I'll tempt her to make a call to the kids, but she

turns down my offer and tells me a bit later. So, we sit in silence for a while as I watch her sip her wine. I go for my second bourbon, sit on the couch and put my arm around her for comfort.

I know she's hurting, but specifically, I don't know why, and this is not the time to ask. "Would you like to change your clothes and take a nap, my darling?"

"Okay."

"Are the clothes in that bag dirty?"

"Yes, I always wore filthy clothes, except for your visits."

"Oh, I didn't know that, and it's pretty awful. I will wash all of them a bit later, but I think we should go upstairs after you finish up your wine, and I'll help you find some comfy things to put on, okay?"

"That would be nice. I didn't sleep well there; I am very tired."

"Would you like a nice warm bath first?"

"No, I just want to sleep."

"What time did they wake you in the morning, hon?"

"I don't know. There was no clock."

"Okay, my sweet, let's move slowly up the stairs, and I'll help undress you and put a robe on you, one of your cozy ones."

We walk gingerly up to our bedroom; at least I made the bed today, so it looks pretty neat.

Viv goes to the window to look outside at the street. She looks from side to side for about five minutes. I just watch her. I have no idea what she is thinking. Then I go to her closet and find a fluffy robe for her.

She turns from the window and allows me to de-robe her nasty clothes. I then go to our bathroom, wet a washcloth, and softly wipe her face, neck, and her back. After that, I stop washing at her legs, as not to hurt them.

"I really need to sleep, Pete. My body aches."

"Okay, Viv, I'll pull down the covers, and you can get yourself comfortable in bed. I'll bet you missed your favorite pillow and those lovely silk sheets. You always would wrap yourself up in them, like a mummy. Are you too warm? I put the fan on. I'll come check on you in an hour or so, but sleep my darling as long as you like."

I wait, watching her eyes close slowly. When her breathing gets a little heavier, I know she's sound asleep. I smile at her, but I am worried sick. Something is amiss. This is not the Viv I know.

I understand she's been through hell and back, but I've never seen her so weak and silent, even at our visits. She's hiding things, and I don't want to make her tell me what's bothering her too soon.

I may have to make a special phone call to the Boss to get to the bottom of any wrongdoing by his guards, but I'll get it out of him one way or another, even if I have to call Lopez myself.

46

VIVIAN

I awaken in the early dawn. Just a peek of light through the window. At first, I don't know where I am. I pull open my drawer and get a small flashlight to see where I am. I think that I am still at the Boss' dungeon; my vision is blurry.

I try to go back to sleep because Pete is still snoring quietly. I close my eyes, and all I can see in my mind's eye is the dungeon, the women pacing back and forth, some sleeping most of the day, the guards changing places at different times, the nights noisy as some are awake murmuring, or asleep snoring.

I remember having nightmares that someone would sneak up and knife me or rape me. Then I would sit up in bed in a heavy sweat. We only slept about five to six hours per night. Our breakfasts were some slop that looked like oatmeal, then lunch was something like a bologna sandwich with apple sauce, and dinner was some kind of mystery meat with lots of gravy to hide the contents.

Before we went to bed, they did give us an ice cream cone, like giving a treat to a dog.

I open my eyes again. It's light outside this time, but Pete is not next to me. I pull down the sheets, and to my ghastly surprise, there is a spot of blood on my sheet, right in the position where I was sleeping.

My breathing gets heavy, and I'm starting to panic. Did they do something to me? Or is it just my normal period, but it's not that time, so that it couldn't be.

"Pete! Pete! Help, come upstairs quickly, please!"

I hear him rushing up the stairs.

"What's the matter?"

"Look, Pete, there's blood on my sheet, and I don't have my period."

Pete examines it and starts pacing the room, not saying anything, but I know he's thinking something. I get out of bed and go to the bathroom; a little blood on the toilet paper. My hand starts shaking, and then my brain begins to lock in, trying to put some pieces together.

I remember one of the guards was eyeing me a lot, smiling at me, and trying to chat with me. Of course, I ignored him as just an idiot, but now that I'm thinking about it, he could have been the one who woke me up one night and tried to get on top of me.

I kicked him, and he jumped on me, then I kicked

him again, and he kicked my legs, put his hand over my mouth, and got on top of me. I must have passed out from fright because I don't remember anything after that until I woke up in the middle of the night and called the guard.

He said he didn't see anyone in our sleeping quarters. Maybe it was him.

"Viv, Are you okay? "

"I don't know, Pete; I'm so mixed up and exhausted that I can't think properly."

"Just please tell me if you think you were raped by one of the guards?"

"Yes, I think so because I do remember being hurt, kicked, and gagged in the middle of the night."

"Oh my God, Viv, that's awful, horrific, and we'll get to the bottom of this right away. Now I know why you had bruises on your legs. You couldn't talk last night, because I think you are were in shock, and I don't blame you. Are you in any pain right now?"

"Just my legs are sore from the bruises, and I feel dirty all over."

"Before we do anything else, Viv, you need to take a bath. I'll help you and put some of those favorite oils in the tub. Then I'll scrub you down, so you're squeaky clean. I want you to relax in the warm water, and I will take the sheet with the bloodstain and keep it for evidence."

"Why are you doing this, Pete?"

"Because I want to know which guard hurt you. They only have about four of them, and they rotate shifts. Will you be able to identify the guard? Because then it makes things easy."

I don't answer Pete right away; I am thinking about what he says, and I need to relax in my bath first to collect my thoughts. I don't want anything to do with that slimy Boss again. I need to get checked by a doctor, just to make sure there's nothing wrong with my privates. I don't need Pete making another fight with the Boss.

"Pete, the warm bath is so wonderful; can you wash my back?"

"I'll be delighted, Viv. Anything else?"

"No, just my back for now. I'm trying hard to relax."

"That's what I want you to do. But while you're relaxing, shouldn't you see a doctor? I mean, it's no big deal to do that, right?"

"No big deal, Pete."

Pete leaves the bathroom, and I luxuriate in my bath. But, in a way, Pete's right. Why should one of these slimy guards get away with this? What he did to me perhaps is a crime. Who knows?

If it proves to be rape, the guard will most likely go to prison, or he'll get shot by the Boss. He doesn't fool around. I've heard stories about him while I was kidnapped, that if you cross him the wrong way, you get knocked off. I'm surprised he's been so lenient with Pete, with the killings and all. That's why I'd like to end this incident as soon as possible.

"Viv, I just called the doctor, and you have an

appointment later today; he thinks it's important that he examine you as soon as possible. Does that work for you, dear?"

"Yes, of course, it works. But then what, Pete?"

"Well, we'll see what he says and what we should do about it. But in any case, I'm keeping the blood-stained sheet. Do you want me to wash your hair?"

"That would be lovely. Here's my shampoo."

Pete is so sweet and gentle with me, not that he wasn't before, but it seems more genuine now; he probably feels sorry for what I've gone through, but I'm not complaining. I'm a little frightened about seeing the doctor; I'm almost embarrassed because of what happened to me.

She might think I'm some kind of criminal or weirdo. I know she will ask me these specific questions, and I don't want to keep repeating them as they disturb me. So I'd like to forget the whole thing.

I want to see my kids, yet I don't feel quite ready to do that yet; I should want them to jump into my arms right now, but somehow, I feel very vulnerable and scared; I don't want them to see that in me. Instead, I want to be happy and loving when they see me.

"Hi, darling, are you finished with your bath?"

"Yes, I am; could you help me out of this tub. I'm still feeling a bit weak."

"Of course, my dear, be happy to. Now hold onto my arms, and I'll pull you up. There, we did it; here's your big bath towel. I'll dry your back and get out of your way."

"Pete?"

"Yes?"

"Will I ever get over this fright, these nightmares and fleeting thoughts that I have?"

"Yes, Viv, you will. But it takes time; it just doesn't disappear like that. Now you get dressed. and I'll make us a nice breakfast; would you like some coffee?"

"Yes, please, that would be fine. I wonder what questions the doctor will ask?"

"The usual, but he will want to know what happened to you, and you have to be truthful. After the doc visit and he determines that it is rape, then we'll call the Boss. We must tell the doctor not to report this to the police; that we'll take care of it."

"I know, but I hate that you must speak to the Boss so soon."

"The sooner, the better, Viv; it has to be aired, and now is the time. You said that you could identify the guard who jumped on you, correct?"

"Yes, I suppose so. But then what?"

"You don't have to do anything except remember him. Then you're out. The Boss will take care of the rest, believe me. So, please don't panic, sweetheart; I know this is difficult for you, but hang in there a little longer, and it will all be over. I'm going downstairs to make breakfast for us."

Poor Pete, he's always in the middle of a mess, and to have to deal with that scumbag is awful; I feel for him. He's such a great guy and can outsmart that idiot; that's my only consolation.

"Hello, I need to speak with the Boss."

"Who is this?"

"Tell the Boss it's an emergency, and I must speak now."

"Hello, Pete, what's up?"

"What's up? I'll tell you what's up! My wife may have been raped by one of your guards, and I'm more than furious!"

"Whoa, take it easy, Pete. How do you know this?"

"I know because there were bloodstains on her sheets last night after we got home. And, she told me that one particular guard had been flirting with her constantly; then one night he jumped on top of her, bruised her legs and had sex with her, and the doctor found evidence of rape, Boss."

"Can she identify which guard? We have four who rotate, but not always the same shifts. I'll see who it was on the night that it happened. Does she remember who it is, what he looks like?"

"Yes, I believe she remembers who did it."

"Well, then we'll have to bring her down here, and if she can pick him out, we'll take care of him. I'll need verification from the doctor that she was raped."

"Oh, absolutely, Boss, I'll have it."

"Okay then, bring your wife down with the doc's note."

47

PETE

The doc visit was okay, in the sense that Viv took the news pretty well. It was, in fact, a rape and the doc is able to prove it. She was told to rest for a few days and wait to see the kids until she is better.

I feel so badly for her. First, they kidnap her, and then they rape her. Whoever did this is going to pay dearly. I'm sure the Boss agrees with me on that score.

Viv is a real trooper; another victim might have a nervous breakdown. She had a minor traumatic experience, but it didn't last long. The kids have called several times, and I keep putting them off.

I hate doing this, but I'm following the doctor's orders. We all know that rape is an evil crime, but we ensured the doc hushed it up; we told him we'd take care of it. I've missed a few workdays, but my manager is kind and knows Viv well.

I am not telling him about the rape; I'll just make up something else. Now it's time for me to make dinner for the two of us. I'm so happy she's home. I keep pinching myself.

"Hey, Viv, you almost ready for dinner?"

"Yes, Pete, I'm starving. Do you need some help?"

"No thanks, hon, I'm just making meatballs and spaghetti."

"That sounds mouth-watering. I'll be down in a minute."

"Wow, that smells amazing. Are you sure you're not poisoning me, Pete? I know your cooking ability."

"What do you mean? I cooked in the army, silly."

"Yeah, but that was slop, right?"

"I'm afraid it was slop, dear."

We sit down at the kitchen table; Viv still looks thin and pale, but I'm not surprised. The first thing she does is she sips a glass of red wine. Maybe she needs some booze in her to taste my food. We have a few minutes of silence.

I think about ending all this stuff with the Boss during that time. But, unfortunately, I haven't heard about a replacement, so I don't know what's happening. I can't deal with the alibis until Viv recovers, and I can go back to work.

I just want all of this to end, period. I don't care who is in charge of that mansion. I just want out. Some of us are still working for Lopez because we need good protection. Or, like Sylvia, we could be in the witness protection program. I'm still confused.

"Don't tell me my food is awful, please. At least you know I try, Viv, gotta give me credit for that, right?"

"Listen, you, the dinner is great. The meatballs are a little over-cooked, but the pasta is perfect. Got any dessert?"

"Well, my dear, in fact, we do, and it's cannoli's; I got them from the Italian bakery and kept them in the freezer; didn't want to tell you."

"You're an angel, Pete. You know I love them."

"I know, and you can have as many as you want. You're way too skinny, and we have to fatten you up."

Phone rings.

"Hello, this is Pete; Oh, Boss, yes, what do you want?"

"You're supposed to be coming down here with your wife to identify the guard. When can you come? Cause I gotta get them all together, so she can pick the right one."

"The doc says she has to rest for a few days. But we'll be down there as soon as she feels up to it. Rape is no joke, Boss, and we're not taking this lightly. Don't worry, I told the doc, we'd take care of it; in other words, we told her not to tell the police, and she won't."

"Okay, then, get down here as soon as you can. And, Pete, we're not finished with the alibis either. Don't think for a minute that I forgot my men getting knocked off. Somebody did it, and you know that as well as I do. I still think you're hiding something, but we'll have to see, very soon too."

"Got it, Boss, we'll get everything settled as soon as possible. Do you think I like dealing with you? Well, I don't. I want out, and I want to live my life as clean as possible; so, don't pull any more tricks on me; I'm done."

"Now, Pete, don't get rough with me; you think I'm old and crabby; I may still be crabby, but I got a lot of punch in me, so don't pull any stuff, just get your ass down here."

"Well, that was a lovely conversation with the Boss; he's getting antsy and wants you down there, Viv. He also wants to find the killers of his men, you know, the alibi stuff."

"I think you should call the damn Boss now and tell him we're coming down tomorrow and to get the men lined up."

"Yeah, except you're supposed to be resting, Viv, that's what the doc says, remember?"

"Pete, I want to get this ordeal over with; I can make it down there, then I'll come home and rest, okay?"

"Are you sure you're up to it, Viv?"

"Yes, I'm sure; now call the Boss back and tell him. I'm feeling good enough to come down tomorrow and to get all the guards lined up; I'm sure I can identify one."

"If you think you're okay, I'll call him."

"Hello, it's Pete. I need the Boss right now."

"That was fast," says the Boss. So, what's up?"

"Me and Viv, my wife, are coming down tomorrow morning, so get all the guards ready. We don't want delays. She's not feeling one hundred percent yet, but wants to get it over."

"I'll have them all here by eleven am."

"Okay, see you then."

"We have an important date with the Boss tomorrow at eleven am. Don't put on any makeup. I want the boss and the guards to see you the same way as when you left. Now, the guard who hurt you may try to disguise himself a little, put on some makeup, cover a scar, or shave his head, but try to recall as much about him as possible. Look carefully, through all that stuff, and look at his physique too. Many who are suspects try to hide certain distinctive features."

"I understand, Pete, but you have to remember it was in the middle of the night."

"Yeah, but you told me someone was eyeing you before the incident, right? Was that in the daylight?"

"Yes."

We turn in early tonight cause we know tomorrow will be stressful. I'm worried about Viv and her mental state, but she's a trooper, and hopefully, she can handle this. I count sheep, and we both conk out.

TOMORROW

"Okay, Viv, let's have our coffee, 'cause we gotta run. We overslept a little; you need that sleep, Viv."

"I don't want to be late, so let's hail a taxi, and we'll drink our coffee in the cab."

I'm getting nervous, and I look over at Viv and see sweat beading on her forehead. She takes out a tissue and wipes it. We must do this right. This guard, whoever he is, deserves to die, and it's up to Viv's memory that we get the right one.

"Greetings, Mr. Pete. I'll escort you to the Boss' office.

"Thank you. I think I know where it is by now."

"Come in, Pete and Mrs. Valenti, please sit down. We will have the guards ready in a few minutes. I hope you are feeling a little better now. My guards are hand-picked; we screen them pretty well, so I am very surprised that one of them attacked you. This is the first time that I have known about an incident like this, and I am very shocked."

"Mr. Boss, the guards are ready."

"Okay, James, we'll be there in a minute."

"Are you ready?"

"Now, Pete, you will stay in my office, and James will take Mrs. Valenti to the viewing room."

"But…"

"But nothing Pete, this is the way we operate here, just relax. She will be fine."

"Come with me, Mrs." says James, "I will see that you are comfortable before I bring the men in. They will be behind a glass wall, so no worries. Please sit down, and the men will walk in slowly and stand there for as long as it takes you to recognize the one.

Here they come now, so look carefully at each one; take your time, no rush. And, when you see someone, please point."

"That big one, with the black curly hair and he had a mustache, but it's gone now, but that's still him, I know it. He had that same smirk on his face, I'm sure of it."

"Okay, Mrs. I'm going to ask them to leave and then mix them up, and they will come back one more time in a different order, okay?"

"Yes," says Vivian with a panicked look on her face.

"Here they come again. Take your time, Mrs."

In a trembling voice, "That one, the same one with the black curly hair. You can't fool me. I remember him. He hasn't changed that much. He's big and strong and jumped on top of me; you rat, you no good piece of shit; if I had a gun, I would kill you now for what you did to me. You shamed me; you hurt me physically; see my bruises, you miserable son of a bitch."

48

THE BOSS

I'm still here with Mr. Pete, waiting on James to bring the wife back. Pete's been pretty quiet since she was taken away to identify her rapist. He has a disturbed look on his face. I can't say that I blame him. I'm trying to make conversation, but he's not talking to me at the moment.

I'm anxiously waiting to see who the guard is because he's in real trouble with me. I hear weeping coming close to my office in another minute or so. Pete jumps up to listen. It sounds like his wife is distraught.

Pete starts moving toward the door. James opens it, and the wife runs into Pete's arms, still weeping. I tell James to step to the side so the couple is not disturbed.

"Oh, Pete, it was so painful, I can't even explain it. He stood there staring at me, the big guy with curly hair. All I want to do is get out of there, I can hardly breathe, and then they brought them back a second time in a different order, which makes it more distressing to me."

"Just keep still, Viv, with your arms around me and breathe deeply; I can imagine the scene. We're in the Boss' office now; I think we should step outside. Let me tell him what we're doing; keep holding, my darling. Hey Boss, we're stepping outside your office to have a private moment; is that okay with you?"

"Yes, but please make it fast because I need to speak with your wife. Go ahead."

"Okay, Viv, we are in private now, don't be afraid to speak."

"I feel disgusted, Pete. I want this guy put away. I can't look at him anymore."

"You won't have to see him again. It's over for you, Viv. Now, it's the Boss' problem as to what he will do, not ours anymore. Come, let's go back into his office so that you and or James can tell the Boss who it is. Are you ready? Or do you need more time, sweetheart?"

"I'm ready, but I need another tissue. My nose is a faucet." She laughs for a moment.

"Okay then, let's get this over with."

"Boss, I think we're ready now."

"Good, please sit down. I understand, Mrs. Valenti, that you and James were together when the guards came in, twice in different orders. Is that true?"

"Yes, that's true."

"How long did it take you to pick out the guard who you know hurt you?"

"About one minute. There were four guards there, and he is the tallest with dark curly hair. He definitely stands out in a crowd. There are no mistakes here. He is the one who stared at me and jumped on top of me in the middle of the night. I tried to fight him off, but no one came to help. As you can still see, I am bruised on my legs and raped according to my doctor, and you have the papers that Pete gave you."

"James?"

"Yes, Boss"

"Is she telling the truth?"

"Yes, Boss; that's why I made them come in twice in a different order, just to be sure, and each time she picked out the same guard."

I can feel my face turning red with anger. I think I know which guard is the target.

"Okay, you two; I think I know who it is, and Mrs. Valenti, I apologize to you for this terrible incident. I may be mean sometimes, but not this time. I hope you recover well. You may leave, and I'll be in touch. James will take you to the front door. Hey, don't forget, we're not finished here. I'm still waiting for your alibis for killing my men. Remember that, Pete."

"I know about it, Boss, and not to worry, it will be done soon enough."

"Okay, Boss, they're gone," says James.

"Sit down, James, and tell me again, was she correct in her identification?"

"I don't know, Boss, it's her word, and she said it twice without hesitation. So, yes, I believe she's right."

"Okay then. Here's what we have to do. We don't put up with guards like that, you know? He's gonna have to get knocked off. We have to think of a scheme to get him quickly and then replace him. Got any ideas, James?"

"Well, we could catch him in his car as he drives into his driveway at home. We could have two hitmen hiding and waiting for him and just blow him off in the car. We'd have to have a car and driver waiting for us to get away quickly. The only problem with that idea is we should really do it in the dark."

"What shift is he usually on, James?"

"Usually, he's on the night shift, so that's to our benefit. He's here at about ten-thirty pm, so he probably leaves his house around ten pm, so that shouldn't be a problem. When do you want to this, Boss?"

"As soon as possible, James. Why don't you look at his shifts? Then let me know the first one that comes up at night."

"Yes, Boss, I'll be right back."

This is what I don't need right now. But it has to be done. We don't tolerate bad choices here. I have enough problems with other families annoyed with me. Some want revenge, I'm old, and my heart is weak.

Yet, I don't know if James is ready to take over; he's not knowledgeable about the gangs and corruption. He's a little too clean shall we say. But I guess he could be trained. Enough of this, I think I'll light up a cigar and put my feet on the desk, that is, if I can lift them. I'm getting very stressed about this job.

Oh, here comes James. "Okay, Boss, tomorrow this guard is working the night shift, and I very casually got some information on him for our job."

"And what is that, James?"

"Well, he's supposed to be here shortly before eleven pm to get ready; then he's actually on shift at that time. So, he told me he leaves his house and takes the rail at about ten-twenty pm."

"Perfect, James. We get two hitmen stationed at the house, hidden, of course. And one driver in a getaway car. So, as the guard is leaving the house, bam, we knock him off, then run. It will be dark, and no one should see us. Shall we plan that for tomorrow night?"

"Yes, Boss, I can arrange it. Let's hope we get him in the heart or the head."

"Report back to me. I'll be waiting up. And make sure the getaway car is close by; I don't want any mistakes, James."

"Boss, there won't be any mishaps, I assure you. My job is on the line. I know it."

"Can I offer you a cigar, James? In the early eve, there is nothing better than a cigar. Now, if you would get me some bourbon, I'll be all set."

I cross myself and hope that this knockoff is a success. If I botch it, I'm in real trouble. I am just thinking that I gotta call Eddie; I haven't spoken with him in ages, and he hasn't been checking in like he usually does. I wonder if he's up to no good. Sometimes he can be sneaky.

"Hello, Eddie? This is the Boss; I haven't heard from you in a while. What's up?"

"Oh, nothin', Boss, just working hard, you know, following my people and collecting dough, as you told me to do, that's it."

"Well, I think it's time we compared notes on exactly who you're following. Why don't you come to my office tomorrow and we'll talk?"

"Sounds good, Boss. Hey, I heard that Mrs. Valenti was raped in your mansion by one of your guards."

"Yeah, how did you hear it?"

"Oh, I can't remember; I guess one of the family members told me. I'm so sorry about that, Boss."

"Yeah, well, keep it to yourself, Eddie; I don't want rumors to get out of hand, understand?"

"I do, Boss, and I promise not to mention it again. Hey, do you want me to bring a list of who I follow?"

"That would be a good idea, Eddie. Okay then, see you tomorrow."

James comes in with my bourbon and one for

himself, which is strange. I guess he's feeling his oats now that I've promoted him. He gives me my glass and then takes his own; we toast to tomorrow's job well done. Then James takes a seat across from me.

"So, Boss, how do you think I'm doing in my job with some new responsibilities?"

"I think you're doing quite well, James. The thing is, you really need the experience to be the Boss here. It's a matter of making the right decisions, you know?"

"Yes, Boss, I do know."

"I mean, you gotta have the guts to do mean things, especially if they are done to you. You can't pussyfoot around and feel sorry for these people; you gotta act on your hunch and get the job done. So, if you're really and truly pissed at someone, get your people together and do what you have to do. Unfortunately, it's an eye for an eye and a tooth for a tooth; there ain't no fooling around; you're learning the ropes, don't kid yourself."

49

PETE

We are getting close to the end of our interactions with the Boss, I hope. Vivian is home, still furious about that guard but slowly calming down. She's just about ready for the kids to come home.

It was a harrowing ordeal having to identify the rapist; It upset her. The Boss is supposed to call me sometime today to let me know the guard's punishment. I have a feeling as to what it will be. Now a couple of things are left: the alibi for the killing of Alex and Garcia.

I'll have to speak with Eddie to see if he met with the Boss about that. And for Viv to talk to the kids and get them back to us to be a real family again. I pray every day that she will be ready to do this, but I won't pester her.

"How's my beautiful wife doing today?"

"Getting better each day, Pete, and you are the

hero, in my mind. You're always there for me in such a supportive and loving way. I don't know what I'd do without you, dear."

"You are doing just fine all on your own; you are a strong woman, Viv, and I love you for that. I'm just a helper, but you do all the healing on your own."

"You know, Pete? I think I'm ready for the kids to come home. I really mean it."

"Wow, Viv, that's the best news I've had for weeks, other than you coming home, of course. When should we pick them up? I'm so excited for both of us."

"Why don't we call them now and speak to Margaret and see what kind of mood they're in; does that sound okay?"

"That sounds great, Viv. Do you want to call Margaret?"

Viv thinks about it for a few seconds, then smiles.

"Yes, I'll call."

"Hello Margaret, this is Viv." Margaret is speechless. She's so happy.

"Viv, I'm so excited to hear your voice. It's been so long. Welcome home, my dear. We've all missed you so much. I mean the whole family. They keep asking about you, and now you're finally home, so wonderful. I can't wait to tell Ted and the kids...you do want to speak with them, don't you?"

"Of course, Margaret, but first, I need to know how they are behaving and if they're in a mood to speak with me. I don't want to frighten them."

"Oh no, Viv, never think that way. They've missed you, and they talk about you every day. I think it would be fine to say hello at this point, yes, absolutely yes!"

"Okay then, put them on the phone, please."

"Hi, mom," they both squeal at once.

"Hi, my darlings. I hope you are well and ready to come home."

"YAY," they both scream together.

"When are we coming home, mom?"

"How about we pick you up tomorrow after school. So, you need to pack up. I'm sure aunt Margaret will help you. I'm so excited to see you both."

"We are, too!" shouts Michael. "Are you feeling better from your rest in Colorado, mom?"

"I sure am, and I want to hug and kiss you guys all over. I can't wait 'til tomorrow, kids."

"We can't either, mom. We'll start packing now, so excited."

Okay, we'll see you and have sweet dreams."

"Well, I think that went very well, Pete, don't you?"

"I couldn't hear them very well, but you sound great, Viv. I think they're super happy to get home, so we can be a family again. Come on, let's have a drink. I'll get us some bourbon."

Phone rings.

"Hello, oh yes, Boss, what's happening?"

"I called to let you know that we took care of the

guard who raped your wife. No mistakes, he's gone. Tell your wife she has nothing to worry about."

"Thank you, Boss, for taking care of that. I know she will rest easy now."

"You're welcome, Pete. By the way, I had Eddie down here today, and something smells fishy. I never told him to follow you, as he says. He has a list from me, and you and Frankie are not on it. So, what the hell is going on here?"

"I have no idea, Boss; all I know is somebody is following us, 'cause we've heard gunshots in our neighborhoods, and it's usually at night. So, we know someone is watching both of us."

"Well, Eddie tells me that he has been following you for some time, that sneaky bastard. So, when I ask him about your being home the night of Alex and Garcia's death, he tells me you were home because he saw you through the window with the lights on. And, the same holds true for Frankie; he was home too. So, I guess that takes care of your alibis. Now, we just have to check with your bosses to see if you were working the day before and the day after, right?"

"I guess so, Boss."

"What do you mean "I guess so, Boss"; of course, we have to check on that, and we will."

"I don't think that will be a problem for us. We were both at work before and after. Just call our managers. They'll tell you the truth."

"You want to know something, Pete? I think you, Frankie, and Eddie are all lying to me; this little deal stinks of an ugly prank. I say you connived Eddie into this, so you would have a good alibi. Wait 'til I wring Eddie's neck!"

"Boss, actually, it was my decision to have Eddie follow us so he could help us with an alibi, got it?"

"I got it alright, and I am furious at all three of you for crossing me like this. Somebody killed those men, and it wasn't me. Why would I want to knock them off? No reason, they didn't cross me like you guys just did."

"Boss, please don't hurt Eddie. He's been a loyal worker for you for many years. He felt sorry for us, but he didn't do anything bad. He didn't maim or kill anyone; I asked him to help, that's all. He's still devoted to you, I know it."

"Yea, but he crossed me, Pete, and you know what happens then, right?"

"But this is me who is responsible. Eddie has been with you for twenty-five years, Boss, have some regard for the man, geez."

"Look, the three of you are in trouble, as far as I'm concerned. I don't care if Eddie worked for fifty years. He crossed me. You crossed me; watch your step, buddy, that's all I have to say, goodbye."

I put the phone down slowly, my heart beating fast. I just sit there staring into space. Now what? I put myself in jeopardy for what reason? To save Eddie? A lowly servant? What on earth did I do this for? I could have blamed it on Eddie.

Yeah, but I would still be in the wrong, according

to the Boss, because I allowed Eddie to do it. Oh God, have mercy on me; I'm too nice of a guy, and then I put my whole family in a mess. What will the Boss do now?

There's no telling, but I need to do more work for Lopez to keep my bodyguard. I need to make some drug deals so I can profit from them. Sometimes, I'm stupid; my kids are coming home, and I don't want Viv or the kids to know this.

I will do some deals on my breaks from work. I don't want to die, and I don't want Eddie or Frankie to die. My tears are falling fast as I grab a tissue to wipe my face to look normal as Viv enters the kitchen where I was talking.

"Hi, Pete, you were on the phone so long. Is there a problem?"

"No, dear, no problem, just chatting with the Boss over some things, the most important of which is that the guard you identified is gone, killed."

"I hate that Boss. His only recourse is to kill someone, except for me, of course. What else did he say?"

"Not much, sweetie. That was the main thing. Let's talk about the kids. Should we make a welcome home sign for them?"

"That's a wonderful idea," she smiles and claps her hands. "What should we make it out of?"

"I have a roll of paper down in the basement. We could cut it to size and then use colored markers to write on it."

"I can't wait for tomorrow, Pete. Now I realize how much I missed those kids."

"Come here, Viv, let me hold you tight for a minute. You're missing your hugs from me."

"I know. I need to recoup them quickly."

Phone rings.

"Hello, oh hi, Frankie, how's it going?"

"I just got a call from the Boss. He's not too happy with us and Eddie. In fact, he was screamin' at me that it was our fault, and we better watch out, and on and on. I think we're in big trouble, Pete. He says we crossed him, and you know what that means. I'm workin' nights for Lopez guardin' certain sketchy neighborhoods at night when I don't have the kids. I'm glad for that cause he's givin' us protection which we desperately need now."

"Listen, Frankie, don't say a word to any of our family. I don't want them to worry. Just play it cool for now. My kids are coming home tomorrow, and I want everything to be completely normal. Viv is so excited to see them, and I don't want to spoil it."

"Yes, and that's great news. I'm so happy for all of you. At last, a family again."

"Yes, Frankie, at last. By the way, have you heard from Danny, Tommy, Ted, or anyone recently?"

"Just a few days ago, I spoke to Danny. He's in 'la-la land' with Doris and seems very happy, thank God. I haven't spoken to the others in a week or so."

"Okay, let's keep this under the table. Maybe you and I should go to church together and pray for our souls. We need every prayer in the book."

"Great idea, Pete. Let's do it soon."

50

THE BOSS

God damn those crooks, I'm fuming. I have a splitting headache, and I'm sweating all over.

This rage is not good for my heart nor my nagging arthritis. I have three jerks on my list, and I have to hire another guard. What the hell should I do about Eddie, Pete, and Frankie? They crossed me, so I guess they all deserve to be knocked off.

I'll think about my plan, but first, I need to speak with James about hiring another guard and finding out who Eddie is supposed to follow.

"Hello James, could you please come to my office. I need to speak with you about a few things. Also, could you please call my massage guy and tell him I'm desperate for a massage. Every bone is aching at the moment cause I'm very upset."

"Yes, Boss, I'll call the massage place and get Richard over here, and then I'll come to your office."

Why would Eddie try to turn against me like that? And why on earth would Pete take the blame to save Eddie, a lowly servant of mine for years? Pete must have something up his sleeve. Maybe I should call Eddie and see if I can get some garbage out of him before James comes in.

"Hello, Eddie."

"Yes, Boss, what can I do for you?"

"You can tell me the truth about this fake alibi you dreamed up to protect Pete and Frankie."

"Well Boss, I did nothin' wrong really. I just decided to change my route of following certain people who may have it out for you, that's it."

"Eddie, you know damn well that when I give you a list of people to follow, you stick to that list and do not wander off wherever you please and change your route."

"Sorry, Boss, I didn't mean to do no harm. I feel sorry for Pete and Frankie; they've had enough beaten around, you know? They're really good guys who suffer cause they lost their brother; his wife was threatened by you, and her guard was knocked off; so, she had to go into witness protection. And, now they'll never see her again. I just feel bad, and I know you'll be mad at me. You know, Boss, I'm gettin' old and just about ready to retire, so if you could spare my life, I'd appreciate it. I'm the one you should blame, not Pete. It was my decision to help them."

"Is their alibi for real; were they both home the

night of the killings and at work the day before and after?"

"Yes, Boss, to my knowledge, that is true. So, if you're going to knock off someone, it should be me."

"Okay, Eddie, Bye."

Geez, that Eddie is an idiot. You can't turn against me. That's it. I need to talk to James.

"Come in, James, sit down and have a cigar. I'm not in a very good mood now. Did you call the massage place?"

"Yes, Boss, they're coming later today. By the way, Boss, I got a call for a guard's position. The man sounded good over the phone, but who knows. He tells me he has experience with other mob families and wants to come and interview with you."

"Well, that's interesting. How did he find me?"

"I took the liberty of putting an anonymous ad in the newspaper, Boss, 'cause I know you are ready for replacement."

"Good thinking, James. I've been so upset lately that I forgot about it. By the way, do you have Eddie's list of people who he follows?"

"Yes, I have it right here."

"Does it have the Valenti brothers on it?"

"No."

Do you know what Eddie is doing?"

"No, what is it?"

"He's helping Pete and Frankie build an alibi by following them on his night shift behind my back."

"Oh my," says James with a surprised look on his

face. "That's like betraying you, Boss. What are you going to do with him?"

"Don't know yet. I'm thinking about it. I'm mad as hell, and I shouldn't make exceptions, right?"

"Right. He should be treated like every other employee."

"I agree. I'll let you know soon what to do with him. Now back to the guard. I think we should meet him before we hire, right?"

"Yes, Boss, I definitely think so."

"Good, then let's have him come over as soon as possible, perhaps before my massage, if he's free."

"Okay, then I'll call him."

Knock on the office door.

"Come in. Oh, Richard, how nice to see you. I'm a total wreck these days, so your massage comes in very handy. Shall we go to the massage room? I can barely get up out of my office chair these days, Richard. I'm getting old and weak."

"Well, Boss, I'll try to ease the pain a little today, and if you need more massages in the coming weeks, just let me know."

"I'll probably need one every week for the next few months. How's your family, Richard?"

"Just fine, sir; my kids are working, though not for me, thankfully, and my wife is about to retire from her sales job. Thanks for asking Boss. How is your family?"

I'm terrible, but my wife is an angel; I don't know how she puts up with me, but she does. Oh, that feels so good, Richard, but a little harder, especially on the back; that's the bad arthritis but gently on the chest. "

After my massage, I feel better, at least physically, though my mind continues to trouble me. I don't know what to do about Eddie, Pete, and Frankie; maybe I should call my brother Vic and bounce some things off him before this new guard applicant comes.

"Hello, Vic, how the hell are you, buddy?"

"I'm fine, bro, I just got back from another trip, so I'm a bit pooped. What's up?"

"Well, I'm not going to repeat everything, but I've got three people who have crossed me in one way or another, one of them being my employee; the other two are clients who owe me money and who may have killed two of my employees. Now they have alibis, with help from Eddie, I think you remember him. I don't know if I should knock all of them off. What do you think?"

"If they all did this behind your back, then I think they need to go, period. That's my advice."

"Okay, Vic, thanks, I appreciate it."

Then I'll have to make a plan to do this. I'll need James to coordinate this with the timing, the number of hitmen we need, etc. Boy, is this going to be a mess, but aren't most of them?

"James, did you reach the potential guard yet?"

"Yes, and he's coming over for an interview in a few minutes, Boss."

"Good. But I need to talk to you first."

"What about sir?"

"Well, I spoke to my brother Vic, and he thinks we should knock off all three. Are you in agreement? Because you have to set the whole thing up, James."

"Yes, Boss, I will do whatever you want. I think I hear footsteps outside your office. May I open the door?"

"Yes, go ahead."

"It's our guard out front asking permission to let our prospective employee inside."

"Yes, tell the guard to bring him into my office."

I hope this guy is a good fit for our team, especially for the other guards. I need to have four on staff besides the outside guard shifts. After that good massage, I'm getting tired, so we'll make it quick. James has already done some of the work.

"Come in, sit down, Mr..."

"Mr. Ferrara pleased to meet you."

"So, you're looking for a guard position?"

"Yes. My previous Boss passed away, and the family got all new guards, so I'm looking."

"What kind of work did you do there?"

"I was on the night shift, so I actually guarded the Boss' bedroom. I also did some work outside of his personal house. I've been working for five years for him and before that I was just a guard for an Italian Restaurant. So, I have different experiences."

"Yes, I understand. All that is good. I will probably need you to guard a small prison-type quarters where I have several people who are being held for different reasons. I have two shifts there with four guards, and they switch out night and day. Do you have a family?"

"Yes, two sisters, a wife, and three kids. It's a lot to handle, but we're a close-knit family."

"I see. What do you think, James? Any questions you want to ask?"

"Yes, one question; have you ever killed anyone?"

"No, that was left to other employees."

"Sounds pretty good to me. When can you start?"

"Anytime you wish."

A moment of silence before the guard whips out a pistol with a silencer on it, shoots the Boss and James, checks their pulses, and runs from the mansion. Once outside, he utters the words, "Revenge for my brother, the guard, killed by Boss Johnnie."

THE END